ALL THESE SUNKEN SOULS

ALL THESE SUNKEN SOULS,

A BLACK HORROR ANTHOLOGY

EDITED BY
CIRCE MOSKOWITZ

AMBERJACK
PUBLISHING

CHICAGO

Published by Amberjack Publishing
An imprint of Chicago Review Press Incorporated
814 North Franklin Street
Chicago, Illinois 60610
Hardcover ISBN 978-1-64160-837-4
Paperback ISBN 978-0-89733-324-5

The Library of Congress has cataloged the hardcover edition under the
following Control Number: 2023936035

Cover and interior illustrations: Sarah Gavagan
Cover and interior design: Jonathan Hahn

Printed in the United States of America

For my parents, who let me watch all the scary movies I wanted as a kid. Love you, or whateva.

Contents

Lights

by

Kalynn Bayron

What is the punishment for murder? I guess it depends on who you are and how much money you have. If you have the money, you can get away with just about anything. I've seen people with good lawyers and deep pockets get away with all kinds of stuff. Murder is sometimes the tamest thing rich people get away with.

If I get caught, I will not get away with this. I know that already, and it is something I have come to accept. I don't have money or a lawyer. I don't have anything—except this pressure on my throat. It's like an invisible hand slowly tightening around my neck, threatening to choke the life from me. It's been bad for a while now, but it can get better.

I know exactly how to ease this terrible, suffocating feeling. The last time I needed to release the pressure was right after my latest birthday. I'd found a guy living alone in a ground-floor apartment. He'd left the window open. Nobody who valued their safety would ever leave their window open. It was an invitation, and it was so easy. The kill was slow, and the relief was immediate. I was satiated, and the fullness lasted longer than it ever had before. Probably because I took my time with him. I learned in those long moments that if I could prolong the kill, the tightness in my chest and neck would lie dormant for much longer. It's hard to believe it's been a year since then. I'm proud of myself for holding out this long, but I can't do it anymore. I have to relieve the pressure, and I've given up pretending that anything other than blood and agony can ease this precious ache.

I've staked out the house for almost a month. The dad is a cop, but I don't know if he's a good one or not. He looks like somebody who could be hiding a secret. That badge gives him power, and maybe he uses it in a way he shouldn't. The mom works at a bank. She wears the same gray suits every single workday, and she walks with her chin up and her chest poked out, like she's better than me. She makes my skin crawl. And then there's the kid. I don't like kids. There is something repulsive about them—the timbre of their voices, their wide, wondering eyes. He's nine or ten and goes to the same elementary school I went to when I was his age. He doesn't seem to hate the place like I did. He's always got some new thing to share or story to tell when his mom comes to walk him home every day at 3:30 PM. Maybe he doesn't have someone there every single day making him wish he'd never been born.

Dad's shifts are all over the place. He pissed somebody off at work, and for the past month he's been working fourteen-hour shifts instead of twelve. I know because his coworkers don't shut up about it on his days off. Their chatter over the police scanner is endless and annoying, and I wonder if he ever listens in the way I do. He is predictably absent.

The mom works a seven-to-three Monday through Friday. I watch her leave every day. I watch her come home every day. I rotate locations, so she doesn't catch on. It never fails to amaze me: people can be so unaware of their surroundings. They don't stop to think that someone might be watching, that with one small misstep they might put themselves in my path and by the end of the day they could by lying face down in a pool of their own blood. That is what happened with this stupid kid and his arrogant mother and his failure of a father. They strolled right past me on the boardwalk over a month ago. The mother got so close I could smell the sweat on her skin. It stirred that thing inside me, and now I know what I have to do.

Every Tuesday, Mom and Dad take the kid to a therapist, and when they return home, they don't wait until they're inside to talk about how the kid is learning to get a handle on his anxiety and how they're so very proud of him.

They treat the kid the way experts say he should be treated. They don't shun him for making up stories. They don't make fun of him for the things he says or what he feels. They got him some help. Good for him. Not everybody gets to have their mommy and daddy give a shit about what's keeping them up at night. They've tried therapy, but maybe what he needs to make him get his head together is a stiff backhand and a few evenings without food or water. I know I should be moved by the care and concern he's shown by the people who supposedly love him, but I'm not. All I feel is the pressure on my neck and the urge to do whatever I can to make it go away.

I took the bus to their neighborhood the day before, keeping the zip ties hidden in my pocket and the hunting knife well out of sight. I slept in the park two blocks from their house. Now, it's Wednesday. Dad went in late in the day, and that means he'll stay gone till much later. That leaves just Mom and the kid.

I watch the mom from across the street as she gets home and stomps up the sagging porch steps. She goes inside, changes her clothes, and walks to get the kid from school. This is their routine. I know it by heart. Thirty minutes and they're back. I have thoughts of starting early, but I push them aside. I have a plan, and it always works better when I stick to it. I need to be focused, disciplined. I wait until the dark is pulling itself across the sky before I cross the street and enter their backyard through the side gate, which is closed with a rusty latch that doesn't sit right in its cradle. I can easily lift it from the outside and slip inside.

The house is one of those cookie-cutter-type places. Every house on the street looks like a slightly different version of this one: one level over an in-ground basement, stucco exterior walls, an orange Spanish-tile roof, brick pathways, and an asphalt driveway. These houses were probably really nice once, but now they're all in various states of disrepair. They're still houses. Single-family houses, not shitty apartments with no heat and loud neighbors. Unfortunately, there are almost no trees on this street. No cover.

Beyond the gate, there's a square slab of concrete just outside the back door of the house, and on it is a set of chairs and a glass table with an umbrella sticking up out of the middle. There's one tree in the far corner of the overgrown yard.

I stand at the side of the house, just inside the gate but outside the range of the floodlight that is constantly lighting up their backyard. They never turn it off, which annoys me to no end. Do they know that turning off the light would make all of this easier? Are they doing it just to mess with me? My heart kicks in my chest. The pressure on my neck intensifies. I let my fingers dance over the handle of my knife. I want relief from the pressure. I want to be satisfied for as long as this kill will allow. I take a deep breath and sink down in the grass. Patience is something I have had to cultivate. The vise grip on my neck is driving me forward, but rushing means mistakes will be made. I've had two close calls since this began, and they both came about because I was impatient, impulsive; the relief from them was fleeting. No mistakes. Not now.

With my back pressed to the exterior wall, I can hear the muffled sounds of a TV—some kids show with a grating song repeated over and over.

Thirty minutes later there is a soft click as Mom unlocks the sliding glass door and slips out onto the patio to have a cigarette. She does this whenever she can, always when her husband is at work and her son is preoccupied.

I know your secrets. You can't hide them from me.

She smokes because she's one of those people who has trouble settling down. She's constantly on edge. Her husband hates the smoke. I hear him tell her he can smell it on her sometimes, and she denies it. She's a liar and not a very good one.

I don't move or breathe as I listen to her inhale the smoke and expel it in long, soft breaths. From my hiding spot at the side of the house, I can't see her, but I can imagine what she looks like there under the floodlight: average height, warm-brown skin, braids that she usually keeps piled on top of her head. She and her son share the same deep-set eyes, the same round face.

One big breath and another huff. A cloud of smoke wafts into view and lingers in the cool night air. I breathe in, and I can taste the mixture of tobacco smoke and her hot breath. A tapping sound tells me she's put the cigarette out and will probably take the butt inside with her. There are never any used cigarettes on the ground or in empty jars on the patio. No evidence left behind. She's almost as good at covering her tracks as I am, but her husband sometimes tells her he's found the sooty remnants of where she put the cigarette out. I guess that's the cop in him. He found the evidence of her smoking habit but didn't find any trace of me.

I hear the sound of the glass door rolling open, then closed again. No sound of the lock clicking. It's my lucky night after all.

I wait. I imagine her going inside, maybe settling down in front of the TV, the kid at her side. I've seen her do this before. She bottles up that nervous energy around him, probably tries to make him feel like there's nothing she can't handle. It is arrogance, the very same arrogance she displays when she struts around with her chin up.

I peer through the kitchen window. I can see the back of her head as she sits on the couch and flips through the channels. Her hair is long enough for me to wrap around my fist. The kid isn't with her yet even though I thought they'd be sitting together. Maybe she's not such a good mother after all. I catch sight of the kid tracing his hand along the wall as he comes down the hall in his stocking-covered feet. He walks heel to toe in a straight line. The lights in the hallway are on, and much like the floodlight outside, I've never seen them get turned off. Not even when I watched them in the small hours of the morning. Their bill must be sky high, but they don't seem to care. Must be nice having money to burn. I prefer the dark, but there is something in my gut that tells me they think these lights will keep them safe from me. It is a challenge I have willingly accepted, because I need them to understand that they cannot hide. The light will not chase me away.

The kid tiptoes into the living room, and balancing along the edge of the severe contrast of shadow cast by the couch, he joins his mother and leans his head against her shoulder.

In my head I know that seeing a young child sharing a tender moment with his mom should be touching in some way, but I feel nothing. I recall my own mother and how hard it was for her to look at me, let alone hold me next to her on the couch. She said I looked too much like my father and she hated him. The pressure around my throat tightens as the images flash in my mind.

The kid decides on a show, and he curls up amid a nest of blankets. I dig my fingertips into my forearm. This isn't what I want. Walking in under cover of dark won't be an option. They want this to be difficult for me. They think they are smarter than me, better than me. They are not.

Rocks litter the side yard—leftovers from the little stone wall that used to ring a garden long since strangled out by weeds. I palm a small, round one and chuck it across the yard. It smacks against the fence on the far side, and the kid's mom turns her head just slightly, angling her ear toward the noise. The television is on, and a laugh track drowns out the noise just enough for her to doubt what she heard. Frustration flows through me, but I tamp it down.

I pick up another stone, wait for a lull in the TV's babble, then send the stone flying. This time, Mom stands up, leaving the kid on the couch as she goes to the window. My plan is working.

She cups her hands around her face and leans close to the dining room window, which faces the back of the house. The floodlight illuminates the rear yard as she stares out.

I could let her see me. I could walk into the rear yard, into the light, and let her understand that this will be the last night of her life, but I restrain myself because that won't work. Too much time. Too many doors between us. She could slip away, and then I'd be on the run again, and the pressure on my neck would be more suffocating than it already is.

She pulls the curtains in the dining room. Mom says something to the kid, and he shakes his head no. As she stands there, hands on her hips, head tilting to the side, the kid gets up and skips into the kitchen. I duck away from the window for a moment, then slowly peek back through.

The mom has retaken her place on the couch. She reaches for her cell phone, then stops herself.

"You're overreacting," I whisper. "It's nothing. You're safe."

She puts the phone back on the table, and her shoulders rise up then slowly relax.

"That's right," I say under my breath.

The kid grabs a bag of chips from the pantry, standing on his tippy-toes to reach. Just as he's about to rejoin his mother in the living room, he stops and turns directly toward the kitchen window.

I stop breathing.

The lights are bright inside, but the area outside of the window is obscured by enough shadow to keep me hidden—at least I think it is. He shuts his eyes tight, and I duck under the window, my heart crashing inside my chest. Footsteps pad over to the kitchen window, and another light flickers on. The footsteps retreat.

After several minutes I slowly stand and peer through the window again. My heart is pumping, and the rush of blood in my ears is so loud. Mom pulls the groggy kid to his feet and nudges him toward the hallway, and he stumbles lazily into the bright light that never goes off. His mom takes his hand and leads him out of my line of sight.

I quickly move around the outside of the house, skirting the flood-light, and come up on the opposite side. Through a narrow window, whose shade is up just enough for me to look inside, I watch as Mom tucks the kid into bed. He smiles at her, and she touches his face. It makes me physically sick to see them this way. She's smothering him. He'll probably grow up to be just as disappointing as his father.

She leaves the room without turning off a single one of the kid's half dozen night-lights and only flicks off the daylight-bright bulb in the domed light in his ceiling. I grip the windowsill until my knuckles ache. I'm not here for the kid, but maybe I could be. Would two slow kills keep the grip on my neck at bay for even longer? I've never considered it, but here's an opportunity to test the theory. I can almost feel the relief flood through me as I imagine the light leaving her eyes with the kids' dimming soon after.

Several quiet moments tick by, and then he changes position, rolling dangerously close to the edge of the bed. One of his bare feet slips from beneath the blanket and dangles over the side. The kid jolts out of a nearly sound sleep and pulls his knees to his chest. He gathers the blankets around him and rocks back and forth glancing down at the floor.

The kid is afraid of the dark. Not just afraid—terrified.

I put my hand over my mouth to keep from laughing out loud. Stupid kid. There are much worse things to be frightened of. His mother didn't neglect him. His father didn't beat him. He wasn't left to fend for himself.

Pressure on my neck.

I sit my hand under the windowsill and press up just slightly. It doesn't budge.

The kid untangles himself from his nest of blankets and slowly slides from his bed, planting his feet firmly in the swath of pale blue light emanating from a night-light shaped like Captain America's shield. He stands there like a statue, barely breathing, his back toward the window.

I could grab him now if the window wasn't locked. I could get my hands around his throat before he had a chance to scream. But the kill would have to be quick. And that's not going to do me any good.

He takes one step toward the door.

Then another.

He keeps his feet in the wash of light like a gymnast on a balance beam. I wonder what happened to make him so fearful. Couldn't have been as bad as the things that have happened to me in the dark, and this kid has a mom who keeps every light in the house on for him. The kid should suck it up.

He tiptoes to the door and disappears into the hallway. A moment later he returns with a little plastic cup, filled to the brim with water. He gulps it down and wipes his mouth with the back of his hand. He goes to set the cup on his nightstand when suddenly, his trembling hand brushes the cup, and it tips over and bounces to the floor, rolling into the far corner of the room where the glow from the night-lights is obstructed by his chest of drawers. His entire frame goes rigid. He turns his head in that direction, and his mouth moves as if he's speaking. I narrow my gaze, trying to read his lips: *monster*.

"No," I say in a whisper. "Not there. At your window."

His mother abruptly appears in the doorway. Her gaze flits to him, to the shadowy corner, and then to the floor at her feet. She rushes to the kid and gathers him to her chest. They exchange words, whispers I can't hear, but his mouth makes that same shape.

After several moments, he calms, and his mother tucks him into bed. She leaves without retrieving the cup.

I slide down the outer wall and sit in the grass against the side of the house. I do not have time for this. I move around to the opposite side of the house and peer through Mom's bedroom window. She has shades, not curtains, and she's got them pulled halfway down. The lights in her room rival the kid's. She's got a collection of lamps of various shapes and sizes. A tall floor lamp with a gold base stands in the corner, casting a cone of light onto the ceiling. A bedside table cradles a small desk lamp with a dark green shade. The closet light is on. The bathroom lights are on. Every goddamned light is on. Even though the kid rarely ventures into her room after dark, it seems she keeps the lights on for him in there too. She treats him like some helpless infant. It's pathetic.

The mom climbs into bed and pulls a sleeping mask down over her eyes. A ripple of anger courses though me and coalesces into a tight ball in the center of my chest. Just cut off the fucking lights and stop making me play this game. I'm ready to relieve this terrible ache, and this woman, this sorry excuse for a mother, thinks she can get in my way? I imagine choking the life from her with my bare hands. I've never strangled anyone before. I wonder how that might feel.

I press up on the window and find it locked. Mom stirs, and I duck down again. I'm done watching and waiting. The pressure on my neck is suffocating. I need to relieve it. Now.

I return to the rear yard and stand in front of the sliding glass door. The wooden dowel that is supposed to be laying in the track is standing straight up. Mom forgot to lay it back down after her smoke. A pattern she repeats entirely too often. Grasping the handle, I slide the door open, lifting it slightly to alleviate some of the pressure on the track that runs along the jamb. It squeaks sometimes when the kid yanks it open. This way, it glides with only a faint rustle that is masked by the gentle flush of the AC kicking on inside.

After all these weeks of watching from the outside, now I'm inside for the first time. The grip of the invisible hand around my throat loosens just slightly. I breathe deep as a sense of calm washes over me. I'm right where I need to be.

I don't like the brightness—the lights, the off-white paint on the walls—it makes me feel exposed. It smells like vanilla air freshener, with some hint of whatever they had for dinner mingled in. I tread softly into the kitchen and try to flip off a light switch near the refrigerator. My fingers slip over the switch, and I realize there's a piece of clear tape holding it in the on position. A switch on the opposite wall is taped up in the same way. Anger bubbles up again, and I scratch away the tape and hit the switch. The light fixture over the dining room table flickers out.

I turn toward the hallway, but somewhere over my shoulder, from the newly darkened dining room, there is a sound. I glance behind me. There's nothing there. A light from a passing car casts a shadow across the floor under the table, and a wave of fear ripples through me. I pinch the skin on my forearm to distract myself.

Think of how good you'll feel when this damn pressure is off your neck.

I proceed down the hall, taking the knife from my pocket and holding it up in front of me. The kid's door is open, and he's sleeping soundly. His chest rises and falls in a slow, steady pattern. The knife is cool and heavy in my hand. I step toward his room. The suffocating pressure in my neck surges. This isn't the plan. Mom first. Kid last.

I gather myself and continue down the hall. Slipping into the mother's bedroom, I stand at the foot of her bed, watching her sleep. People are so vulnerable when they're sleeping. They're completely oblivious to the world around them. It's not fair. I never sleep so soundly.

Taking care not to make a sound, I move to the head of the bed and put my knife to the side of her neck. She stirs and reaches up to pull her sleeping mask away. This is the first time she's really seen me, but I've been watching her for so long it feels like we know each other.

"What—" She registers the knife. She tenses, glancing frantically down the hall.

"He's asleep," I say in a whisper. "I won't hurt him if you do what I tell you to do." It is a lie, and I think she knows that.

"Who are you?" she asks. "What do you want?"

"Does it matter?" I put my free hand on my neck. I just want to be free from this pain, and killing has been the only thing in the world that has helped. It's a curse, but it's the only way. I reach into my pocket and take out the zip ties. She doesn't struggle as I bind her wrists and ankles, but she pleads for her son.

"He's just a baby," she weeps. "Please. You—you're so young too. What's wrong? Can I help you? Is there anything I can do?"

"He's not a fucking baby even though you treat him like one," I say. "Shut up." I don't have time for this. I can feel the grip on my throat loosening. I'm almost free. With the knife in hand, I eye the targets, places where it can go deep that won't kill her immediately. This has to last if I'm to get any sense of peace.

From down the hall, a thud, then footsteps.

I slide the sleeping mask down, and it muffles the mother's pleas. Now she's struggling, and I can't keep hold of her. I try to grip her arms, but she kicks out with her bound feet and sends me careening into the side table. The lamps crash to the floor, the delicate bulbs shattering, their lights sputtering off. Pain rockets through my back.

"Oh no," the mother whispers through the makeshift gag. "No. No. No."

A rush of anger engulfs me—the lights? Fighting back? No. This is not the plan! She starts to hop toward the hall, but I cut her off, shoving her in the back. She can't keep herself balanced, and she falls into the dresser. Her head strikes the corner with a deliciously sickening crack, and she collapses into a heap on the floor, unconscious, blood staining the carpet.

I slam my hands against the wall and clench my jaw so tight it pops, sending pain creeping up to my temple. Everything is going to shit, and I know what that means for me: long nights on back roads, no sleep until I'm far away. No. No fuckups this time.

I can make this right. There's still time.

I grip my knife and stalk down the hall to the kid's room. My neck feels like it's in a vise. The pressure mounting behind my eyes makes me dizzy but eases just slightly when I see his form shrouded beneath the blankets on his bed.

I rush in and yank away the covers only to find his collection of stuffed animals. Crouching, I peer under the bed. He's got battery-powered night-lights illuminating the underside, but he's not there. I scramble to my feet as a hollow noise sounds from behind me. The kid's plastic cup skids out from under his dresser. It's dented on one side, and part of the lip is missing, leaving a jagged edge. I pause. I cannot take my eyes off the cup. What the fuck happened to it? I scan the shadowy corner of the room, then kick the cup away and move out into the hall. I have to get to the kid.

Down the hall, the lights are still blazing bright. My knife drawn, I come upon the kid, who's standing in the center of the living room. He's flipped on a switch, and a cone of clear, white light surrounds him like the beam of some alien craft ready to whisk him away. The bright lights are overwhelming, and I think of smashing the fixtures but stop myself. I don't want to chase the kid around.

I tuck the knife away and stand very still as the kid trembles. His Spider-Man pajamas are a size too big, and tears are streaming down his face. He's absolutely pathetic.

"Were you even going to try to hide?" I ask. "Or escape?"

He shakes his head.

"Well, that's no fun," I say. "Go. Go hide. It'll be a game. Look. I'll even cover my eyes." I put my hand over my face, but I can still see him between my fingers. He deserves another chance to hide—to at least feel like he did his best to save himself. He skirts around the coffee table and jumps into a square of light cast by a lamp in the far corner of the room.

I sigh and drop my hand. "Why are you so bad at this? Try harder." His inability to find a decent hiding spot stokes a wild rage in me. Does he not understand, or does he not want to do what I'm telling him? There's a coat closet; there's room under the dining room table that's also now shrouded in darkness, thanks to me. He could choose either one of those, but he doesn't.

The kid slides along the wall and stands stock still next to the open closet. I expect him to duck inside, but he just stands there, eyes wide and wet, mouth drawn into a quivering frown.

"Are you stupid?" I ask. "You must be the dumbest kid I've ever known."

His gaze darts from me to the space under the dining room table, then to the door that leads to the basement. My heart kicks up. Yes. Getting him down there will make this easier than it already is. There are no windows down there and only the one door.

I tense my body and flinch at him as he makes a break for the door. He throws it open and darts down into the dark. He must be terrified, seeing as he couldn't even sleep in his own room without his collection of night-lights and lamps.

"Daveed!" the mother's voice calls, hoarse and tinged with fear. "Daveed! Baby!"

"It's okay," I call out to her. She's restrained. She's injured. I'm not worried about her. "Don't mind us. We're playing a little game of hide-and-seek in the basement. It'll all be over soon."

"Don't! Don't go down there! He'll get you!" She stops short. Probably lost consciousness again. I can't help but laugh. The kid is probably too busy pissing his pants to take his mother's sound advice.

Closing the door behind me, I descend the basement stairs. The steep steps groan under me, and even still, I can hear the kid hyperventilating somewhere in the dark. "Don't be afraid," I whisper, gripping my knife. The pressure in my neck is already lifting. The anticipation of what is to come is like a high. I want this kill more than I've ever wanted anything.

As I reach the bottom step, I stop. The kid is standing in the middle of the neatly organized basement. Above his head a single light bulb washes him in a thready light, its long chain dangling so low it brushes against his shoulder.

"Another terrible hiding spot," I say. "I'm sorry you didn't do better."

I glance at the boy. I expect him to be crying, terrified, but he's looking at me like he feels sorry for me—a slight shake of his head as he holds himself around the waist.

"I'm not playing *your* game!" I scream at him. I'm so angry they've lured me into this—the lights, the running, the resistance. "*I* make the rules, not you!"

A rustling sounds from the far corner of the dank, dark space. I whip my head to look, half expecting to see someone standing there. "Who's down here with you?"

The kid doesn't answer. He doesn't even turn his head toward the sound, a sound that grows more defined as the seconds tick by—rhythmic, ragged . . . breathing.

I never encountered a fourth person is this miserable family in all my time watching them. Neighbors stayed away. Even friends and family kept their distance. There is no one else who should be here, and still. I have missed something. I have fucked up somewhere in my planning, and now I will have to adjust course again. Maybe I can make this three kills in one night. That would feed my demons and release this pressure on my neck for a good long time.

I hold my breath and try to quiet the rush of blood in my ears. I hold the knife out in front of me, pointing it into the corner of the room, where the darkness is complete. The dim light of the single bulb does nothing to penetrate the shadows around the edges of the basement, and I'm suddenly overwhelmed by the feeling of eyes on me.

The breathing ebbs, and I wonder if maybe the noises are coming from the boy. I spin around as the noise moves behind me. No, it can't be him. Fear grips my chest, and the little hairs on the back of my neck stand on end.

Something knocks my arm. The knife goes skittering across the floor, and I stumble back.

Outside, a car door slams. The kid's mother cries out, and then there is a flurry of footsteps and a man's voice—the father—from upstairs.

"Somebody broke in!" Mom screams. "He's in the basement with Daveed!" More shuffling upstairs.

My arm aches, and as I hold it up in front of me, I realize that when my knife fell to the floor, my hand was still gripping it, having been separated from my wrist so quickly that my brain could not process it. There should be pain, but I cannot comprehend that the ragged, bloody stump belongs to me.

The kid is smiling when I look at him. I want to scream at him for putting me in this position. "What—what is this?" I stammer. "What are you—who—what is this?!"

I stumble to the bottom of the stairs, still numb, still unable to feel the pain I know should be racking my mind and body, but fear has taken over and allows me nothing but dread. The kid's parents, Mom and Dad, are just standing at the top of the stairs.

"Oh no," the kid's father says. He sinks to his knees, his arms hanging loosely at his sides. The mother steps forward and puts her hand, a zip tie still hanging from her wrist, on the doorknob.

They don't rush me. Their expressions confuse me. Don't they want to save their son? I glance behind me to see the boy just standing there. He doesn't go to his parents. A cold, mind-numbing terror washes over me. They won't come down because they are afraid.

"Daveed, baby?" the mother calls, only the slightest tremble in her voice. "You got your flashlight?"

I look at the boy, unable to speak as grunting and shuffling echo from the shadows.

"Yes, ma'am," the kid says.

The mother sighs. "Stay in the light, baby."

I can't make my legs work. I can't take a single step. Blood gushes from my wound; flashes of light dance at the edges of my vision. The pain finally announces itself like a clap of thunder. I can't keep my body from spasming, bending my back until I'm looking at the ceiling from somewhere below my knees. In one terrible moment, the reality of what is happening falls on me: something has a hold of me. Its hands reach out of the shadows like tendrils unfurling. There is no more pressure on my neck. There will be a death, but it will not be this boy or his mother. I glance at him as something vital snaps in my back and my vision blurs from the sudden burst of pain. He reaches up and grasps the chain hanging from the lightbulb over his head. He yanks it down, and the darkness envelops me.

I lay on the floor as the thing from the shadows fills the darkness around me and begins to devour me. It slashes across my belly, spilling its contents across the cold concrete. The pain comes in like a wave, crashing over me, sucking the scream from my throat, stealing the breath from my lungs.

The last thing I see, before I'm lost to the dark and the tide of pain, is the kid. He's holding his flashlight over his head, and it shines down on him like a spotlight. He stays in the center of the beam as he ascends the stairs.

He was afraid of the dark, and now I understand why.

I am not the only monster lurking here in the shadows.

Be Not Afraid

by

Ashia Monet

I

You won't know her name. She is ageless and ancient, and as we speak, she is being buried alive for the third time.

Not to worry. She has grown accustomed to the sound of dirt dropping atop her coffin. She is used to her limbs feeling wound up tight, used to a sheet of darkness lying in front of her vision regardless of whether her eyes are open or shut.

When one is buried alive, sound is the only remaining sense. That is how she paints the image of what is happening above her when night turns to day and the congregation fills the church that she lies beneath, their feet landing heavy on the floorboards six feet above her head.

She can hear the organs, the chatter. But the other senses she has to imagine: the scent of the incense, the smell of the bodies sweaty from working beneath the southern sun, the taste of the communion wafer.

She can imagine him, too, the man of God who stands at the front, holy and heavy in his priestly robes. From his voice she paints an image of him in her minds' eye. She has seen his face so many times, his image is nearly seared onto her eyes. It is a face she knows well and a face that makes her mind buzz, as if filled with flies.

His was the first face she saw when she arrived here.

II

She first arrived at God's Glory Church in the middle of the night, about three years ago now. She has not aged since then—she has not aged in a very, very long time—so she looked then almost as she looks now: small, with loose coils of hair and soil-brown skin, in a hand-me-down dress stained deep brown with blood. She walked in because she was cold and the church was warm.

The priest's hair was threaded gold. His was a face of sharp angles and eyes wild with intelligence and passion. He regarded her with indifference.

He'd been cradling his palm, bloody, in his other hand. Dropped at his feet were a bloody letter opener and an envelope.

"This place isn't for your folk," he said. "I think you're looking for the Episcopal down the street . . ."

It was not her voice that interrupted him, because she did not speak. His attention turned to his palm because his skin was healing itself.

He watched his flesh patch itself over as if the injury had never occurred. When he looked up at her, his eyes were wide, as wide and as blue as the ocean.

A man of God knows a miracle when he's been sent one.

III

The priest cleaned her up and dressed her in a white smocked dress that was too small, perhaps meant for someone else's daughter.

He coaxed her to sit beneath the altar, hidden behind the cloth that fell like a curtain to the milky-white tile. She tucked her knees in tight. She wrapped her arms around herself. She just wanted to be warm.

Her nose and her ears were the only sensors that remained useful. She heard the priest stand at the foot of the altar stairs, about a stone's throw away from where she lay. She heard him lift a knife, could smell the blood as he cut open his palm.

"Dear God," he whispered when the scent of blood had gone from the air.

The priest left her there, curled up and hidden in God's house. She was alone in that place with its tolling stillness. If she squinted very hard, she could see through the altar cloth. Then she could make out the illustrated faces on the stained glass, hundreds of eyes watching her in uncaring silence. This went on for hours. She was very cold.

When the priest returned, he returned with a flock of life, of noise. She was hypnotized by the music, by the warmth that filled the building, which had felt almost corpse-like in its silence. The church, it seemed, only came alive when bodies filled its pews.

She wanted to drink it down her throat.

That first sermon, the priest's voice trembled as if he, too, were nervous for what was about to transpire. She smelled the blood as he cut and raised his palm before the crowd. The congregation gasped as the flesh healed. A woman shouted; demands were made, confusion turning into stunned amazement.

"Bring me your weak," he told them. "Bring me your lame, your broken. Through the power of Christ, I will make them whole."

Behold the power of the Lord.

IV

The priest called her the angel. He did not ask her name, nor did he give one to her.

Many of his people spoke of how they considered the church their home. She would, too, she supposed, if she saw any of it. Her home was beneath the altar, behind the cloths that shifted with the seasons.

Everything in the church changed shape and color over time, except for her. She did not need to eat nor relieve herself in restrooms. She could sit beneath that altar like another piece of furniture and the priest was content to leave her—and treat her—as such.

Only once was she ever introduced to someone. One evening, the fabric was suddenly raised by the priest. Behind him was an old man, wrinkling his nose. Later she would recognize his footsteps as those that went around sweeping, cleaning, and changing the lights.

His voice was like crunching gravel. "Where did it come from?"

"Don't matter," said the priest.

The old man did not believe an angel would choose a body, a form, that looked like hers.

"God works in mysterious ways; it is not to question," said the priest. "'Be not afraid,' the angel Gabriel says. Perhaps this appearance is why."

The priest explained that the congregation would not understand. To keep from frightening them, she was to stay hidden as the priest channeled the power of the Lord to his people.

The language was dizzying to her: from the metaphors to the quotes to the meanings piled upon alternative meanings. It was difficult to piece together why people kept coming and going, coming and going. Healing neither drained nor hurt her. She could feel nothing when the priest's "miracles" transpired; she relied entirely on the reactions of the churchgoers to help her understand.

A sister brought her younger brother, who'd sprained his arm, and he raised it high when it straightened, whole again. A wife helped her husband inch his broken leg toward the priest. He nearly ran down the aisle when it was healed, knocking over one of the candlesticks. The most dramatic of all was the woman who burst in, halting the Ave Maria, crying in the middle of the aisle. She'd been cured of cancer, she explained.

That was when the congregation began to grow too large for the church to contain. Money poured in from tithes, overflowing in the golden buckets that were passed around until folded bills peaked over their edges, floating to the floor.

From the opening and closing church doors, the girl would get glimpses of large vans outside. Well-dressed women with microphones stood in front of cameras with wide lenses, gesturing toward the church. She heard a certain phrase more than once: *the home of miracles.*

The priest had made headlines. She knew because when she stuck her head out—as she was wont to do when the church was empty and quiet—she saw a paper discarded in the pew that the old man had not yet cleaned away. On the front page, the priest had his arms raised high, to heaven.

New faces began to arrive, with different features. Sometimes with darker hair, sometimes not; sometimes rich and sometimes poor. But always, the girl noticed, fair skinned like the priest and the old man. None that at all resembled her.

Time went on in this way. Her body was growing stiff, and her mind was growing tired. One night, when darkness fell and all life had drained from the church again, she left in search of someplace better than this building that had begun to bore her.

Soon her wandering mind and feet brought her to the vast, emerald greenery of a park. Though there were chittering squirrels and singing birds, more interested was she in the small scatterings of people. Best of all, there was warmth.

She sat, removed from prying eyes, hidden in a small thicket of trees and bushes, her bare feet dug into the dirt. No more haunting quotes. No more statues. No more candles. Just the warmth she could drink in with her eyes, watching these mortals live.

Then there was a shout. Then there was the old man.

He snatched her to her feet. He dragged her from the park. A picnicking family looked twice but turned away as the old man tossed her into the back of a dark car. He drove so quickly the trees outside blurred. The vehicle only stopped when the tall steeples of the church loomed in front of the windshield.

The priest berated her as she knelt before him. It was the second time he'd spoken to her.

He paced, each footstep landing heavier than the last. His voice shot into her ears like spears. "An angel exists only to do good, to proclaim God. What more could you need than what is already here?"

A vessel. A tool. An angel.

V

They tied her under the altar with heavy silver chains. Cold. She hated the cold. She shifted her bones around inside her skin until the ropes slid loose, and she slid free.

They dragged her back.

This time they nailed her to the floor by her hair. She shifted form into something that did not need a scalp and returned to her thicket in the park, leaving her hair behind.

They dragged her back.

The priest and the old man were growing frustrated with her slipperiness. They called her names she could not discern the meaning of, names they did not call each other. Names that were meant to be degrading.

This time when they shoved her back beneath the altar, they began to discuss in harsh, sharp tones what to do. "The Lord said, 'Be not afraid,'" the priest was saying. "You must trust him; you must believe him."

Words could be very powerful, she had realized. After all, those were the words the priest used to convince the old man to bury her.

She heard the floorboards crackle like logs of firewood as the old man snapped them up. She heard the shifting of the earth as his shovel dug and dug, heard the old man's grunts of effort as he traveled farther and farther into the dark world beneath.

The priest watched silently as the old man wrestled her from her hiding spot and tossed her into the coffin. When the lid was shut and the world was lost to her eyes, she heard the heavy, thudding sound of nails being driven into the lid.

This, ironically, was familiar to her. Not the worship, not the language of the church, not the brutality, but this, the desperate burying, as if she were something to be locked away. Though she'd never been buried for *this* reason before, she'd faced a similar fate due to other motivations. Fear, yes. A misunderstanding of what *immortal* meant, yes as well. Perhaps this small novelty is what satiated her, what made her lie still as they piled dirt on top of her and replaced the floorboards as if a girl had not disappeared here.

And she listened, still, when the church came alive as the priest stood atop her and worked his miracles—her miracles.

The whole cycle was beginning to bore her, but the being buried alive and forced to perform miracles bit, that was intriguing. How long, she wondered, would they leave her here? When the priest and the old man died and she was still here, would they have initiated others in their place? Or would she be forgotten, the memory of her disappeared along with their fleeting lives?

She was pondering these many, flowing thoughts when she heard the church swell into an uproar. Shouting, demands being made, and words thrown—words the girl recognized as the same words the priest and old man had called her earlier.

"Please, please," a voice begged. It trembled across the words, desperation clinging to each strangely accented syllable. "It's just that—the doctors don't know what's wrong. I'm the only one in my family who can work, and I can't be sick, I just can't—"

The masses overpowered the person's pleas. The same insults were delivered just as sharply above a begging, a shouting, a crying that became quieter and quieter as the person was driven from the church.

The church moved on. The girl did not.

She had not realized they treated others as they treated her. She thought they knew what she was, hence their rudeness. She thought, perhaps, they had invented things to call a monster such as her. But to call another breathing mortal such vile words? To treat them, someone who had spoken so desperately, so imploringly, as the monster she was? She had never heard anyone in the church speak with an accent such as that. And she had never, not once, healed a person with skin as dark as the skin of the human figure she used.

Something broke in her like a dam.

And now,

Now.

VI

She closes her eyes and presses on the coffin above her until her bones begin to crack. Her shoulders first dislocate and multiply beneath her skin, sprouting into two limbs, then four, six, eight. Then she opens the skin along her limbs until all her eyes pop open, lined like goosebumps up her multiplying legs, up the many arms birthing from her torso. All of her looking upward, to freedom.

She presses and presses until dirt fills the coffin, fills her rows upon rows of waiting, hungry mouths and teeth that swallow the dirt. The mouths across her neck and face work the quickest, moving like starving animals, moving pounds and pounds of dirt down her many throats. The dirt tries to close in on her, but she is too large, too fast. Her body swells and grows until the wooden planks of her coffin bend and then burst, too full of her. And her body grows still, clearly no longer something that can be called a girl. Her now hundreds and hundreds of limbs swell upwards, all-seeing with thousands of eyes—cracking, finally, through the floorboards of God's Glory Church.

She rises through the floor, shattering the pews and the massive organ beneath her. Now she can breathe, now she *is*—though *what* she is truly is sinew and limbs that whisper of an ancient, forgotten power.

Beneath her head that sits somewhere near the ceiling, the candlelight ebbs and sways across her form, which slithers in the shadows, crushing the church beneath its weight.

She has taken on a form that is not meant for mortal eyes. And the whole church screams.

Behold. *Behold.*

She catches the congregants who try to run first, sweeping them up in her tentacles and crushing their bodies like berries in a toddler's palm. Blood spills to the floor. And they scream and scream and scream, a symphony emphasized by pews and bones snapping in half.

There are no survivors. Of course there aren't. This is a massacre. This is a rapture.

Ahead of her, at the altar, the priest and the old man—so tiny now, so insignificant beneath her—crane their necks back to behold her, gone white as the sheets they wear.

The priest gapes silently, stumbling backward as her tendrils pry the old man apart, reveling in the warmth—finally warmth—of life, of thought, of the capacity only mortals have, to love. Every wound he has ever sustained opens back up; every cut reappears; every bruise marks his skin black again. His bones snap out of place; his nose breaks again; his left eye blackens. She drinks him whole until he is a husk, something gasping and frail but not dead yet.

And the priest.

The priest.

Cosmic energy sparks and splits, and it feels like the entire earth has been made bare and screeching before this priest, as if universes are dying and lighting in her multitude of ravenous eyes. She is nothing short of rapture.

She moves toward him. He scrambles back, chest heaving. He is sweating. His mouth trembles as he beholds her.

"But," he begins. "But you are an angel."

Her mouths open. She speaks her first words. "No," she says from her many throats. "You named me that."

She spears him through his chest, then five times through his arms, legs, and finally through his stomach and drinks him down until she feels him in the pit of her stomachs, warm, warm, warm.

And she feasts on it all—his memories, his pain, his hopes, his beliefs, his suffering—drinks it, drinks it, drinks it. She is nowhere near full—she could devour universes and never be full—but his body has withered, the skin plastered to the bone with no muscle left, the eyes rolled free from their sockets, the hair turned gray, and so she discards him atop a broken pew.

And when this is done, she folds herself up small, in her pretty, brown, four-limbed body, with its spiral dark curls, in her old, stained dress.

She goes walking. She moves barefoot through the dirt to find somewhere warm, some other town where, perhaps, they will know better than to think her an angel.

Leaving this place means very little to her. After all, this church is no longer warm.

All My Best Friends Are Dead

by

Liselle Sambury

After

Something is wrong with us.

There's a silence at our table of four, made more obvious by the buzz of the cafeteria. The sounds bounce off the white brick walls and the dotted ceiling squares with sharpened pencils stuck in them and stop short of where we sit, like there's something physical separating us from everyone else.

It's been like this since the sleepover.

And every day it gets worse. I come out of class, and no one is waiting for me to walk together to the next one. Our group chat is basically dead. And everyone's solution is to say nothing.

Finally Nova stops scrolling on her phone and looks around at us. Her newly dyed black hair is pulled behind her ears and makes her already pale-white skin look even paler. I tense and play with the ends of my braids to try and look casual, like I'm not ready to hang off her every word. "I think that I'm going to stay with my dad until graduation."

"What the fuck?" It slips out of my mouth before I can stop it. Nova's dad lives five hours away. She would have to switch schools. Besides, we're only sophomores—she would be gone for *two years*. Maybe even more if she ended up really liking the place.

Vicky puts down the chopsticks she was using to pick at the Korean side dishes her mom packed for her. I turn to her, expecting a joke that doesn't come. Her voice is flat when she says, "No, but actually, what the fuck?"

"I've been talking with my therapist—" Nova starts to say before Lea cuts in.

"About?" Lea says carefully, closing the bio textbook she was clearly using more to avoid conversation than to study. Her tight curls are pulled back from her face, and her eyes are at attention behind her oversized glasses.

"About the fact that we had a sleepover a month ago, and I can't remember any of it, and I feel fucked up now. She thinks the move may be good for me."

I swallow and look around at the others.

Lea presses her fingers to her temple. Her edges are wild and free. I like mine like that, but she usually slicks hers down. It's like she can't be bothered anymore. "It's not that serious. Why would you move?"

"Isn't it?" Nova pushes.

"Your mom is fine with that?" I ask. There's no way. This is too extreme.

She shrugs. "My dad always bugs her about wanting more time with me, and she's busy with her own stuff. It's just a couple years."

No.

I can see it already: Nova moving. Lea leaning into her study groups and away from us. Vicky spending more time at volleyball and less time hanging out. And where will that end?

With just me.

The new girl who no one wants to hang out with.

Alone.

Again.

I grasp onto Nova's hand and she flinches. I blink at her. We used to do things like this all the time, but now it's strange and alien.

"Sorry," she mutters. "You just . . . just surprised me."

I feel her trying to tug her fingers away, but I keep a hold of them and meet her eyes. "We should do something together. Like, you can all come over to my house again." I jerk my eyes around the table from one girl to the next. Both Lea and Vicky avoid my gaze. "We haven't hung out in forever. And if Nova . . ." I pause to swallow, not wanting to say the words. "If Nova is leaving, we should do something."

We haven't actually spent any time together since that day, not outside of school. Maybe if we did, Nova would be reminded of everything she would be leaving behind. Maybe the girls would remember how we used to be. It could fix everything.

The bell rings.

Everyone stands like the conversation is over.

I grab onto Lea's jean jacket and hold her in place. The others continue on without us. Maybe they haven't even noticed that we're not following. She looks at their retreating backs and then at my hand, still curled in denim of her jacket. "Come on, Maddie. Let's go."

I try not to sound desperate. "If you tell them the sleepover is a good idea, they'll listen. This could be really great for us, don't you think?"

Lea was the one who first reached out to me when I was new at school. She complimented my braids, and we ended up talking about the best ways to make the style last and our favorite products. And because she brought me in, the other girls accepted me. It would be the same with this.

"At your house?" Lea doesn't look at me as she speaks.

It could be at any of our houses, anywhere really. But I do want it to be at mine. I don't know what went wrong last time, but it was supposed to be my chance to show I belonged with them. And I can't pretend that I don't want to make up for it.

But I would give up that chance if it meant the girls would hang out with me. "It can be anyone's house. I don't mind."

A shout rings out in the room as two boys fight over a girl's hand mirror, yelling, "Brenda Butterfingers!" as the girl laughs and barely tries to rescue her mirror.

When I turn back to Lea, she's finally looking at me. "Let's do your house. I'll talk to them." I grin and throw my arms around her, pulling her close to me.

It's like hugging a block of concrete.

Before

Everything had to be perfect.

On the kitchen island, I laid out the paper plates and cups I'd gotten from the party store downtown. They were black with crystal designs. I stared at them for a moment. It looked like I was decorating for an elementary school birthday party. None of the other girls did this much when we went to their houses. They didn't "prepare."

I swept the matching dishes off the table and shoved them in the back of one of the new white cupboards. We could use regular plates and cups and be careful with them. They were brand new sets, just like everything else in the house.

It was completely renovated from top to bottom. All the shitty furniture that used to pack our apartment was sold off. Now that Mom was Mrs. Harrison and I was Mr. Harrison's stepdaughter, we could afford it. It was like I'd become a whole new person. A better one.

Now I could actually stand to have my friends come over. It only had taken a couple seconds in Lea's perfect two-story house to realize that we weren't the same. Vicky had joked that her house was a dump, but she had a pool. And I still remembered how Nova had reacted when she'd learned that I lived in an apartment: "That's so cool! I've never been inside of one!" It was just another way that I didn't fit in with them.

It made me want to fucking die.

But now things were different. I wasn't going to just be the new girl they were nice enough to let into their group. I would be one of them.

The doorbell rang, and I rushed out of the kitchen to the entryway where Mom and Glenn were standing arm in arm as she opened the door. She was in this sparkling sequin dress with a slit up the side, and he was in a full-on suit. Ready for their every-other-Friday date-night thing they did.

Mom smiled at Vicky, Lea, and Nova. "Your friends are here! We'll be back late." She gave me a wink that was mortifying. I glanced at the girls to see their reactions, but they were smiling. I forced out a laugh.

"Have fun, girls," Glenn said. The fade in his hair was immaculate, and his teeth were whiter than our cabinets.

They left and I released a breath.

Vicky walked in first. Her hair was pulled up in her signature ponytail, the dark strands long and glossy. "Dude," she said. "Your parents are hot."

"Agree!" Nova cackled, following after Vicky. It was strange to see her without the dark winged eyeliner and bright lipstick she wore to school. Instead, her face was bare and dewy looking.

Lea came in last. She'd gotten braids put in last week and wore them in a bun on top of her head. It was perfect, nothing out of place. She rolled her eyes at her friends. *Our* friends. "Don't be weird." She smiled at me. "Ignore them. Where are we sleeping?"

I was once again glad for Lea. Not just for bringing me into the group but for helping me fit in. "We'll stay in my room."

I led them upstairs into my bedroom. It was my first time getting to pick the wall color. We weren't ever allowed to paint our apartments and always got stuck with faded pink or off-white. I'd chosen an earthy green for three of the walls and black for the last one. I'd hung up string lights in the shape of stars and dozens of prints of constellations, not to mention a shit ton of plants. I'd bought them all yesterday since I didn't actually know how to take care of them and figured they'd die fast, but they looked perfect for tonight. Then I'd decorated my dresser and desk with crystals and a bunch of random candles and candle holders and teacups I'd gotten from a thrift store and spray-painted black. The final touch was the photos of us, hung up next to the dangling fairy lights.

Nova looked around and said, "Very witchy. I like it."

"Thanks," I said, making my voice sound breezy, like it didn't matter what she thought. Like I hadn't spent hours, days really, arranging and rearranging everything.

"Who do I have to kill to get a pizza?" Vicky whined, turning to me. "You ordered one? Right?"

"Yeah, should be here soon." I even timed it so it would come thirty minutes after everyone got here. "I thought maybe we could do something fun before that."

Lea raised an eyebrow and Nova grinned. Vicky collapsed onto my
bed. "Pizza is fun . . ."

"Shut up, Vicky," Nova said. "What is it?"

"I don't know if you all know this . . . but this house, well . . . Brenda
Butterfingers used to live here." I dropped my voice to a dramatic whisper.
"She died here too."

Lea and Nova exchanged a look. "We know," Lea said.

"Everyone knows," Vicky said from her spot on the bed.

"Oh." Right. Of course. It wasn't like this was a huge town. I was the
new one. And even then, it hadn't taken long for the Brenda Butterfingers
story to get to me—about the girl whose fingers "slipped" and dropped a
knife that fell into her friend and killed her. Really, she was just some sad
girl who quickly became the odd one out when her bestie made a new set
of friends. It was very "If I can't have you, no one can." But someone gave
her a creepy rhyming name and now she was a local legend.

I shouldn't have been that surprised that the girls knew this was her
house. It was fine. I could still make this work.

"I'm not doing that mirror bullshit, by the way," Lea said, shaking her
head. "In case that's where this is going."

"Why?" Nova whined. "It's fun! And it's not real anyway."

Vicky sat up and grinned at Lea. "You're not scared, are you? I thought
your biggest fear was getting a B."

Lea crossed her arms. "Firstly, I would never be afraid of getting a B
because I would never get one. And secondly, I'm not scared. I'm offended.
Saying Brenda Butterfingers in the mirror three times is an obvious rip-
off of both Bloody Mary *and* Candyman."

Trying to get back into the conversation, I said, "It does fit though!
At the crime scene, they found a bunch of mirrors smashed. Apparently,
Brenda couldn't stand to look at herself after what she did."

"I heard it was because she was like super ugly and hated her reflection. Isn't that why she killed the friend? Because she was really pretty?"
Nova said.

"See?" Vicky said to Lea. "There's mostly relevant backstory for the
mirror."

Lea sighed. "Whatever. So, we're doing the same mirror thing everyone does?"

And then they all turned to look at me. I realized that they were waiting for what I had to say. I was running the show, and they were my captive audience.

"We're not going to do the mirror thing." I said, a grin stretching my lips as wide as they could go. "But we are going to summon her."

After

The girls drop their overnight bags on the floor of my room with dull thuds. We stand around, not doing or saying anything. It's somehow more awkward than Mom making a big deal out of them coming back for a visit when she and Glenn left. It had only been a month since the first sleepover, but it felt like forever. Maybe Mom picked up on that.

I notice that each of the girls sits beside their bag, like they want to be ready to leave at any moment. Nova pulls out her phone and starts looking at something on it. Vicky picks at the callouses on her hands. And Lea sighs, looking over at me expectantly.

I had hoped that maybe she would help lead this. But instead, it seems like it's going to be up to me. I play with the ends of my braids and shift from foot to foot before saying, "Um, what does everyone want to do?"

The girls don't reply, though Nova looks up from her phone and Vicky stops picking at her skin. They first look at each other and then at me.

"We could order pizza?" I look over at Vicky who I expect to get excited at the prospect of food, but she's frowning at the floor. "Or we could watch a movie or—"

"Let's play truth or dare," Nova says suddenly, smiling up at me.

Lea throws her a sharp look.

Vicky freezes. Just . . . goes still.

"What?" Nova shrugs and meets Lea's gaze. "I'm making a suggestion because, for once, you seem to have nothing to say."

I look between the two of them. I don't want any arguments. This is supposed to be about us making up and fixing whatever broke us. I'm not excited about truth or dare, but Nova actually suggested something, so I'm not going to say no. I'm happy to do whatever they want to do.

"Fine," Lea grinds out between her teeth. "Truth or dare?" she asks Nova.

"Dare, obviously."

"Let me pick the dare," Vicky says, finally looking up. Her voice is flat. "I'm better at them."

Lea's eyes dart over to me and then to Nova and Vicky. "Okay . . ."

"Okay!" I say, smiling. I don't want this to be awkward. I want it to be fun. I want us to have a good time.

Vicky nods, pleased with the approval. She says, "I dare you to say Brenda Butterfingers in the mirror three times."

The smile slides off my face.

"Vicky," Lea snaps. "What the fuck?"

Vicky turns to Lea, and suddenly she's angry too. Her face is tight. It's like her ponytail, which I now notice is pulled so taut that it almost seems like it's yanking on her scalp, stretching her face back. "What? You said I could pick. That's my dare."

Nova glares at Vicky. "That's a lot for a starting dare, don't you think?"

"I think it'll be fun," she says, her lips pulling into a small smile.

"Lea!" I say, willing my voice not to sound as frantic as I feel. "You do me instead."

"Nova hasn't done hers," Vicky says, and we ignore her. I don't know why she's being like this. Usually she's the laid back one: you feed her and she's happy.

Lea swallows. "Truth or dare?"

"Truth!" I say immediately. Lea never gives upsetting truths or dares. She throws softballs.

Lea licks her lips. They're dry. Her skin too. Ashy, like she's been forgetting to moisturize. "Do you really not remember anything from last time?" she asks.

We never talked about what we did or didn't remember. We just settled on the fact that none of us remembered anything. I wonder if she's asking because she knows something. But then, why not just tell us?

"No," I say. "I know that you all came to my house for the sleepover. But then . . . I just remember us waking up. And we went downstairs and had breakfast."

Silence fell in the room.

"That was too easy!" I laugh, forcing the tension away. "I want to do Nova's dare. I dare you to flirt with whoever comes to deliver the pizza. But it's gotta be, like, really heavy handed."

Nova grins; I ignore how her lips twitch at the corners, like she's fighting to do it. "Okay, but like, if I get their number, you all owe me something."

"We have to find something sexy of Maddie's for you to wear," Lea adds, and she starts rooting through my closet with Nova. I move to join them, but eyes on my back stop me, and I turn around.

Vicky is just sitting there. Staring at me.

When I look back at Lea and Nova, they're practically half-inside my closet, muttering something to each other too quiet for me to hear. Nova spots me watching them and says, "Just making a game plan for the dare."

Why would they whisper about that? And why not wait until I came over? It was my dare.

My face flushes. We're all friends. *We are.* It's okay that they've known each other longer. I'm still part of the group. And this will work. We'll be close after, like before. The Brenda dare was just a little hiccup. They're not edging me out. There's no fucking way that they would do that.

I go over and help lay out some potential outfits for Nova to wear. We're still deciding on the options when Lea says, "We should take a picture." She motions to my Instax camera. I always forget that I have it. It was one of those things that I wanted when everyone was getting them but then, once I had one, it kind of felt like the hype had already died.

Vicky jumps to her feet before I can. "I'll get it!" She grabs the camera, but instead of bringing it over, she says, "What is this?" There's a photo in the palm of her hand, but I missed where it came from. It must have been under the camera or something.

I blink at her. "What?"

Lea is the first to go investigate. She peers over Vicky's shoulder, then gasps. There's something about her gasp that digs at me—like it's too over the top or something.

"Okay, now I have to see this." Nova joins them, taking the small polaroid between her fingers, then whispers, "Holy shit."

I know that I should be going to them, should be wanting to see what they're all looking at. But somehow, I stay glued in place, not moving. This feels . . . I don't know . . . off? I don't want to look, though there's no reason not to.

"Maddie," Lea says, turning around and holding out the photo to me. I swallow and reach out, accepting it. I stare at the tiny picture.

It's us. We're wearing different outfits, but we're in my room, and Nova is holding the camera for the selfie.

Nova, Lea, Vicky, me . . . and another girl.

A girl I've never seen before.

Before

The doorbell rang and I jumped to my feet, taking the stairs two at a time. We hadn't even gotten to start the Brenda ritual yet! The delivery was early. So much for sticking to customer requests.

Vicky was hot on my heels, and as I grabbed the pizza from the guy, she swept in to take the boxes of wings and the plastic bag full of pop. "Yessssss, I am so starving."

I rolled my eyes at her. "You can take it all up to my room. I'll grab the plates and cups."

We met back in the bedroom where we sat in a circle on the giant floor rug.

"So, what are we doing for this summoning?" Vicky asked around a slice of pepperoni. "Like, Ouija board or something?"

I shook my head. "That's so cheesy."

The girls laughed, and I sat a little straighter. They had all been together for so long, since they were in kindergarten. They were used to ripping on each other, so why shouldn't I join in? Like I was always part of the group instead of just the girl who showed up last year.

"We should know the whole plan and what each of us has to do and if there are any, like, side effects," Lea said.

Nova groaned. "Oh my God, Lea."

"Um, maybe you're unfamiliar because of your blue-eyed, Caucasian final-girl status, but some of us would die first in a horror movie and want to know what we're getting into."

Vicky added, "I probably wouldn't even be cast in a Hollywood slasher, so we're already breaking the mold."

"See? We're clearly operating with inclusive horror movie rules," Nova said. "Equal dying opportunity."

"No one is going to die," I assured them, though I didn't think they were being serious. Vicky was never serious, for one. And I knew for a fact that Nova thought ghosts were bullshit. Lea, I was sure, just wanted to take control of the situation and mom it, which I didn't mind.

"Let's do it now," I said. "I'll show you. Just let me grab some things." They'd barely nodded their agreement before I was racing down to the kitchen and returning with a box of salt in my arms and a small knife stuck in my back pocket. "We'll need to move the pizza and stuff."

The girls stopped eating—Vicky very reluctantly—and we moved the boxes to my bed. I unplugged the fairy lights and gave each of them a candle. I pushed back the fuzzy white rug on the floor to expose the hardwood and brought the standing mirror into the middle of the room.

I said, "Everyone move and form a circle in front of the mirror, kind of as if the mirror is part of the circle."

They did as I directed, and I lit their candles, then my own, which I gave to Lea to hold while I sprinkled salt around the mirror and us. The girls were quiet but in a way that felt like anticipation.

I turned off the main light and left us in the dark. Now we only had the candles, whose fire made it look like shadows were flickering across the room.

Vicky made an "ohhh" sound and giggled.

"Shh!" Lea said, but she was laughing too.

Nova grinned and rolled her eyes.

They were enjoying it! I could tell. Meanwhile, I tried to be serious and ominous, which made them giggle more, just like I'd hoped it would. "Okay," I said, stepping into my part of the circle. "Now we drip the wax onto the mirror."

I beckoned the girls forward, and we each tried with varying degrees of success to get it on the mirror. It wasn't perfect, but it was good enough. I pulled the knife out of my pocket.

"Is that really necessary?" Lea asked, looking from the blade to me and back.

I faltered for a moment, but I could tell from Vicky and Nova's faces that they were loving it. "It's just to write her name," I said and carved BRENDA into the wax.

Vicky tilted her head. "Not a lot of room to put 'Butterfingers.'"

"That's not her real name, asshole," Nova quipped.

"Now," I said. "We have to be quiet and join hands, and I'll ask Brenda if she wants to talk to us."

I put the knife back into my pocket, and we all held hands. I put my right hand on the mirror to complete the circle and Lea reluctantly did the same with her left. She eyed me and said, "You know our ancestors are rolling in their graves watching us do this, right?"

"The original instructions wanted us to put our blood on the mirror, so I've actually made it safer."

Lea sighed. "Fine."

I shushed everyone again. "We call on the spirit of Brenda, who once resided in this house. If you wish to communicate with us, please step into the mirror. We invite you to speak with us."

We waited a moment in silence, but nothing happened.

I repeated the words.

Again, nothing.

"Bust!" Vicky shouted and we let go of our hands.

It was fine. I didn't really expect anything to happen. I just wanted to do something they would think was fun and cool. I shrugged and flicked the lights back on. "We can eat now."

"Picture first!" Nova grabbed the Instax camera from my vanity, and we posed.

Just as we were finishing, I glanced back at the mirror. There was a tiny crack in it that hadn't been there before.

I walked forward, and as I went to touch it, it cracked again and sliced the tip of my finger. "Shit!" I pulled my hand back, watching as a bead of blood stuck to the mirror.

"Okay, that's actually kind of creepy," said Vicky with a nervous laugh.

Lea squinted, adjusting her glasses on her face. "It's probably just, like, heat settling or something. The candle wax we threw on it must have messed it up."

Before anyone could get a chance to respond, the entire mirror shattered.

After

When I look up from the photo, they're all staring at me. I can't guess what they're thinking, but I know that it looks weird that I have this picture that none of us can remember taking with this girl who we don't know.

She's Black with her hair in braids, like mine, but she's added little metal jewels to them.

"Why didn't you mention that you had this?" Vicky says, her voice low.

I shake my head. "I've never seen this before. If I had, I would have said something." I hadn't touched that camera since the last sleepover.

"This is so fucked up," Nova says suddenly, shaking her head. "How could we forget an entire person?"

"Maybe when my mom gets back, we can ask her how many girls she remembers coming by that day?"

"Why not call her now?" Nova pushes.

"It's date night. They both turn their phones off."

"What if it's an emergency?"

"Then I'm supposed to call my aunt, and she'll take care of it." I shrug because I don't know what else to do. "Maybe we can brainstorm or something about who she could be?"

Vicky says, "Maybe she's Brenda Butterfingers . . ." It should be a joke, but she doesn't change the tone of her voice at all.

"Ha ha," I say, but no one laughs.

"For fuck's sake, Vicky," Lea mutters, shooting a glare at the other girl. "I can't be in this room right now." And then she leaves.

Just walks out of the room.

Nova follows her.

Vicky too.

And it's just me.

Alone.

My mouth opens and closes, but I don't know what to yell after them. What am I supposed to say? Clearly, something happened at the last sleepover. Something bad. Something none of us can remember. And now there's this mystery girl.

I don't care about her. I don't care who she is or why she's in the picture. The only thing I care about is fixing whatever is going on between us.

I grip my hands into fists. We are going to be best friends again.

No matter what.

Before

I chased the girls down the steps, nearly sliding down the slick hardwood, the image of the mirror shattering replaying in my mind. Lea and Vicky's bags bounced against their shoulders, hastily zipped up and grabbed.

This couldn't be happening. They couldn't just *leave*.

"Guys!" I shouted after them. "I'm sure it's fine. It was just that heat thing like Lea said!"

Lea shook her head. "That was not some heat thing. That was fucked up."

Nova was the only one who hadn't taken her stuff with her, but I noticed the fine hairs on her arms were jerked to attention. She said, "Just chill. There's no way anything supernatural is actually happening."

"Um, did you miss the mirror ominously blowing up into a million pieces?" Vicky asked. "I don't know about you, but I don't want 'Died in a mysterious reflective glass accident' to be on my tombstone."

"I thought you wanted to be cremated?"

"Nova!"

Nova rolled her eyes. "Okay, fine, if you two are so scared, maybe we can go to my place instead?"

I fought a grimace. Her mom always wanted to involve herself like she was "one of the girls" and offered us wine, and it was weird and uncomfortable. Besides, this was *my* sleepover. My chance to show that I was part of the group. If we went to Nova's place, it would just be like I was invading their space. An outsider.

"No way, your mom is so cringe," Vicky said.

"Wow, okay, fuck you."

Lea suggested, "My place?"

"Oh!" Nova said, brightening. "Is your brother around?"

"Gross."

"Don't go!" I shouted.

The girls froze and turned to me. I could feel my chest heaving, and I tried to make myself calm down. I didn't want to look completely unhinged, but I also didn't want them to leave. This was my first time hosting. It was supposed to be *perfect*. I was going to show that I belonged with them, that we were it. Lea, Nova, Vicky, and *me*. I just wanted to be close the way the others were. I felt like they would straight up die for each other. I had never had friends like that. At my old school, we promised we would stay in touch, but we didn't really. We just liked each other's posts and DMed every once in a while. If they left now, my place would always be a reminder of that one terrible sleepover. They would never come back. And maybe they would rethink if I actually belonged in their group.

I choked out, "I'm sorry about the mirror thing. That was a bad idea. But please . . . just stay. We can watch a movie. We can sleep in the basement even."

Then I burst into tears.

And I immediately hated myself for it.

Lea sighed and dropped her bag on the ground, coming over to pull me into her arms. "It's okay, it's cool. Don't get upset. It's nothing to do with you. We just got kind of freaked out."

"Yeah, it's fine. We can watch something funny. Laughing will cheer you up." Vicky added.

Nova pulled her pajama sleeves over her hands and wiped the tears off my face. "It's all good, we'll stay. Don't cry."

I wanted to disappear into the ground. The whole persona I was supposed to have when I moved was this chill, cottagecore, witchy vibe. I had gotten the aesthetic down, but coming across the way I wanted was harder. The last thing I needed was to be seen as pathetic and desperate. I'd already unintentionally done that at my old school. I didn't want a repeat. But here I was, in tears, having to be comforted.

I managed to spit out something like a thank you, which felt just as pathetic.

We went into the finished basement with its leather armchairs and projection screen, and Nova and Vicky got to work figuring out how to get a movie playing. Meanwhile, Lea grabbed one of the spare blankets and draped it over both of us.

"Don't worry about it," she said to me. "If you haven't seen your friend cry, are you even friends?"

I laughed a little despite myself. I appreciated Lea. And we were all together. They'd stayed. But not because they wanted to. Not really. They did it because they felt sorry for me.

And that was the worst sort of friendship to have.

After

I make my way downstairs to find the girls. First, I poke my head into the kitchen, but it's empty. Next, I try the living room, but it's deserted too. I gnaw on my lip. They didn't . . . leave, did they? No. Their stuff is still upstairs. So where are they? Finally, I wander down to the basement.

There are soft murmurs coming from inside the room, and I find myself slowing down, making sure my feet aren't making obvious sounds.

How did they even know to go down there? Did they remember going there last time? Is that something we did? And why would they come down here without me? It's not like stepping out of the room to get air. They *chose* to come here together and leave me upstairs.

I think of the question Lea asked me—if I really didn't remember anything from that night—and now, I wonder the same thing about them. I press against the basement door and listen.

"What now?" Vicky says. "The whole memory jogging thing is a bust."

"Because you've been so much help with that." Nova sounds like she's talking while grinding her teeth.

Lea adds, "But she's right. We need to do something else. It's time for plan B."

What was plan B, and why hadn't they told me anything about it? Besides, since when was the point of this to remember what we forgot? I thought we were just spending time together. I lean harder against the door, and it pushes in, just a bit. I freeze.

They fall silent. Lea says, "Maddie? Is that you?"

I push open the door, swallowing as I enter. "Hey . . ."

"Hey," they echo back as one.

They were down here, planning something, without me. I grip my hands into fists and then forcibly release them. But honestly, what the fuck? What the actual fuck? We're supposed to be friends. All of us. But now they're pulling this bullshit. What is plan B? I want to scream at them and ask what exactly is going on. Instead, I smile. It's tight, but I can't manage anything else. They *are* my friends. We *are* friends.

"What were you guys talking about?" I say, my voice stiffer than I want it to be. But it's pleasant, which is good enough.

They all look around at each other. None of them saying anything.

Finally, Vicky says, "Fuck it," and shoves me.

Shoves. Me.

The back of my head slams into the basement door, and I fall onto my butt.

"Seriously?" Lea snaps at her. "What happened to plan B?"

"This *is* plan B."

Vicky hurt me. She. . . hurt me. I stare at her, incredulous, but all she does is look back coolly. "Vicky . . . What?"

Nova stares down at me with the same detached look. "Great, now we'll have to drag her upstairs. Thanks again, Vicky." And then she reaches out, grabs the front of my shirt, and tugs. *Hard.*

I cry out, and she pulls me down to the ground. Tears prick at the corners of my eyes, and I look over at Lea for help. But she isn't looking at me. She's pulling a knife out of her pocket, one of the ones from the kitchen. "Hold her," she tells Nova. Then she comes up close and presses it to my throat.

A croak falls from my mouth. I can't find any words.

"I'm so serious, if you do anything other than exactly what we tell you, I will cut you," Lea says. "I'm not playing."

The tone of her voice matches her words. Lea has never spoken to me like this. She's always been sweet and caring. Whenever we hung out, she would check in to make sure I was having fun and felt included. If I was sick and stayed home from school, she would text to make sure I was okay and ask if I needed anything. She even asked when my birthday was and said she would plan me a party. Only Mom had ever done that for me before.

But when she looks at me now, there's none of that kindness in her eyes.

Vicky and Nova yank under my armpits, pulling me to my feet, and they drag me up the stairs to the main floor.

"Why are you doing this?" I finally manage to choke out. "I'm your friend."

Nova laughs. "Oh my fucking God."

"Ignore her," Lea says, grabbing a box of salt from the kitchen on our way up the stairs leading to the second floor. There's something familiar about the salt.

I jerk in their grip. Lea kicks me in the back, and my face slams into the staircase. There's a crunch that turns my stomach. I whimper.

"Holy shit," Vicky cackles, dragging me back up.

My blood is smeared on the hardwood.

This can't be happening. They can't be doing this to me. What did I do wrong? I've done everything right—everything. This was supposed to be perfect.

We get back into my bedroom, and Lea starts making arrangements as the other two girls hold me. She pulls the rug off the floor and drags in a mirror from another room. The girls tug me closer to it while Lea draws a circle around us with salt.

I squeeze my eyes shut as my head pounds. There's something about what they're doing . . . it's like déjà vu. When I open my eyes again, Lea is pouring candle wax on the mirror and writing something in it with the knife.

Nova and Vicky drop me, but before I can scramble up, Vicky plants a foot in my back. When I'm down, she digs her knee into my spine, pressing all her weight on top of me.

I jerk my head up to Lea, and she's looming over me, her face set in a grim line, fingering the knife in her hands.

Finally, I can read what she's written on the glass.

BRENDA.

Before

I sat huddled in the blankets and tried to laugh along with the others while we watched the movie. I could tell that they were doing their best to act normal after my break down, to pretend like everything was fine.

For me.

This was all my fault. Because I wanted to impress them with this creepy Brenda Butterfingers shit. But I could fix it.

"I'm gonna go pee," I said, peeling myself off the recliner and setting aside my blanket. The girls looked up and nodded. Vicky made a request for me to bring popcorn on my way back.

Leaving them, I walked up the stairs and out of the basement, but instead of going into the half bath on the main floor, I continued upstairs to my room and dug around in my things.

Finally I found it, the cleansing stick that I had bought along with the crystals and other stuff I got from the new age store downtown. I still didn't understand how everything worked, but I knew that the cleansing stick was for dealing with bad energy.

I was searching for a match when the sound of cracking glass reached my ears.

Slowly, I turned toward the broken mirror.

I screamed.

After

I shudder as Lea runs the knife across the skin of my cheek, drawing blood. Tears leak out my eyes, and that just seems to make her angry. She takes the knife over to the mirror and smears my blood on it.

"Why are you doing this?" I make a weak attempt to buck the girls off me, but they stay firm.

Lea grabs a handful of my braids and jerks my head up. "Give us back Maddie!"

"I *am* Maddie! What are you talking about?!"

Vicky digs her knee harder into my back. "No, you're not! You know everything about her, and everyone acts like you are, but you aren't!"

I grunt from the pain. My nose is throbbing. My back aches. My cheek stings. But what hurts the most is the fact that they're doing this to me. It's like I can barely catch my breath. Everything has been torn from me by these people who are supposed to be my friends. My *best* friends.

Lea tugs at my braids again. "Give her back!" She pulls out the pola-roid and shoves it in my face. "See this girl beside Nova? *That's* Maddie. This bitch on the end? We don't know her! That's you! And it was just in your bag, lying there for anyone to see. And I did see it. And all the memories came back. The same thing happened when I showed it to Nova and Vicky. We remembered—remembered that you took our friend!"

They were wrong.

I'd never seen that photo before tonight.

But if it wasn't mine and Vicky "found" it in my stuff, that meant they planned that whole moment of pretending they were seeing it for the first time. Why?!

"Stop, please stop," I sob, trembling, and shaking my head. "I don't remember anything."

Something slams into the back of my head, and my face smashes onto the floor. My already damaged nose cracks more, and I scream.

"Yeah, we're starting to get that. Convenient for you to forget too. We thought if you remembered everything, you could also remember what you did," Nova snarls. "Do you know how disgusting it was to be around you and act just friendly enough to keep you hanging on while we planned everything?" My face slams down again. Snot runs from my nose and mixes with the blood. I pant, struggling to breathe properly. "Maybe that will help jog your memory."

I wonder suddenly if Nova was ever actually going to move in with her dad, or if it was all just a part of this plan to get back here. This entire time, they were playing me, and I fell for it.

"What are you going to do? Kill me?" I ask. The snot and blood reach my mouth, and I spit the mess out onto the floor.

Vicky snaps, "If that's what it takes."

These girls aren't my friends.

Maybe I should have realized that earlier. But I didn't want to believe it. I would have done anything for them. Everything would have been fine. All they had to do was be my friend.

But now, the image of Maddie I saw reflected in the mirror of my mind is shattering, and I can see myself.

Can see who I really am.

And I remember.

A soft sigh escapes my lips.

I just didn't want to be alone again.

Before

What is a memory, other than a story that you tell yourself?

And what does your memory matter when everyone decides what the story is on their own?

The knife slipped.

It was an *accident*.

But no one would have believed me.

I would have done anything for my friends. Even knowing that she was pulling away from me, that she was going to dump me soon for those new girls. I tucked her into a crawlspace with me and stayed with her, even though I knew it was too late.

I couldn't let her be alone. I knew how terrible that would be. Even if that was exactly what she'd planned to do to me.

But it took them so long to find us. Dad was gone for work, and when he texted, I said everything was fine because I didn't want to tell him what I'd done. The neighbors didn't bother to call about the smell until it was too late. And she did smell. It was unbearable. But I wasn't going to leave her for anything.

And then we were both gone, but I was still around in a different way. Alone. Moving in the mirrors that I smashed because I couldn't stand to see what I'd done.

By accident. It was an *accident*.

Those girls called to *me*.

I *understood* Maddie.

She would do anything to avoid being alone too.

I just wanted a little of what she had. And with her blood, I could see her story, those memories, bleeding through the glass into me, soaking into my skin. I pulled myself out of the mirror, and I shoved her inside. I took the picture from her pocket and smiled as I appeared in the frame. It was the only thing I had to remember from when we were all friends.

I liked that, so I kept it. I didn't want to push Maddie out, but I needed her spot.

The girls rushed into the room.

I didn't look like Maddie, but it didn't matter. I could see the way their memories were morphing as they stared at me; I watched as the photos on the walls changed Maddie into my image.

"You screamed . . ." Lea said, her voice trailing off.

I smiled. "I'm fine."

And I let my memory become the story that I wanted.

We would be friends. I would be their *best* friend. I was a good friend, no matter what anyone else thought. They were better than the girls I had been around before. I could tell. I would do anything for them. And they would do anything for Maddie, for *me*. I felt that. I really believed that.

But sometimes, bad memories reappeared when you didn't want them to.

After

I smile at the girls as they laugh over a video. We're all leaning in, lunches pushed aside, grinning down at the screen.

"That's so depraved, honestly."

"Then why are you laughing?"

"Because it's also funny."

A news bulletin flashes at the top of the screen, and I frown.

"Hold on, tap that."

I wish they wouldn't.

No New Leads in Sleepover Massacre Case

The accompanying photo is the front of Maddie's house, with her mom and stepdad clutching each other while multiple body bags are wheeled away.

Four to be exact.

I let them have Maddie back in the end. Friends should stick together, after all. Those girls deserved each other.

"People are saying they sacrificed each other to Satan or whatever."

"Fuck off, that's bullshit. They were acting weird for weeks. Sometimes this shit happens. People just snap."

"Or . . . maybe it was Brenda. They were found in front of a mirror."

"No way, we did the Brenda Butterfingers summoning thing last week, and nothing happened to us, remember?"

This time would be better.

I'm a good friend.

Always have been, always will be.

The Teeth Come Out at Night

by

Sami Ellis

SATs (three times): 1 waiver + $136 (I should've got a good score the first time, but $68 x 2 now = a $4K merit scholarship come award letters)

Don't everybody know how to hustle to make money.

With Mrs. Ackerman rifling through her purse, every card number and security code flashing at Akeela's hungry eyes, that much was obvious. People who work hard protect their asses. "The thing I love about you, Alana, is that you can always make last minute work," Mrs. Ackerman said.

"Of course, Mrs. Ackerman," Akeela said with a light laugh. She didn't even blink at the false name. "You don't gotta tell me twice. *You* just worry about relaxing at the spa with Mr. Ackerman. I'll handle Bryson until you get back."

"And you won't have any problems staying here until midnight? It's not the most fun you could have on a Friday, you know?" Mrs. Ackerman's upper-crust Charleston accent was a harp to Akeela's banjo.

"Absolutely not. I could use the study time; I still need to revise a few college admissions essays." What she needed was extra cash—something good quality that she could turn over to the Docter within the week.

"Heaven sent. Just heaven sent!" Mrs. Ackerman praised Akeela, tucking her seamless blonde weave behind her ear. "For the lateness, we've bumped you up to fifteen an hour—but don't get mad when it goes back down to ten next week."

Akeela laughed heartily. "Of course not," she replied.

Cheapskate.

"And *call* me if anything happens—the security people won't come in to fix our system for at least another week."

"Yes, Mrs. Ackerman."

After what felt like three hours, Mrs. Ackerman *finally* started heading out the door. Akeela followed close behind to close it, trying not to seem too eager—but really how long could this go on?

"And don't forget!" Mrs. Ackerman shouted, halting in her footsteps.

Akeela damn near stepped on her foot.

"Bryson is missing a tooth. We put it under his pillow for the tooth fairy, but I know you said you like to go all out for that kind of thing."

"Yes, I do," Akeela said. She'd been plotting on that tooth long before Mrs. Ackerman noticed it was gone. She flexed her fingers at her side while she maintained her pasted-on Homecoming Queen smile. Once she got her hands on that tooth, she'd text her aunt and tell her to come over.

Mrs. Ackerman leaned in, lowering her voice. "He also has a few other stubborn sons of bitches in there," she said. "But those ain't comin' out easy. We'll have to do the door trick for them probably."

Not on Akeela's watch. But, of course, she was more inclined to be delicate with the merchandise.

It was surprising Mrs. Ackerman even noticed anything about Bryson at all. Out of all Akeela's clients, the Ackermans were the least involved in their child's life. Beyond ensuring that Bryson was in one piece, Mrs. Ackerman never seemed to care.

"Don't worry, I've got it," Akeela finished.

It was a wonder Mrs. Ackerman ever left. She resisted every nudge Akeela gave, to the point that Akeela was about ready to shove her out the door. But when the moon was high up and all the stars were crystal clear, the owner of the house finally set foot on the front stoop.

Akeela gave her a slight wave. "Don't worry about me and Bryson. I'll send you pictures and check-ins until you get back," she said.

"No need to do that . . ." Mrs. Ackerman hesitated. She stopped herself whenever she realized others might see her as a Bad Mom. "But if you insist."

Akeela's fingers curled around the wood of the door as she gently guided it closed. She didn't turn away from the thickly painted frame until she heard Mrs. Ackerman's car turn on and the wheels crunching over the cement and into the street.

Then she turned around. The TV was blasting out nursery rhymes. Bryson stood in the entryway behind her, staring at her. The TV light flickered on his back, his silhouette a kitchen-counter-height menace.

But if anyone was the menace, it was Akeela. She stared back at him, crossing her arms. "I heard your tooth fell out, kid."

Bryson gave her a wide grin. The missing hole where his front tooth should have been shadowed over the pink of his tongue, and strings of gummy flesh moved where he pushed at the gap.

Proof in the pudding.

Akeela smirked at him, pinching his chin between her fingers. She eyed the remaining teeth, aching to reach in and test them out for herself—there had to be one more ripe for the taking. She didn't though.

Scaring the kid would do her no good.

"Same deal as always. You get half," she lied. "As long as you don't tell your mom."

⁂

Application Fees: $330 = $70 (fee waiver code didn't work) ~~+ $50~~ (waived) + $60 (my family's too rich to waive???) + $45 (family too rich to waive) + $65 (financial aid office didn't respond) + $50 (didn't know I could ask yet) + $40 (didn't know I could ask yet)

A couple of hours later it was almost time for Akeela's visitor, and she wanted Bryson knocked out by the time her aunt arrived. "Time for bed, kid," she called to him. And not a moment too soon—the droning nursery rhymes were starting to get on Akeela's last nerve. Bryson watched them in rapt attention. At this point, it didn't even seem like he was getting sleepy.

Just hypnotized.

It took him a minute to rip his eyes from the TV, the first time he had in hours, but as all her kids did, he ended the night following her up the stairs with his head hung low. It only took about a half hour for him to start snoring, and Akeela sneaked back downstairs.

A knock at the door two hours later stopped Akeela in the middle of her admissions essay draft. She was alone in the HGTV-wannabe kitchen/living/dining room.

Calmly, Akeela grabbed her book bag off the couch, pulling out the deep black blanket that she kept folded inside. She unfolded the cloth, laying it out neatly on the kitchen island to keep Mrs. Ackerman's "antique marble," as Mrs. Ackerman always made a point to call it, clean from bits of flesh and blood. Then she pulled out a puffed-up envelope from her backpack's front pocket.

She dumped the envelope's contents onto the center of the blanket, staring at the objects with her bottom lip between her teeth. This had to be enough.

There was another knock at the door.

When Akeela finally opened the door, the porch light flickered on like distant lightning. Her aunt stood on the doorstep, a stuffed tote over her shoulder and an impatient look on her face. "If it ain't my favorite niece," Aunt Mickey greeted.

Her headwrap bobbled to the side when Akeela moved out of her way, locs peeking from beneath. Shining gold bands jangled around her wrist. Aunt Mickey wouldn't have been caught dead outside with anything other than real gold. The thick, metallic ropes could fetch her over five hundred bucks easy—even from that racist shop in the south side that always underpaid. Aunt Mickey's whole set couldn't have been worth more than $2,000 altogether—that was just thirty days in jail.

Akeela ached to swipe the jewelry. But the possible $1,000 fine kept her hands to herself.

As if reading her mind, Aunt Mickey flexed her fingers around her wrist, rubbing the wrinkled skin as she walked inside. She wasn't new to this—she was Akeela's mom's sister, so Aunt Mickey knew Akeela definitely wasn't to be trusted around the valuables.

Still, her smile hadn't left her. "Movin' on up to the east side, are we?" Aunt Mickey asked. "This is the fanciest house I've ever seen you in."

"Only for three hours a week," Akeela responded.

Her aunt made a beeline for the kitchen island. Her eyes were narrowed on the black cloth, and she sat on the breakfast stool as if it were a throne. She crossed her legs beneath her form-fitting yellow maxi dress.

"Your brother asked me for some money last week," she said. She peeked over her oversized glasses, the frames sliding down her nose a little. "I'm guessing you ain't tol' him about our . . . arrangement."

It was Akeela's flawless talent for performance that kept her from laughing in her aunt's face. "You know, I've been meaning to, but then I took a few extra jobs to make up the cash. Ended up just forgetting."

"*Mmm*hmm." Her aunt's eyebrow arched in a smooth lift, eyes narrowing. "You been staying outta trouble?"

"Yes, ma'am." Akeela felt like she was in the damned hot seat. But, thankfully, her aunt didn't press her any further.

Aunt Mickey just raised her eyeglasses back squarely on her nose and got down to business. She leaned toward the blanket, furrowing her brow as she ran her fingers along the edges.

Beneath the delicately placed rows of teeth.

"You got anything good this time?" Aunt Mickey asked.

Akeela clasped her hands before her, trying not to sweat. If her aunt was asking that, she obviously wasn't seeing nothin'. The teeth were simple and small, varying in colors of yellow. Some broken, some animal. Some human. Akeela swallowed hard while her aunt picked up one of them with a thin cloth.

"How much they payin' today?" Akeela asked. She didn't want to take the risk that it was low for the day. The prices changed every so often, and Akeela had learned her lesson once before on selling too low. Sell too low, the prices stopped changing and the Docter started tryna get over on you. He ain't care how hard it was for a teenage girl to get ahold of albino gator teeth.

She was up against real doctors, licensed ones that could shoot her supply out the water. Akeela's only edge was the baby teeth. Most people just threw them away. She was lucky enough to have a consistent, fresh supply.

Aunt Mickey was all business. Her pleasant expression wiped clean as she dropped the tooth onto the blanket. Her cleavage spilled over her dress's low collar. "Five. For quality," she said firmly. "And from what I'm seeing, this ain't quality."

"It was ten last week."

"Last week the Docter had demand. This week we have maintenance. Five for *quality*."

Akeela grimaced, her heart pounding in her chest. She clicked her teeth together as she stared at the collection she had presented. It was garbage. She knew that. She couldn't wait till the prices went back up. She needed to sell now. Those due dates were fast approaching. Emails were comin' in with exclamation points in the subject line. Everything told her she was in a hurry.

Money now.

With a last huff, Akeela ripped her book bag off the ground, digging in the front pocket again. This time she pulled out a glass jar smaller than her own palm. Her aunt watched her with a solemn expression. Didn't question when Akeela poured the teeth onto the table, letting them sprinkle and bounce on impact.

Some were chipped, broken, shredded. Some were sharp.

All of them were from a child's mouth.

It was the only reason she hadn't been phased out of the business.

"Hundred fifty for the bunch," Akeela said directly.

Aunt Mickey didn't look satisfied. Even with Akeela's signature supply, she knew the extra fifty was a gamble.

"This is way less than you usually give me," Aunt Mickey said. "You usually have at least ten. And you want *more than* a hundred for four?"

Akeela swallowed. "Aunt Mickey."

"If you're running out of supply, can't you just pick up more babysitting jobs?"

"Aunt Mickey."

"The Docter isn't going to like this at all."

"Aunt Mickey!"

"What is it?" Her aunt finally looked up from the table, meeting Akeela's gaze. Something in her expression halted, and for a flicker, she was no longer all business. For a moment, she was just Akeela's aunt.

Then, Akeela spoke. "There was a problem," she said.

That got Aunt Mickey's attention. "What do you *mean* a problem?" she hissed. Her eyes almost seemed ablaze as she clenched the island countertop. "You didn't get caught, did you?"

"Of course not," Akeela snapped. Her aunt only gave her one rule: don't get caught stealing teeth. And it wasn't just her aunt who forbade it. So did the Docter.

Akeela couldn't afford to jeopardize this job. She focused too much on school to work a regular job. She couldn't build up experience, and jobs weren't flexible enough. After she got out of juvie the first time, she'd let all her grades fall to the point raising them back up to respectable took most of her time. She didn't have much choice but to take the babysitting jobs the Docter gave her, her hoodoo auntie the only thing that kept her afloat.

Akeela dug her fingers into her pocket. Little pellets at the bottom danced around her touch, and she pulled them out to sprinkle them on the table like pepper.

Aunt Mickey stared at them blank faced, watching the reddened teeth roll around the good ones. Silence filled the room as her aunt flexed her fingers.

"What," her aunt gritted out, "the *hell* is this?"

"I don't know," Akeela said simply. "The teeth all turned red."

Red was an understatement.

The deep burgundy color that sprinkled the table was not a simple red but an absence all together—as if, for the space of the loose teeth, for the moment they were in her vision, nothing existed but blood and rot.

Akeela tried not to stare at them, but she couldn't meet her aunt's eyes either. "The last couple of weeks, they all turned that way after I stole them. After I *touched* them," she said. "By the time I get home, the teeth are always turned."

An athlete's teenage protégé. A billionaire's daughter. Akeela babysat throughout the richest neighborhoods and got called all kinds of "thief" and "jezebel" and "addict" and "charity case." Her clients didn't know about her record—didn't know her real name even. Just from the way she looked and the way she talked and the scuff marks on her sneakers, they decided she wasn't worth the respect they gave their Pilates instructors.

Akeela put up with all of it just to supply the Docter with those teeth, to hold up her end of the bargain. And now they didn't even last a second in her possession.

It happened one job, and then again a few jobs later. And then a couple later. It started happening more and more often. It used to be she could manage to get up to twenty teeth to sell. Now she was digging in her bedroom drawers for four—four teeth she'd held on to weeks after she'd discarded them for quality control.

Aunt Mickey picked up one of the bloody kernels, squeezing it between her fingers as if it would disintegrate. It didn't. It didn't even leave behind a red smudge, though it seemed like it should have. "What am I supposed to do with damaged teeth?" she asked.

"It's all I can find."

"Can't get money for rotting teeth."

Akeela said nothing. Her heart pounded as she watched her aunt's fingers. Their every flex. The pattern on the fingerprints.

The tooth *roll, roll, rolling* between her index and thumb.

Her aunt pinched the tooth harder. "If I was the Docter, I'd fire you. I'd tell you, 'Don't come 'round no more. You got cursed hands.'"

Akeela's heart sank.

If Aunt Mickey were the Docter, Akeela would have some blackmail of her own to drive up her cash outs. But she wasn't.

"Are you?" Akeela blurted. She swallowed, looking at the tooth with glazed eyes. "Firing me? Me and the Docter got a deal; you can't do that." Akeela cursed the way her voice cracked. It wasn't smart to lose her cool. Even if Aunt Mickey was family, she worked for the Docter.

Not even a month after she got out, Akeela got caught stealing bikes for cash. Since she already had a record, she thought there wasn't any future for her at that point. But while she was under arrest at the precinct, waiting to hear if she was jail-bound or juvie-bound, Aunt Mickey showed up as her guardian. With a man Akeela had never met.

A man who smiled with his hands in his pockets, his long coat smelling of smoke and incense.

The Docter.

"A gooba like you too smart to be so hopeless," he'd said to her.

It was the beginning of the deal. If she worked for him, he'd supply her with middle class babysitting jobs until she graduated high school. And if she used her sticky fingers to supply him with baby teeth, he'd get her record expunged. A new slate. A future she thought she'd lost.

And she would *not* let whatever the universe was doing to her teeth take it away from her.

"I'll have more Friday, Aunt Mickey," Akeela said quickly. She still had the Davenports later tonight and a few other houses throughout the week. It didn't matter if she couldn't touch the teeth. She'd just find a way not to. She made shit work—5¢ or $500.

Although her aunt didn't look convinced, she put the red tooth down and nodded. Then she pushed away from the island, lowering her glasses again to give Akeela that dead-on gaze. "Not these," her aunt said in no uncertain terms, gesturing at the animal teeth. "Baby teeth are the ones that are really worth a damn. If you can come back here with six clean, *fresh* baby teeth? I'll talk to the Docter about this tooth, and about your . . . problem." She squints down at the opaque red in her fingers. "I'll see if I can get you twenty each for something better."

"Seventy-five."

"Forty."

Akeela nodded. Her mind was already on the end result. She'd long calculated that this would be an offer she could not refuse. She internally catalogued the houses with children who she'd babysat at over the past month, trying to recall each individual kid's two rows of teeth. She had a few jobs this week. There was a chance.

"And Akeela?" Her aunt's voice interrupted Akeela's thoughts, and she realized Aunt Mickey was staring at her still.

"Yes?"

"You *cannot* get caught stealing teeth."

Akeela nodded solemnly. "Yes, Aunt Mickey."

Enrollment Deposit Due:
- *School A: 3 days*
- *School B: 5 weeks*

Just a few more weeks of this deal.

If she kept it together for the Docter just until December, he would expunge her record in time for early applications and for her to qualify for federal aid.

She could not afford to mess this up. So what the hell was she gon' do now?

After Akeela waved her aunt out of the house and cleaned up the carnage on the Ackermans' kitchen island, she could only sigh to herself. This was a whole lot of making it work, not a lot of things actually working. Except her.

On top of that, she'd been hoping to get a hundred for the teeth. No teeth cash-out today meant no enrollment deposit by the deadline for her top state school.

She'd be down to only one collegiate choice if her extension request fell through.

Her brother hadn't been happy when she'd decided to go off to college in the first place. He thought it was a white ideal of success—something to keep them in debt, not bring them out of it. But ever since Akeela had gotten her second chance from the Docter, she'd known this was the way for her. She'd just hoped to soften her brother up by going to a cheap one nearby. That tactic was looking more hopeless by the day.

Creaaaaak.

A slow, low whining sounded from upstairs and snapped Akeela to attention. The creak seemed to go from one side of the ceiling to the other: one groan in the wood, two groans, three. Like long, dragging footsteps.

Akeela rubbed her forehead, checked the lock on the door, then turned to the living room. The shadow of the dark upstairs cut the steps into halves.

"You ain't asleep yet?" she shouted up to Bryson. She cleaned up the rest of her business and stuffed it into her backpack.

Bryson never went to sleep when he was supposed to. But it was 10:00 PM now, and even with his favorite song, "The Wheels on the Bus"— the one he always played louder than a Beyoncé concert—he didn't make a peep. Nothing else sounded from upstairs.

Akeela furrowed her brow.

It was weird, too, now that she thought about it. She looked back over the stairs. The darkness from the upstairs hall was almost too deep, like pitch black dripping down the walls. There were no windows up on the landing, and it often got too dark up there with Mrs. Ackerman's Premiere Blackout Curtains in every room. But Bryson was so, so scared of the dark.

He never used to go to bed without the bathroom light on. Peeking up the steps, Akeela saw cuts of the landing in their outlines and shadows. She started climbing up, moving slowly as each carpeted stair moaned beneath her. The decorated wall of pictures crawled over her shoulder just as slowly. Following her even. All of Mrs. and Mr. Ackerman and Bryson—the picture-perfect family of Black elite.

Akeela wondered, sometimes, if her mom would have bothered to stick around if they'd had money. Maybe she would've. She'd be flighty and neglectful like Mrs. Ackerman, but she'd still be here. But just as quickly as Akeela wondered about it, she eliminated the possibility. There was no universe where people like her mom had money. People like herself, her family—they scraped and saved and worked two and three jobs, and at the end of the day, they just had enough for tap water and a roach-infested apartment.

People like the Ackermans don't have to work hard to live well. It was what the universe had dealt to them, and they gladly accepted the gifts, the Teslas, and the six-figure salaries.

Yet they still paid trash.

At the top of the stairs, there were only four doors. The parents' bedroom door was behind her. Open. The bathroom was open too, and the laundry closet doors were slid wide apart. Only Bryson's door, decorated with ribbons and photographs from soccer teams past, was cracked slightly.

The soft carpet shushed beneath her socks. There was a little light, now that she was closer, from outside. Bryson's room faced the street, and she could see the lines and crosses of the windowpane stretching across the hallway ceiling.

Akeela half expected him to jump out from behind his door and scream in her face, as he liked to scare her. He'd seen an old Jason movie while Mrs. Ackerman was drowning herself in wine and imported cheese, and now he was going through a rather forced horror phase. Despite clearly being scared shitless and having no point of reference beyond the single film, he insisted he loved horror.

And annoyance and all, Akeela dealt with it smiling. "Oh, garsh, isn't he just precious," she'd tell Mrs. Ackerman—piss not even dry yet on the thighs of her pants.

When Akeela went into his room, he did not jump out. Actually, it seemed there was nothing to worry about. The walls, as always, were a soft blue, even in the dark. The posters that lined the walls were a mix of too-babyish and too-grown: the ABCs and *The Fast and the Furious*.

And in the middle, Bryson was under his covers, sound asleep. A car drove by outside, its motor muted white noise against the silent bedroom. Akeela watched as the light from the window slid across the wall, then the bed and to his bedside dresser before resetting after the car fully passed.

On that dresser, Akeela found a hastily drawn picture faceup. Its crayon letters were drawn so heavy handed, she could still read it in the dark.

Dear Tooth Fairy

Thank you for the money.

Damn near every letter was backward—even the *o*'s in "Tooth Fairy," somehow. Poor boy.

But if this to-the-point letter was how Bryson handled a check, then maybe he was a kid after her own heart. No, he *definitely* was—because directly to the left of his note she saw two teeth.

She went to pick them up with her bare hands—and then stopped herself. The grin stiffening her cheeks faltered before she delicately scooped the teeth up with the cloth of her T-shirt. They were beautiful; she couldn't help but notice. Blood still lined the inserts, and gunk stained the cotton as she rolled it between the cloth. Definitely worth forty bucks a pop.

She looked over to Bryson burrowed in his comforter, then back to the teeth. She placed her free hand on his covered shoulder. "You're still good for something, kid," she said.

After she pocketed them, she left him five bucks, strictly out of the goodness of her heart. Her smile didn't leave her face even when she went back into the hallway. Her footsteps did pause, though, at the sliver of light that cut through the landing.

The curtains in the parents' room were cracked open, a thick line of porch-light yellow stretching toward Bryson's closed door. There was nothing but silence, not even the slow, low creaks she had heard minutes ago.

Two Enrollment Deposits:
- School A (early admission): $200; best choice for network (get more money later on)
- School B (early admission): $100; best choice for low cost (pay less money up front)

The Ackermans didn't return until 1:30 AM.

"I'm so, *so* sorry," Mrs. Ackerman said, shrugging off her jacket in the doorway. Mr. Ackerman stood behind her, looming like Death. "It turned out the massage parlor wasn't the kind we thought it was. We ended up with a little bit more commitment than we wanted," she said.

Akeela was already late to the Davenports' house. She maintained her stiff smile. "That's fine."

"Such a blessing," Mrs. Ackerman sighed. The term was getting old when Akeela still had no "blessing" money to speak of.

Mr. Ackerman shuffled into the house, his coat and shoes still on. His eyes drooped in the corners, the red in the whites crackling like broken concrete. His movements were sluggish as he slunk toward the sofa. The nursery rhymes were set low but still playing as Akeela forgot to turn off the TV. Their cheery voices were overprocessed, wailing in chords that had a digital edge to them. It grated on Akeela, making her grind her teeth a little. But Mr. Ackerman parked himself right in front of the screen, rapt with attention.

Akeela kept it professional as she hurriedly slapped her backpack like it was a timed Olympic sport. "No worries, Mrs. Ackerman," she said brightly, slipping on her shoes. "Just give me my pay and I'll—"

"It's so dark in here," Mrs. Ackerman interrupted, scratching at her wrists.

Flaky skin of a scab peeked from between Mrs. Ackerman's fingers. The folds of her wrists glistened with moisture, as if liquid seeped from the seams. Mrs. Ackerman scratched at them absentmindedly, unaware Akeela could see.

"My pay?" Akeela said slowly.

Mrs. Ackerman didn't turn her way.

"Bryson's been in bed since nine. We had dinner, but he didn't eat much." She had spent most of the time writing backup state application essays. And coming up with ways to make that enrollment deposit with only three days left.

"Oh, Alana, I know you prefer cash," Mrs. Ackerman said, and she slid Akeela a twenty with a smile. "But we were way too busy to stop at an ATM this time. We'll send the rest through the app."

Mr. Ackerman just sat on the couch, blankly watching the preschool channel.

If Akeela got her pay through the app, she'd have to first check if her bank account was overdrawn—which it was. Of course it was; her account was constantly in the negative.

The wealthier clients didn't like it when she checked her account in front of them. She'd just have to live in the anxiety of knowing the bank would gobble up the little scraps she'd gotten. "Thanks, Mrs. Ackerman!" Akeela said in a forced-cheerful goodbye.

With Mrs. Ackerman still spaced out, Akeela broke into a full sprint for her car. The night air was brisk, and her little hand-me-down sedan was dim in the street across the manicured lawn.

The next house was the Davenports'. By the time Akeela got there, the kid was already asleep—and he ain't have no good teeth.

"He lost his two front teeth earlier today," their neighbor said to her. The old lady had agreed to look over him in Akeela's absence, but it was obvious she wasn't about to sacrifice a *whole* good night of sleep. "They're right over there," the lady whispered over his sleeping form.

Akeela looked at the teeth but didn't touch them, now that it was causing her issues. People didn't like when she did that anyway—the actual, bare-handed touching of children's teeth. So she kept her distance, staring down at them, gaze unwavering.

And when she finally neared enough to look down on the fleck of white, she saw it wasn't two teeth but one—one tooth, broken in half. *Fuck.*

"I told him to stop skateboarding all the time, but you know that's how he got 'em knocked out. Carryin' on up and down MLK." She waved her hand wide, gesturing out of his street-facing window. "I watched him bust his whole face open from my garden."

Akeela pulled out a dollar and a napkin from her pocket. "Don't worry, Mrs. Greene," Akeela said, pocketing the teeth. "I'll watch out for him."

She talked as if it wasn't a bust. Broken teeth ain't go too well with Aunt Mickey the other day, but Akeela'd try for it anyway. Not like she had a choice—her pockets were past the point of picking and choosing.

She stayed at the Davenports' without complaints—at least not out loud—until the kid's aunt arrived. And by the time Akeela got home, the sun was already rising. She walked into the flickering hallway of the apartment complex. The lights hadn't been fixed in months, and she doubted anybody had called maintenance. They probably wouldn't do anything if somebody asked anyways.

No one was awake when she entered her apartment. She saw her brother's long legs hanging from the back of the couch. A couple of bills rested on the glass side table. She put the twenty from Mrs. Ackerman there as well.

Nothing in their house was free.

She'd rather pay some of the bills than have their electricity cut off in the middle of a school paper again. It made it harder to pay off all the enrollment deposits and the application fees, but she couldn't get any fee waivers after the ones she'd gotten for the SATs. When she asked her teachers, they didn't even know what fee waivers were and came back later saying her family made too much money for her to qualify.

⸺◦◦◦⸺

NABA Membership: $35 (fucking score—that's a schol-
arship in the bag if I ever seen one)

The farmer's market was in full swing this early on a Saturday morning. Food trucks and carts and foldable tables and chairs lined all sides of the church parking lot until it was a maze.

Sss . . .

A sizzle caught Akeela's attention, and she glanced to the next table over where a chalkboard sign advertised freshly caught fish. Akeela could smell it: hot oil, a fresh crust, and some peppers and seasoning that would burn the tip of her tongue just so. It made her mouth water, but all she had in her pocket was her small glass jar.

Akeela cut her gaze away from the damned menu, lest she "accidentally" spend ten dollars of application fee money on a fresh fried platter.

Aunt Mickey's shop was right at home between a basket-weaving stall and a waist-bead maker. Despite her aunt's eclectic inventory, there was a steady stream of older men and women who stopped by her table before bouncing off to get somebody's good-smelling food. Aunt Mickey was basically the Incense Lady.

If you knew, you knew. If you didn't, you had no business by her table. The skirt of her black tablecloth flowed in the soft breeze, and the dried flowers on the tabletop whipped against the paperweight that held them down. Along with fresh lavender, sage, and a few other herbs Akeela couldn't name by sight, the table was covered in neatly organized jars filled with dried herbs, dirts, and pickled limbs from pigs' feet to frog legs.

Aunt Mickey thrived at the market. "Hopefully we have better luck today," she said to Akeela when she saw her niece shuffling up on the rocky pathway.

DOCTER was all her sign said.

"The red teeth turned to dust when 'e Docta got his hands on 'em," her aunt said in a low voice. *Well damn, right down to business.* Her aunt slid her glasses down, glaring at Akeela. "The deal was for you to deliver baby teeth, so I did convince him to give you another chance. You had any luck yesterday?"

Akeela sighed heavily. At this point, she didn't even want to pull the jar out of her pocket. By the time she woke up this morning, half of them had already turned red—even the ones she hadn't touched. Some were okay; some were smudged and muddy. The jar glistened in the sunlight, reflecting patterns of silver from the lid onto the black cloth of the table.

The red that rubbed against the clear glass was smeared up and around the walls, as if someone had tried to paint a human heart with watercolors.

"I'll take them for a lower price," Aunt Mickey said.

Akeela clenched her fist at her sides, thinking about the money she'd lost out on yesterday. She couldn't take a lower price. Two days left until the enrollment deposit was due for the state school that gave 90 percent of its students at least $20,000 in financial aid.

If that wasn't the fucking answers to her prayers on a platter, she didn't know what was.

She couldn't afford to lose income.

"Do you think it would work if they were fresher?" Akeela asked.

Her aunt sat in her chair, plopping down with her legs crossed and running her fingers along her locs. "I don't know," she said. "Docter used to take pliers to a drunk's mouth, but it's not like you can do that anymore. Plus . . ." She didn't finish, but Akeela knew what her aunt wanted to say.

Akeela worked with children.

It didn't make her feel *great* thinking about pulling out children's teeth with pliers. But a lot of the children had teeth that could be removed. She didn't want to hurt her kids, to be clear. She just wanted to get what she needed and give them a little help on their adult dental journey.

She swallowed. "I'll bring you something better," she said, collecting the glass jar with her eyes closed. "Just make sure you keep the prices up."

And with that, she left. If she was going to get fresh teeth, she couldn't be on the clock. And that meant lying a little.

<hr />

Two Housing Deposits:
- School A: $150
- School B: $55
(I'll cross this road when I get there—enrollment deposit is top priority)

The light from the Ackerman's house shone brightly. It leaked into the night like pools, glittering in the grass as dew settled at the tips of the blades. Akeela's sneakers thudded like boots as she hopped up the porch steps. Everything was so quiet.

The sound of the doorbell echoed.

Akeela's stiff smile ripped at her chapped lips as she stood on the doorstep, a chill breezing through the air and beneath her thin jacket. She was used to the cool of night, bringing some relief after overly hot days. For a Charleston night, though—it was cold. Colder than normal.

Akeela pressed the doorbell again.

"One second!" Mrs. Ackerman yelled from inside.

Good. Akeela—or, Alana for the next few minutes—bounced on her toes once, twice. She straightened her shoulders, brightening her smile and setting her teeth even more rigidly. She heard the locks click in a slow tempo—one . . . two . . . three—and then the front door opened.

It was a miracle Akeela didn't flinch.

Mrs. Ackerman stood in the doorway of her fancy brick house, the porch light flickering on before her and illuminating her brown skin. The scars that had started at her wrist were now up to her cheekbones, long tiger stripes pasted with white and gold and red. The woman had a towel around her neck, which dripped onto her T-shirt.

When she made out Akeela, a furrow hit her brow for a brief moment. It cleared—but she didn't smile like she usually did. "Atlanta, we didn't schedule you for tonight!"

Action.

Akeela smiled softly and brightly, as if Mrs. Ackerman hadn't gotten her fake name wrong. She pressed her nail into her hand to keep calm. "I know, Mrs. Ackerman—I'm so sorry, but I might have left my cell phone in Bryson's room yesterday. The last time I had it was when I sent you that update pic of him sleeping." The lies came out so smoothly, like they were written ahead of time. Should she change her major to acting?

Of course not—not enough money at the start.

Mrs. Ackerman's frown returned. "Last night?"

"Yeah, sorry. I couldn't call ahead . . . no phone."

This time, the furrowed look didn't leave the woman's expression. It was a faraway one, and Akeela imagined Mrs. Ackerman was going over all the possibilities in her mind of what could happen if she let the terror of Unexpected Company in.

Eventually, Mrs. Ackerman must have decided the possibilities weren't too dangerous to risk. She smiled at Akeela softly, standing to the side as all the welcoming warmth from the inside flowed out to the foyer.

Akeela felt like she walked into a holiday movie, the kind where the moral was that everything was all about family. The smell of cinnamon and ginger wafted from the kitchen. Strange.

Why was it so bright in the house? The paintings that adorned the back walls, the paintings of the Ackerman family, stared at her as Mrs. Ackerman led her inside the house, chattering away. It was around 9:00 PM—she'd had another kid she babysat across the city, a toothless one she couldn't cancel. She couldn't get here earlier.

Akeela turned to the kitchen, and there was a half-eaten meal left on the stove. She looked over to the living room. The television was still on that preschool channel; Mr. Ackerman was still in front of it. But he slept on the floor, the remote in the same place it had been when she left the previous night.

"The Wheels on the Bus" played yet again, though the words were unfamiliar, the beat slightly different.

"Let's hurry up and wash it off, wash it off, wash it off!"

The cartoon kids gathered around a sink with bright smiles and wide eyes as red splotches seeped into their clothes.

"He's really tired," Mrs. Ackerman cut in, leaning against the sofa and blocking Mr. Ackerman from Akeela's vision. The woman started scratching her wrists again.

"Sorry," Akeela said again. "I wanted to get here earlier, but I had another house I had to babysit at."

"The Thompsons," Mrs. Ackerman supplied.

Akeela's smile went even stiffer. "Yes, Mrs. Ackerman."

Scratch, scratch, scratch.

It seemed like the more she scratched, the rougher it sounded and the slower her responses. The lower her eyelids. Mrs. Ackerman kept her nails to her wrist, her gaze settling just above Akeela's head. "You can go upstairs and look for your phone," she said. Her tone was almost normal. It was *almost* there—just . . . hollow. "Try not to wake Bryson up. He has some kind of sleepover birthday party nonsense tomorrow. I don't want the little shit's mom getting pissy and sending Bryson back early."

"Yes, Mrs. Ackerman," Akeela said slowly.

The mother followed Akeela's steps, captivated as Akeela moved toward the stairs. She tried not to focus on Mrs. Ackerman's uncharacteristic words because she'd always known Mrs. Ackerman felt that way about kids. Even Bryson.

She'd just never *said* it. Lord, she'd never said it *out loud*.

Akeela paused before she climbed the first step. None of the lights were on up the stairs. Again.

It was a stark contrast to the kitchen and living room, where it seemed like it was damn near daytime.

"And he's sleep?" Akeela asked Mrs. Ackerman.

Mrs. Ackerman didn't answer. She was still standing in the living room, leaning against the sofa. She scratched at her wrists, and her eyes glazed over, focusing on nothing in the direction of the kitchen.

Okay. Akeela was going to do this quick.

She hopped up two steps at a time, ignoring the creaks and the rustling picture frames as she pushed to the landing faster than she ever had. The thin sliver from Mrs. Ackerman's room was no more, and Akeela was starting to convince herself she hadn't even seen Mrs. Ackerman's curtains opened that night.

At the top of the staircase, her thighs felt a little tingle. The light from downstairs was a warmth on her back, but the darkness of the landing was a cool breath on her cheeks.

Bryson's door was wide open.

She could see him huddled under the covers, buried in a pile of clothes and comforter—the same way he'd been when she left him the previous night. The floor squeaked with her every footstep as she approached his door. She got closer, flexing her fingers at her side as she walked into the dark room.

A dark stain colored the top of the comforter like a runny egg yolk.

While there wasn't a smell, Akeela found that she couldn't breathe deeply. Could barely breathe at all.

The teeth, she reminded herself.

She needed to get the teeth. Digging into her pocket, she pulled out a pair of pliers that gleamed in the moonlight from the slits in the blinds.

Her pulse pounded in her wrist, and she swallowed. She could see it. She could see her skin pop and flatten, pop and flatten, every time her heart beat. She reached for the bedding.

"*Do not pull the covers.*" A voice. The corner of the room.

She shrieked, dropped the pliers, and bumped into the bedside dresser as she whipped toward the reading chair. The corner was enclosed in shadows. There was nothing there but a small figure—a child, whose eyes gleamed in the dark.

She could see their breath puff out before them, obscuring their form like a thick fog.

"Do not pull the covers," the child said. "Those teeth are mine."

"Is everything okay?" Mrs. Ackerman's voice echoed from downstairs. And just beneath, Akeela heard rattling. Shaking.

It was her hand on the dresser, trembling and rustling the metal handles.

She didn't turn away from the reading chair. The child's eyes didn't leave hers. Its silhouette was darker than night, an emptiness in the low-lit room.

"Do not pull the covers. Those teeth are mine," they said again.

Then Akeela bolted. She ran as fast as she could—pliers left behind, Bryson left behind, Mrs. Ackerman's calls on her shoulder as she abandoned her mission and popped out of the door. No one chased her.

<hr>

State Scholarship ($3,350):
- 1200 SATs (done)
- 3.5 GPA (3.4, waiting for approved AP chem makeup that doesn't mess with babysitting schedule)

Akeela's breaths came out like ragged gasps, one hand trembling around the steering wheel as the other clenched tight around her phone. She was just at the side of the road, away from the Ackermans' but nowhere near far enough. Suburbia stretched before her as the dial tone hummed in her ear. Her eyes kept darting into the shadows, looking for . . . something.

Her knee bounced in place, the engine revving as her toes pressed in and out of the gas pedal. It was fine. She was parked.

Finally, the dial tone stopped. A huff sounded over the receiver. "You callin' me this late you better be dead," Aunt Mickey deadpanned.

Akeela did not care about the cold reception. Her mom and Aunt Mickey grew up together, but they weren't close. Akeela didn't meet her aunt until high school, and even then Aunt Mickey would only step in to help with bills or parent-teacher conferences every once in a while. It was a bare-minimum kind of thing.

This night, it didn't matter.

Akeela gripped her phone like it was her lifeline. "There was something there," she breathed. "There was something in the room."

Something in her voice must have rang true. Though small, there was a trace of concern in Aunt Mickey's voice when she spoke. "What's wrong?"

"I need you to tell me what I saw," Akeela said. She told Aunt Mickey everything that had happened—the weird behavior, the oozing scabs, the stained bed.

And the figure in the corner of the room.

Aunt Mickey didn't say anything for a while. Didn't say anything for so long Akeela checked if the call was still connected. They were. It was that bad.

"Aunt Mickey, I'm scared," Akeela said.

"Are you?"

Ah, there it was. Her aunt's sarcastic tone was back in full force, the shock of whatever Akeela had witnessed wearing off.

"Akeela, you were the one that made the deal with the Docter. You had to know you were messing with things you had no business messing with."

Akeela grit her teeth. "Well, what the hell am I messing with?"

"You don't want to know," Aunt Mickey told her. "Because you want to get out of here someday. You don't want to know more about this world."

No, no. Akeela needed answers. "Aunt Mickey."

"Why did you make a deal with the Docter that day?" her aunt asked. Her words came out harsh, like a hiss. "Was it to learn hoodoo? Or was it to survive?"

Akeela clamped her eyes shut, the sound of her breaths rattling around the car. She'd made a deal with the Docter because she was desperate. Because she thought it was her *only way* to survive.

"You lucked out," Aunt Mickey said firmly. "You made a deal with a devil and you didn't get burned. But, Akeela, make no mistake—*this is not your world*. Keep surviving. Don't buck if you don't knuck."

It was clear at this point that Aunt Mickey wouldn't be giving Akeela answers. Whether that was for her own good or not, Akeela was undecided. The plastic of her phone crackled under her tense grip. She straightened her back. She took a deep breath, picturing a life on a campus away from a shitty apartment and red eviction notices. A campus with a lawn and trees that shed leaves on a path that was cleaned every day, where dead rats didn't decompose in the open when the temperatures warmed.

"Do you know what I saw?" Akeela asked directly.

Once again, Aunt Mickey took a moment to answer. "Of course," she said. "But you don't want to know what you saw."

Akeela swallowed.

"Can I kill it?" she asked.

"If it is what I think it is, it could kill you." Aunt Mickey let out a deep chuckle. "Hell, it could kill the Docter if it decided to."

And Akeela knew the Docter was the most powerful man she'd ever met. She was in over her head. "Is it worth it?" she asked.

Aunt Mickey didn't say anything for a while again. Akeela heard a long drag on the other side of the line, and she cleared her head enough to realize Aunt Mickey had been smoking this whole time. "I'm sure the

Docter appreciates your efforts thus far," her aunt said. "Just focus on the teeth, Akeela. As long as you get him his teeth, nothing else matters."

Total Money Out of Pocket per Year (with scholarship (because you can't afford to not get it)):
- School A: $8,420
- School B: $4,380

Minimum Working Hours as College Student:
- School A: $10/hr, 30 hr/wk (doable, still get the scholarship, tho)
- School B: $10/hr, 15 hr/wk (easy, turn in this enrollment deposit first)

It was rare for Akeela to see the Ackermans' house during the daytime. The way the sun hit the eaves and bounced off the windowpanes, raining sparkly rainbows on their manicured lawn, wasn't something she had to stomach at night. She didn't expect to find their van in the driveway.

Akeela got out of her car, walking around the driveway to the front door. The baseball bat clutched in her hand seemed a little silly in the sunlight, so she leaned it on the porch steps' rail as she knocked. The plan was simple: They weren't home, and she didn't know much, but she knew their security didn't work. It was a workday, so none of the neighbors were around, either.

So she had the perfect opportunity for some *light* home invasion.

She wasn't planning to really steal anything. She knew from experience that that was way more trouble than it was worth. But Aunt Mickey was right: all that mattered was the teeth. And all Akeela wanted to do was finally get some of Bryson's loose teeth that she had left behind, and maybe leave a note for the kid to believe in himself or whatever. She wasn't warm and cuddly, but she felt sorry for him.

Akeela looked up, realizing she'd knocked a while ago, and there was still no answer.

Despite the van, as she thought, they weren't home. They must have carpooled together or something. Grabbing her bat, she went down the porch stairs in one leap, feeling the force of her feet hitting the ground up in her calves. Curling around the front of the home, Akeela winced at the long hedge's prickle against her forearms.

The side window was mostly out of view. The high fence kept her shadowed; the bushes kept her covered. There was nobody watching. There were no cameras.

But the best thing was that the Ackermans didn't even know her name. Even if it was traced back to the babysitter, how would they find Alana-No-Last-Name? She stared at her reflection in the window, watching her silhouette move from side to side as she rested the baseball bat on her shoulder. This was going to be a mistake. She was going too far.

But.

There was only one thing she wanted. She inhaled deep and swung.

The window crashed when the metal hit the glass, shards raining as it crumbled and hit the floor. The short sleeves of her T-shirt shredded just a little, light freckles of blood peppering her bicep, glass pushing into her skin.

She paused before the open window, taking another inhale. Music from inside drifted toward her in slow monotonous tones.

"Babies get scared in the dark, in the dark, in the dark!"

It was "The Wheels on the Bus" again, and Akeela wouldn't be surprised if the show was on its hundredth verse. She cleared away more of the glass, laying her tooth blanket from her bookbag onto the bottom half of the sill.

Her knees ground against the thick shards like gravel, her jeans ripping in small bits as she shoved into the kitchen. When she fully stepped onto the tile, immediately she felt the heat. It actually seemed like the heater was on. She looked up at the air vents, and sure enough, hot air blasted out of the ceiling, way unwelcome in late May.

Her sneakers crackled against the tile as she tiptoed through the kitchen, the floor tacky like Velcro. When she looked down, a thin layer of brown lined the white, deep in the cracks, in the grout. Looking around, she saw it stained the woods of the counters too.

It was as if someone had spilled sewage across the whole of the room—and just let it evaporate.

When she got to the living room, she saw the cartoons in full view. Now "The Wheels on the Bus" burrowed into her ears, hypnotic to match her slow, measured steps into the living room.

It was empty.

All the rooms downstairs were. No one was on the couch, but the TV was still on. All the lights were still on. The air was still on.

But there was no one in the Ackermans' home.

Akeela gripped tighter onto her bat and reached down to the floor with her other hand, grabbing the longest shard of glass that had popped from the window. It cut her hands, but she didn't care if she got cut. The tiny grains burned into her palm, and she let it keep her present—alert. Akeela stayed silent as she straightened her spine and her resolve.

She was going to get what she wanted.

She wasn't going to die for it.

She was going to fight for it.

Once again, the hallway was cast in shadow, and she found herself going up the steps alone with the high-pitched creaks bouncing around the landing above her. The dimmer upstairs was finally lit, the sun casting on the walls that fought away the encroaching darkness. Mrs. Ackerman must have opened her curtains.

She released her breath, swallowing one good time.

She approached Bryson's room, checking over her shoulder. No one would come up from behind her. She knew that—but *were* the Ackermans at work? Why did it look like they had disappeared the moment she left last night?

When she entered Bryson's room, there was no one in the chair. Sunlight trickled through in a thin streak from a crack in the blinds, slicing across the floor. The comforter was black, still in that messy pile that sloped as if in silhouette. It had been blue before. She remembered it that way, at least, from when she'd seen it before. It felt like a year ago at this point.

But now it was dark and damp. Akeela stared at the edges of the fabric and the slick sheen on the bed frame where the bedding brushed against it.

Her hands trembled as she reached toward the top corner.

Gripped it.

It made a squishing sound under her fingers. But even though she didn't want to see red, and she hoped to not see red, she looked at her palm.

She saw powder. Deep burgundy—nearly black—powder.

Whatever it was, it wasn't blood.

She whipped the comforter away from the mattress. She yanked with all her strength, twisting and tossing the blanket away. It hit the wall with a *slop*, and her eyes went wide.

Akeela screamed at the top of her lungs. Roadkill.

That was the only way to describe it.

Flesh and hair and bones twisted around each other in a carcass that seemed tortured in its pose, midlife, half-shredded from whatever killed it. Her hands shook as she looked at the wisps of hair at the top of its head and saw the full-grown row of teeth, unharmed inside the skinless mouth of the creature.

Mrs. Ackerman.

She didn't know why it was her first thought. Maybe it was because of the thinness of the blonde, or the teeth themselves.

Akeela took a step back, her hands shaking around the glass she still held as she stared at the corpse before her.

This was something she didn't know how to handle. This was something she hadn't expected.

Aunt Mickey was absolutely right. This thing—whatever *it* was—it could *kill* her.

But there was no one there. The house was empty. She knew that. She knew she should leave too.

But what she knew, most of all, that this was her chance.

The mother's teeth were all there in a tight row. They gleamed in the brief slash of sunlight in the room, only slightly tarnished by that redness, that deep color that bled over the edges of her molars. Otherwise, they were untouched. All thirty-two of them.

Mrs. Ackerman was already dead. And Akeela already had pliers. What was the risk *really*?

What was the risk compared to how shitty everything already was? She'd already committed to clawing her way out of this paycheck-to-paycheck hell. Akeela was fighting, fist first.

Akeela's hands calmed as she grabbed her brother's large pliers from her bag, approaching Mrs. Ackerman with blurry vision. Her breath was so short and so fast it bounced against the walls. She could hear it as she leaned closer.

Dear Tooth Fairy
Thank you for the money.

The paper was still on the bedside dresser with another tooth from Bryson. Though she had no clue where the child was, she hoped that he was somewhere with his father. That he never saw what happened to his mother.

But most of all . . . she hoped that these fucking teeth were worth something.

Akeela clenched tight on the pliers, fastening them around the bottom tooth that stood in the center of the corpse's mouth. Mrs. Ackerman had always warned Alana to never underestimate the importance of braces.

Akeela yanked from her bicep. Burgundy gunk spurted over the flesh of Mrs. Ackerman's chin. The tooth popped out, and Akeela's hand jerked. She watched the liquid spill to the floor like smoke, and she swallowed.

Footsteps sounded behind her.

She whipped around—but there was nothing there. The taps faded into quiet, low and distant, as if they were just a recording. Or just in her mind.

Akeela looked at the tooth in the tip of the pliers. She sighed.

Touching these was not an option. She didn't care if the teeth still turned when she ain't touch them—she was taking every caution she could. Without getting the tooth in contact with her skin, she popped it straight into the glass bottle. Through the blinds, the sun's gleam twisted over the hood of a car driving by. It made the shadows of the doorway dance.

She turned back to Mrs. Ackerman, working faster. She didn't have time.

She had drive.

And I always will.

Thump. A door shut somewhere behind her. She ignored it as she pulled canines, digging the pliers so deep in the flesh she gagged as she tugged, then dropping them into her glass jar.

Molars. Twist. Gag. Yank. *Plop.*

Incisors. Screw. Gag. Rip. *Tink.*

Nothing else mattered. Nothing else would stop her. She'd gotten herself this much, and she refused to let *anything* keep her underwater. She would never drown.

Thirty-one teeth. It was unquestionably enough to put her over—she could divide the money, get all her applications, *and* pay her two enrollment deposits before it was too late.

The gunk pooled in Mrs. Ackerman's mouth and on Bryson's bedside carpet. It dusted her fingers, feeling more like chalk dust than a liquid. By the time she was on the final tooth, her fingertips were stained dark purple, and her pliers were slippery and hard to grip.

"*I told you not to pull the covers.*" A child's voice.

Akeela contorted, snatching up her bat. Didn't even think about it. The voice was nearly in her ear. The metal weapon went right through the doorway, through the "boy" that stood there—who vanished in a breath, like a ghost.

Akeela screamed, whirling with the bat again. The fog remained, but no one else formed in the doorway. Akeela flexed her fingers, using the plyers with one hand. By the time she put the last tooth into the glass jar, her hands were shivering, like she was hypothermic. But she was done.

She dropped the tooth in her jar—and then caught eyes. Too soon. Too soon.

The silhouette in the corner was back.

"*Those teeth are mine,*" they said. "*I told you.*"

The shadow jumped out at her, a long strike of night. It smelled like rotted meat and char. Its weeping canines burrowed into Akeela's chest, her shoulder jerking with its bite. She screamed again, swinging her bat wildly as her back hit the ground. The metal vibrated under her palms. She was making contact. But it held onto her shoulder like it wanted to take the chunk off.

Mrs. Ackerman's teeth did not belong to it.

They were hers.

Her scream ripped from deep within her, burning her throat as the flat of the metal bat hit right into the creature's skull. Liquid ashes oozed onto the ground as she stood. Her skin shredded in its teeth. Blood gushed from her arm to her fingertips.

She looked down at her hand laying limp at her side.

The smell in the room thickened and deepened. The stench shoved itself into her mouth, clogging her throat until she felt her lungs in her chest, pulsing for air. This . . . this *thing*. It was like a snake, with scaley, thick skin that was rough to the touch. But brown skin dotted in thick patches up its neck and hips and feet. It had human ears.

Akeela took a step back as she looked at its exposed flesh, and then she took out the shard of glass. Her screams were inhuman now, and she burrowed the shard into the monster's mouth, screaming with all the air she had left. She stabbed at its teeth in wide swings, over and over.

Until its chest no longer rose and fell.

Flesh dangled at the end of its last tooth in chunks, shreds of red and thickness swaying like the fringe on a dress. But her hands were already so dirty. She grabbed it bare, palming the large canine and shoving it into her bag. Her screams were short shrieks now. High pitched, tinny. Staccato in one breath, gone the next.

As she put tooth after tooth in the bag, she realized she wasn't screaming at all.

She was laughing.

Standard adult teeth for twenty dollars. Current rate for baby teeth: forty dollars. She knew she should have left a long time ago. Staying was stupid—she could have gotten caught, or killed.

A monster. A rarity. One tooth—one hundred dollars, maybe?

She was glad she didn't leave, though. She didn't get caught. She didn't die at all.

She made it work. And she'd *earned* every bloody drop of cold, hard cash she got.

So she laughed with joy.

I Love Your Eyes

by

Joel Rochester

The first time he saw them, Adam joked that Frey's eyes were the ones that would belong to his lover: a rich dark brown he could gaze into for eternity. In return Frey remarked that Adam's eyes were the blue of an ocean tide, a great wave that could move their life into a new direction. From that moment the two had been inseparable, bound by an invisible string of fate. Frey saw it as a sign from some cosmic force—as though their parents had delivered Adam on the anniversary of their death, a wish for Frey to be happy. They were happy with Adam; they were in love with him.

He was their opposite yet their parallel. Even though Adam's preference of crime and sci-fi didn't match Frey's interest in fantasy and romance, they still watched *Game of Thrones* together, and even tried to come up with their own alternative ending. Frey attended a three-hour orchestra performance, despite hating classical music, because Adam loved one of the cellists who was performing. Frey even found themself crying when the orchestra played the Tchaikovsky Pas de Deux. And Adam said strawberry was the best ice cream flavor when the correct answer was mint chocolate chip. But they both enjoyed horror films, sharing a keen eye for how wrongdoings are always punished in slashers. Their love lay in the differences as well as the similarities.

Now, as the couple approached their three-year anniversary, Frey smiled in reverie at the wall of photos in their London apartment, all memories that they had made with Adam: The late-night study sessions when Adam worked on numerous essays for his biomechanical engineering degree and Frey gazed at him, providing constant tea, cuddles, and snacks. The ceremony where Frey won a grant for Black people in tech with an article they had submitted on improving the accuracy of real-time location tracking. Adam had bought the biggest bouquet out of anyone at that ceremony. They were academics first, lovers second.

Of course, Frey had been planning something special for their anniversary: a candlelit dinner, all prepared by them, in a rented cabin in the woods. Completely unplugged, cut off from the rest of the world, they would only have each other. It would be delicate, intimate, and perfect. Often Frey and Adam talked about their desire to run away, and this would give them the opportunity to do just that.

"Do you ever feel the desperate urge to leave behind everything that ties you here?" Frey once asked, snuggling up to Adam in bed. "Though, love, I just realized that is probably way too deep for a 2:00 AM conversation."

"It's not like we've never done this before. At this point, we may as well call you Frey, late-night-philosopher extraordinaire," Adam joked, bringing Frey closer to him as they lightly bit his shoulder at that remark. "Ow—okay, okay! Well, I guess I do. Sometimes, I have this desire to create my own little world to live in, with the people I create to be there. But is it wrong to play God? Or have we made ourselves believe we are too powerless for such a role?"

"*Oookay*, Socrates," Frey said, surprised by the direction of Adam's response. "You've clearly had enough philosophical thinking for one night. You're just desperate to play *The Sims* right now, aren't you?"

"Something like that, yeah."

It was often the smaller things that Frey loved about Adam. He always remembered to thank them for cleaning the kitchen, and he never forgot their go-to coffee order. Everything he planned was done meticulously, like when he arranged a private dinner for their first anniversary in the bookstore where they first met. Adam brought to life such grandiose ideas that made Frey's heart swim with glee.

Despite the happiness Adam brought, there were times when Frey saw something in him—rare moments that made them doubt their relationship. Each time he returned from a work trip, he would be especially agitated, confused, and conflicted. He claimed his trips often consisted of stressful work, analyzing some new breakthrough in technology or visiting hospitals to conduct research. Once Frey saw blood on his shoes, but when questioned, he explained they were from an intensive surgery where he'd forgotten to wear shoe covers.

Though he gave these explanations and reassurances, Adam's heart would turn to ice, the very tension of Frey's apartment becoming so tight they refrained from taking any steps toward him. It was at these times that Frey craved for Adam to open up; it had been almost three years and they still felt he carefully guarded parts of himself. But before the air between them could suffocate Frey completely, he would return to them as the Adam from before, the Adam they knew, the Adam they loved.

It would be okay though, as Adam only had one research trip left, and after that, he wouldn't have to leave again as he would write up his findings. The idea of always having Adam where they could see him, always having him close by, Frey liked that. They liked that very much.

Twilight skies emerged as Frey waited by the apartment window for Adam to come from the lab. The week leading up to their anniversary had been a complete disaster. The cabin Frey had booked cancelled their reservation due to a sudden and raging woodboring beetle infestation. To make matters even worse, their favorite *Great British Bake-Off* baker was no longer able to make the anniversary cake that Adam had been excited about for months. Unlike Adam, Frey was drowning in the stress of now having to plan something completely new with such short notice. It was not their forte. They preferred long-term planning, plans that took years to enact.

At the apex of their stress, they felt the hairs rising on their skin. Frey withdrew the gold-plated Zippo lighter from their pocket, rubbing their father's engraved initials and set it ablaze, embracing the warmth it provided. This lighter was the only thing that Frey kept after their parents died. It reminded them of how the lighter brought them together. Holding it tightly, Frey reassured themself that they would make their parents proud. All the pair had ever wanted for them was for them to do what their heart desired; Frey could achieve that and so much more.

The front door unlocked as Frey finished lighting some candles to set the mood. Adam walked into their flat, throwing himself down on the green velvet couch. Although he didn't live with Frey, he very much acted like it was his home.

"God, I am so, so happy to be finished with today." Adam smiled at Frey, who was nervous to mention anything about rearranging their anniversary plans. They had managed to find some alternatives, but they wanted to gauge how he felt about a change in plans.

However, any attempt Frey would've made to broach the subject was completely negated by a singular sentence: "For our anniversary, I'm taking you to my parents' manor in North Wales."

The room was silent, the crackling flames growing louder as Frey stared blankly at Adam. "What? Your parents have a *manor house?* No. No, that's not what we're doing. We both agreed I'd make the arrangements this year."

"They haven't exactly worked out."

"Oh, I know they haven't worked out. But I was working something out. I had alternatives and spreadsheets and—"

"I really do appreciate that, but you know how special this would be for me. It's what my parents would've wanted, and maybe yours too."

Frey recoiled slightly. The mention of their parents on his tongue felt foreign, unrecognizable. They took a deep breath, trying to stop their hands from shaking.

"I— You're right. Thank you, I guess." They tried not to sound ungrateful, but they wished Adam had at least asked first, not that he ever did. It was something they noticed slowly at first: Adam assumed what they would think instead of asking for their opinion. With a Starbucks order it was cute, but it hurt more when Adam got Frey a chocolate cake for their birthday, knowing full well it was *his* favorite rather than theirs.

It always led to either Adam apologizing by cooking his famous French onion soup or Frey conceding. Giving in. Submitting.

In this case, Frey decided they would go along with Adam's plan; they had to.

"I guess I can still make it work. But let's not skip over the fact you're an heir to a manor? After three years, you're still keeping things from me. In North Wales too!" Though Frey and Adam were close, his family history was always a touchy subject. Once, they had both opened up over a bottle of wine about their messy family histories. For Adam, it was his abusive father. For Frey, it was the manner of their parents death: saying that their parents died was, in fact, avoiding the fact that they were murdered. But when Frey tried to press further into Adam's past, with his family or any potential exes, he would close up and become reclusive. He was a private person, so Frey took his desire for them to see his family home as a sign that he wanted to share a bit more.

"We used to hike up parts of Yr Wyddfa," Adam said. "Before they died and I was left with their inheritance. It's not something I like to talk about, Frey. Living with them was a dark time in my life. And after they died, I was so lonely, so afraid. And that's when she came to m—" Adam stopped, paralyzed as if he were a statue. Frey knew they shouldn't push any further, but there was a desire to know more, about him and about her.

"Who?"

"No one. Forget I said anything."

"But—"

Adam rose, putting his coat on as he made his way to the front door, Frey tailing behind him. "I'm gonna head off, but be sure you're packed by Wednesday morning. I'll come pick you up at nine." He kissed Frey's forehead, leaving without eating the dinner they had made. As moments passed and the apartment grew darker, moonlight spilled into the room where Frey stood alone in silence.

It would be dishonest if Frey said they were enthusiastic about going to North Wales with Adam. It was all very sudden, and they'd had no say in the change of plans whatsoever—their voice lost. Frey felt their chest quicken as they paced around the room. They slumped against the hall bookshelf, anxiety creeping across their skin. The walls closed in on them, and the clock ticked loudly across the room. It was in these moments that Frey remembered what their mother had taught them. As Frey took a deep breath and opened their eyes, their fears began to quiet.

With her herbal remedies and powerful words of wisdom, Frey's mother often knew exactly what was needed, even when Frey didn't know themself. Now with her gone, Frey felt the calming exercise gave them an added sense of power, as if she were right there with them.

"I can do this," Frey told themself as they stood, feeling renewed as they ventured over and withdrew their suitcase from the back of their wardrobe. For their parents, they would do this. Because there was something about Adam that Frey was so drawn to. He had his flaws and his moments, but love, to Frey, was accepting those flaws. Ultimately, no one else understood the hunger they shared, the desire to seek what is yours, to claim it for yourself. And Adam had claimed Frey, as they had claimed him.

———

At 9:00 AM the following Wednesday, Adam arrived in his black Tesla Model S. This was one of the few times Frey had seen Adam's car, as he often preferred to take public transport, or the rare Uber in case of an emergency. However, today would be the first time Frey actually sat in it.

Frey readjusted their seat numerous times, as though their cheap gray sweats would ruin the leather of such an expensive car. Sometimes it was these differences that made Frey wonder whether they truly fit together.

As Adam drove, his phone noted it would take six hours to reach North Wales. Frey was glad they had peed beforehand as Adam didn't like stopping midroute, preferring to head directly for any goal in mind. Often this meant Frey found smaller details he missed.

Frey had, once again, packed at the last minute and hadn't gotten much sleep last night, so they attempted to make up for it during the first two hours of the drive. Later in the journey, the pair debated if one of Adam's friends was attracted to one of Frey's, which, like most of their conversations, led to too many tangents and, inevitably, the discussion of academic research. Whereas Adam explained his professor's hypothesis for machine-assisted bioregeneration, Frey spoke about the potential to code technology into jewelry.

Eventually the hills of the Welsh countryside soothed Frey to sleep again. It was only when Adam turned the ignition off that Frey awoke to the sight of a large iron gate, which presumably led to the manor. Darkened clouds plagued the skies. The trees that paved the way shook violently, and the overgrown ivy reigned over the stone walls surrounding the manor. The ivy didn't reached the gate itself. In fact, it looked like it had been cut wherever it closed in on the gate, which Frey thought was interesting for a place that hadn't been visited in years.

Down the road from the village of Beddgelert, the manor itself was tucked away in a cozy part of North Wales near the mountain Yr Wyddfa, or, as it was known in English, Snowdon. Adam had explained on the drive that the manor was built during the Victorian period, passed through the generations until it eventually came into his possession. The pair hopped out of the car to pull the iron gates open, the scent of rusted metal covering their hands. Afterward, Adam drove them down the winding road that eventually led to his family home. Frey took in its architecture, the way the wood and stone supported one another in harmony. Its many windows were many doorways into a part of Adam's world. Frey had no idea how they would fit into it, or if they could. The sheer size of the manor and its effortless grandeur intimidated them into still silence. It was the windows that drew them in, the windows that acted like eyes, the windows that bore directly into Frey's soul.

Frey's hand shook, but when Adam held it, they felt themself calm, the raging ocean subsiding to a calm sea. He was always like this, his cool nature able to calm the fiercest fire, the strongest storms. Frey was thankful for his presence, for he reminded them what was important.

"Your family home is quite big, y'know? I . . . Our childhoods were very different." Frey squeezed Adam's hand, who returned the gesture and gazed at the house, with a look that Frey couldn't quite decipher.

"Funny, I've always found it quite small. You couldn't hide anything, not even secrets."

As Frey turned toward the front door, they found a footprint in the mud, of a similar size and print to one of Adam's shoes. They were musing over this when Adam stepped into Frey's vision. He must've guessed Frey's thought process because he explained, "Oh! I stopped by here on the way back from the work trip in Bangor. It helped me realize that I wanted to take you here. In a roundabout way, I took the Airbnb being cancelled as a sign this was the time."

Frey laughed; it was just a strange coincidence, just another one of his strange coincidences. But how many strange coincidences does it take until it's stranger than a coincidence?

The couple entered the manor together, and the coldness seemingly intensified indoors, stillness permeating the air. Both contributed to what Frey's mother would describe as a "strange aura of tension," a vibe that made them feel on edge. The darkness of the interior was uninviting, the shutters on every window closed, emphasizing that this was an atmosphere devoid of any life or happiness.

White sheets covered the furniture. A clear layer of dust coated the oak floors. Adam noted there was limited electricity, the main sources of light coming from gas lamps, which Frey remarked was "very eccentric" of Adam's parents. The interior of the house groaned, providing nothing but an echo to every thought and every feeling as the pair uncovered fragments of the vast living space.

As they removed the sheets, Frey began to construct an image of Adam's parents. The red velvet sofa combined with the lacquered oak table indicated a couple who was refined in their taste—perhaps pretentious and *too* perfect. Frey knew he had been unhappy here, and the layers of dust echoed that.

"Your parents were definitely Tories," Frey joked as they removed the sheet from an old bone-china tea set.

"That, I can't even deny. But this is my parents' house, so show some respect." Frey watched Adam examining the furniture, looking as though they were ghosts coming to haunt him. What once were characteristics of his family home were now nothing but articles of a faded past.

When Frey examined a faded photograph of Adam and a woman Frey didn't recognize on the wall, the slightest whiff of lemon wafted through the air. Frey wretched, the clinical scent bringing back images of the hospital room where their parents lay dead on their beds, their marriage fingers cut off as some sort of murderer's signature. As they had learned to do, Frey took a deep breath and regained stability. Then they turned to Adam.

"Do you have a secret sibling you haven't told me about?" they joked as Adam came over to glance at the photo. Any slight happiness he might've had dropped from his face.

"Oh. That's Penny—Penelope. My ex-fiancée."

"Ex-fiancée? This is the first time I'm hearing of her—was the breakup that messy?"

Adam remained silent for what felt like a minute before he coldly said, "She died."

"Oh. Shit. I'm so sorry, Adam." Frey had ripped open a deep wound, and they noticed the watery glaze of Adam's eyes. He would either withdraw and ignore them for the rest of the night or proceed as if nothing had happened.

"It's fine. I'm sure that soon I won't be sad about her being dead." Adam smiled at the picture of Penny, gently touching the photograph. Frey felt hot in the face. Adam never touched them that gently, that lovingly, and yet this photograph reached something in him in an instant that Frey couldn't in three years.

"Losing a loved one is tough, but things do become easier," Frey responded, moving away to take in more of the manor. "You find ways to live on, which can fuel you for many years."

While Adam strolled through the manor, Frey felt increasingly on edge. Their chest grew heavy with dread, and they felt like Adam's parents were watching their every move, the furniture becoming loyal spies with a mission to make Frey unwelcome.

At that moment, Adam's hand enveloped theirs, and Frey turned to smile at the man they loved. Maybe they could get used to being inside such a massive house. But would it always be like this between them, always on the edge of being too different?

"So, can I have a look around? I want to be a little nosy." Frey tenderly squeezed Adam's hand as they pointed down one of the many corridors.

"Actually, I'd prefer to give you the grand tour. I'd rather not let you loose in my family home so easily." Adam moved his hand to Frey's shoulder as he squeezed it. Frey nodded, their elbow hooked around Adam's, who led them through the house.

There were numerous things Frey noticed as Adam showed the many rooms of his past. Though the house was very old, with much of the wood either rotting or breaking away, there remained a timeless quality about it. As Adam would tell them, whether it lay in the crimson velvet curtains or the echoes of the hardwood floor, there was a character and personality to this house. But Frey couldn't quite decipher whether that personality actually liked their presence.

As they returned to the living area, Frey was drawn closer to a brown gilded door near the back of the room. Footprints lay in the dust facing toward the door; they looked fresh though neither of them had approached this door all day. Before they could investigate further, however, Adam took Frey's hands and spun them away.

"You do not want to go down there, not yet anyways," Adam smiled, guiding them to one of the uncovered sofas.

"Oh? Someone's been down there recently though." Frey nodded over to the footprints, resisting the urge to narrow their eyes at him. Perhaps the front door hadn't been the only place Adam had inspected during his last visit.

"You're a little Sherlock Holmes, aren't you? Yes, I did go down there when I came back last week. I was checking that the oil for the lamps was fully stocked. The basement is a mess right now, but I'll tidy it up for you." Adam caressed Frey's cheeks as he leant forward, placing a tender kiss on their lips. It made Frey realize that this was perfect and what they always had imagined for their anniversary: remote and secluded, away from the world that pressured them so heavily.

But as Frey embraced Adam's warmth, behind the lingering lemon scent, there was a hint of a deeper smell. The faint smell of something putrid arose, as though rot lay beneath the floorboards. Frey couldn't help but wonder: Was this the house's way of welcoming or warning them?

On the morning of their anniversary, Frey stood at the base of Yr Wyddfa. Small pockets of snow covered the peaks like little white blankets. As the happy couple prepared for their guided hike, Frey looked forward to creating more memories that they'd cherish. They knew it was hard for Adam to open up, yet Frey hoped going somewhere so deeply connected to him would change this. Otherwise, things wouldn't look good for the future of their relationship.

"Need some help?" a deep, masculine voice asked as Frey turned to a kind face smiling at them, green eyes filling them with comfort.

"Th-That would be great. I've never hiked up Yr Wyddfa before, but there's a first time for everything, right?" Frey smiled, watching as the man approached and checked out their hiking gear.

"You're so right about that. Sometimes it can be scary to go through with something new, but nine times out of ten, you feel much better afterward." These were words of wisdom that Frey so desperately needed, and they appreciated what this new friend had to say. "Well, it looks like you've got great gear for the hike. I'm sure we'll have a great walk together, alongside everyone else who's joining us today. Name's Kai, by the way."

Kai held out his hand, which Frey shook. "I'm Frey! And you're too kind. I would love some help if you're ready to provide it."

"Adam." He spoke from behind Frey, as though he were their shadow looming over them. "I'm sure you've prepared an adequate route for my partner to climb up?"

"Partner? Oh—of course! It's a great scenic route for beginners." Kai smiled, as he began to lead the group up the Welsh mountain.

Kai opted for the Llanberis Path, which Adam grunted over, noting that Pyg Track would be much faster. Nevertheless, the path Kai led was

filled with scenic views of the countryside, the lush greenery only separated by small streams leading to glistening lakes. It was mesmerizing,
and Frey's small conversations with Kai only enhanced their enjoyment of
the walk; he was fascinating to talk to and really took an interest in Frey's
life. However, any attempts to enjoy this hike with Adam were spoiled by
his cold demeanor. He barely interacted, apart from a few grunts whenever Kai spoke.

As they reached a fork on the path, Adam finally spoke up, "We
should go right. It'll be scenic and much faster than the left."

"That's true, Adam. However, the right is also steeper, and as we have
some older walkers with us, the left is the more ideal path," Kai responded,
ushering everyone toward the left path while Adam remained. "If you
would rather, you can take the right path and meet us at the summit."

Frey stood between the two men, unsure of how to proceed. They
wanted to continue their conversation with Kai about their favorite horror books, but they couldn't let Adam out of their sight, especially in the
state he was in. Frey could feel the storm brewing within Adam's mind,
and ultimately, it was a tough decision to make.

"Frey. Let's go," Adam coldly instructed. As always, the decision had
been made for them, and there would be no point in arguing with him.
As Frey turned to leave, Kai gave them a slip of paper.

"To let me know when you've reached the top." He winked, and with
that, Frey left with Adam.

As they took the right path to ascend Yr Wyddfa, the less-than-happy
couple remained in silence. Despite the increasingly beautiful scenery,
Frey, feeling Adam's animosity, couldn't enjoy it as much as before. It was
times like these that Frey would reach for their father's lighter, fiddling
with it while Adam processed his anger and prepared to take it out on
Frey.

They hated these moments: never knowing when Adam's rage was
going to arrive. When they approached the mountain's peak half an hour
later, Frey realized it wouldn't be long before Adam would burst. Just as
they were messaging Kai to tell him they had made it to the top, the wind
roared and Adam turned to face Frey.

"What the fuck was that back there?" Adam demanded, his cheeks flushed red hot. Never had Frey seen such an explosion from him.

Frey's hand shook as the fierce winds blew on the mountain peak. They couldn't believe that, once again, Adam was trying to pin this on them. They sought out the lighter in their pocket for comfort, "What do you mean? You're the one who embarrassed me. I made a new friend, and yet you tried to prove you were superior."

Adam moved toward Frey, who struggled to breathe as the coldness sharpened. Slowly, almost imperceptibly, their attempts at moving away from Adam had forced them to creep closer to the edge of the mountain-side. "Adam, step away from me."

"No, Frey, we're going to settle this right here, right now."

Besides Adam, they were completely alone, in an unfamiliar place. Frey had never thought Adam was the type to get physical, but if he decided to push . . . The cold winds ate at Frey's thoughts, the hairs on their neck rising as their heart began to race.

Then, just as suddenly as his anger had risen, Adam turned away, sighing deeply before he said, "I thought this vacation was going to be just us, away from the world?"

"It is! It definitely is! But meeting new people isn't exactly a bad thing. I know it's hard for you to make friends given your aloofness, but—"

"Aloofness?" Adam whirled around, pressing even closer as the rocks behind Frey's feet rolled down the mountainside. "You think I can't be friendly?"

Frey gripped their lighter, clinging to the comfort it provided. Adam could do anything in this moment, and no one would ever know. Frey knew he loved them, but had they gone too far this time? Despite every fiber in their body telling them to, Frey resisted the urge to scream.

Continuing to fiddle with the lighter, Frey took a deep breath and said, "It's not that. You know you can be hard to get along with some-times. But lately, it's been worse. You're so absent from what is going on right here, right now. It's like I'm spending our anniversary with a brick wall. I don't know, do you still want me anymore?"

"Don't be stupid. Of course I want you."

Frey scoffed, "Then show it! You literally showed more affection to a photograph of your ex-fiancée than—"

Adam gripped Frey's wrist tightly, painfully so. His icy gaze bore into their eyes, a chilling warning. "You have no idea what powers you're messing with."

Frey couldn't move, despite fear clawing at them to run, to scream, to hide. The warmth from the lighter wasn't enough. But there was something inside them, a lone flame Frey had repressed for so long. The flame turned white hot, and that warmth was inviting to Frey, an irresistible urge to let go. And so, they did.

"No, Adam. YOU have no idea who the fuck you're messing with." Frey's eyes ignited, staring at their partner with a new intensity. And, with their father's lighter held tightly in their fist, Frey punched Adam square in the face. A stone-cold silence hung in the air thereafter. Frey had snapped, and as Adam recovered, realization dawned on his face.

"Oh shit." Adam immediately let go of Frey, dropping his face between his cold hands, rubbing gently. "Oh shit, oh shit, oh shit. I . . . Frey, fuck. Frey, I deserved that. I really became my father's son. Just . . . I'm so fucking sorry, I can't—not again. Fuck."

Frey stared at him, watching the tears fall down his face and the blood seep from his nose. "Baby, it's okay. Well, it's not—you're literally bleeding—but we've both apologized. We can put this behind us, can't we?" They smiled as they pulled Adam into a tight, warm embrace. Frey felt reassured in that moment: they couldn't lose Adam; they wouldn't let go of the one person they needed. Not yet.

They sat together on the summit of Yr Wyddfa for what felt like an eternity. The silence this time was not one filled with malice but one of calm and contentment—as though the recent past no longer mattered and they were here as two individuals, linked together by an invisible string. Frey felt they had connected, that maybe their punch had unlocked something in him. In a way, Frey felt good about committing the act, not that they'd ever admit it.

"For a moment there, I thought you were going to push me off the mountain." Frey laughed as they snuggled in closer to Adam's embrace.

Slowly Adam cocked Frey's head toward his, and the pair stared into each other's eyes, those memorable eyes, deeply.

"What would you have done if I had?" Adam asked plainly, holding Frey tightly as they mused over their response for a short while.

"I'd have dragged you down with me. I would have my revenge," Frey joked, poking Adam's chest as the pair laughed together. This was it, what Frey had always wanted in their relationship. And yet, the feeling of power from punching Adam lingered in the back of their mind.

"Tell you what," Adam said. "I'll cook us my famous French onion soup tonight. You go pamper yourself, dress up for dinner, and together we'll have a feast that only the *Game of Thrones*' Red Wedding can rival." Adam smirked and Frey chuckled, squeezing him tightly as they placed a kiss on his forehead.

Snow crunched. As the couple heard approaching footsteps, Frey quickly moved to wipe the blood off Adam's face. This way, no one would see what they had done; no one would know of Frey's moment of anger.

"Hey lovebirds!" Kai shouted, leading the rest of the group to the mountaintop. "I'm glad you made it up safely!"

As they watched the sun slowly begin to set and storm clouds gather in all around, Frey realized they had fallen into this routine again. But this time—this time it would be different. After tonight, they wouldn't need to worry about anything anymore. All their worries would be behind them, and Frey would finally be happy.

—∞—

After returning from their hike, Frey prepared for dinner in the groaning manor. The cracks in the wood had grown larger, the moans of the house louder. Goosebumps prickled on Frey's skin at the creaks in the floorboards. The storm outside whistled, assaulting the glass windows with its cries. Frey could've sworn the wind was screaming a single word, one they couldn't quite decipher. They gazed in the mirror as they fidgeted with the lighter once more. And they finally descended to the dining hall, the manor bathed in the darkness of night.

They looked beautiful, a flicker of flame in the darkness. They opted for a high-neck satin shirt, red, with volume in the long sleeves; black trousers with a gold belt; and oxblood brogues, providing the perfect finishing accent. They also wore the gold mother-of-pearl necklace Adam had given them for the couple's second anniversary. This was the outfit—minus the necklace—Frey had worn when they'd first met, the day when everything in the world had unmade and made itself. It was when Frey realized that everything happens in cycles and the time had come for them to end what Adam had started.

As Frey sat at the dinner table across from Adam, the lamplight illuminated the delicious French onion soup between them. Here they were yet again: Adam apologizing with his favorite meal and Frey conveniently forgetting anything had happened. The cold crept up Frey's skin as their eyes stared at the man who shifted between Jekyll and Hyde, night and day, hot and cold. The doctor whose eyes were a warm river exuded a tenderness and consideration toward Frey that made him a man many would desire. But then would come Mr. Hyde, who allowed no life or air to thrive, leaving Frey to fend for themself, alone. They couldn't take this duality anymore, and so Frey had vowed it would end.

Tonight.

The pair consumed the soup, the familiar flavor filling Frey with warmth. They placed the lighter down on the table, noticing the lamps were slowly dimming. Frey rose from their seat and delivered a small gift box to Adam. "My gift to you, my love."

He opened the box to find an assortment of ethically sourced spices and seasonings from around the world. Included were handmade recipe cards Frey had spent so long creating, working with artists to make them just right. It wasn't elaborate, but it was intricate and exactly Frey. Adam smiled at the gift, shuffling through the cards as he examined each recipe.

However, Frey couldn't help but notice how Adam's hand shook while he held anything. His foot tapped a repeating rhythm on the hardwood floor. The echo of the taps made Frey consider the almost porcelain quality of Adam's actions tonight. Despite his smiles and kind eyes, he was on edge. The room grew steadily darker as the lamps began to dim.

"Do you think the lamp oil needs changing?" Frey suggested, signaling over to what they believed was the way to the basement. "Maybe I should go down and get more?"

"No, I replaced them just before dinner. Why? What's up?" Adam placed his hand on Frey's as he smiled up at them.

"N-Nothing. It's just a bit dark, that's all." Frey felt light headed as they made their way back to their seat. They couldn't be ill, not now. Not while they were celebrating their anniversary.

Finishing his soup, Adam proposed they make a toast—glasses filled with his parents' favorite wine.

"Tonight, we toast to how we should continue to do everything for the ones we love. Happy Anniversary, Frey." And after Frey sipped the wine, Adam brought his hands together. "That is why my present to you, my love, is a sacrifice for the greater good."

"What is it? Are you making me give up those red velvet cupcakes I get from Martha's?"

"No, no, no, my love. Simply, you are going to die tonight. And what I take from you will be used in such a better way. For you are undeserving. You are weak."

Frey was taken aback, not only by what Adam was saying but also by the way he was saying it. They had never heard this tone of voice from him before. With such intention, such conviction. Their hands were shaking now, their feet jittering under the table, ready to run, waiting for what Adam would do next.

Frey felt the walls crowd around them as though they'd been sentenced and every inch of the manor wished to see the predetermined verdict. The truth didn't matter. Frey would always be guilty—because Adam would always be Adam, and Frey would always give in.

Adam relaxed back into his seat. "Let's face it, this was an awful relationship. I did think once that we could be happy together, that I could forget everything I had tried to do for Penny. But you were so goddamn annoying, always wanting my attention, always bickering with me. I couldn't leave you though. I needed you. You were the final prize I needed to win, the final part of my masterpiece. For that, you needed to be happy, and I did what I could to make that happen despite how hard it was to be with you as the years went on."

"In that case, why don't we just cut things off now?" Frey asked, the room growing so dark they could barely see. They felt their limbs becoming weaker as they tried to protest. They refused to believe that this was the man Adam was underneath it all. "You don't need me; you can go be in someone else's life."

"Alas, Frey, the only life I need now is yours. But we'll talk soon, my love. Have a nice rest. The soup really had a great spice in it today, no?"

Frey glanced down. A residual powder laced the bottom of their bowl. The soup had been tainted. This was the man Adam truly was, the phantom beneath the mask. The darkness around them only enhanced the fear growing inside Frey, but they couldn't move from their seat, and they slunk back in their chair. The manor walls pulled back into sinister smiles that rose from the crevices as they watched Frey struggle. The fireplace behind Adam began to fade, prompting Frey to use the last of their energy to reach for their father's lighter. However, their body wouldn't respond to the desperate calls to hold this source of comfort. For malice has no warmth, and it was intent on consuming Frey completely.

As the cold wave swept them to slumber, everything they had known fell apart. And in that moment, as Frey grasped the lighter, they finally understood what the wind had been trying to say.

Run.

The familiar warmth of consciousness washed over Frey as they opened their eyes, their vision beginning to clear. Frey looked upward, greeted by the light coming from the brown gilded door of the basement—the other side of it. They must have been carried down here. The place was so much larger than their London apartment.

The heavy stench of decay overwhelmed them. It permeated the air as they felt the roughness of the rope that bound them to the back of a green velvet armchair. They struggled against the bonds, the flashes of Adam's sinister smile popping into Frey's mind.

"Adam?" they called out, slight urgency in their tone. Every inch of this room was alien to them, from the loud groan of a fridge in the back corner to the rattling bottles of lamp oil on the wall. They couldn't reach their father's lighter, and so they tried their mother's breathing exercise. Nothing helped the growing unease and disquiet they felt. Their trembling limbs were laced with the frightful truth that something was very, very wrong.

As Frey focused on the refrigerator, the inside revealed the body of a woman. Not just any woman though; this was the same woman from the picture: Penelope, Adam's ex-fiancée, who died. And she definitely looked dead. There was something oddly constructed about her. Parts of her body were stitched together with parts that didn't belong, as though she were some kind of puzzle that Adam was trying to fix.

And as their eyes descended from her straw-like blonde hair to her skeletal hands, they spotted her marriage fingers, stitched with fingers that had their own wedding rings. Frey attempted to leap forward, but their bindings held them in place. Staring at Penelope, their heart swelled with grief for what Adam had done to them. She didn't deserve this, and neither did Frey.

The floorboards above creaked as footsteps descended the steps, each footfall filling Frey with dread. As Adam came into view, they could no longer find the man they had grown to love. There remained no love in his eyes, replaced instead by that insatiable hunger—the hunger Frey knew all too well, belonging to a predator gazing upon their prey in delight.

"I'm so sorry it has come to this, my love." Adam caressed Frey's cheek, smiling softly as he paced around the armchair. "But you see, my glorious plan is almost complete."

His tone was sinister, with a blasphemous self-righteousness that twisted Frey's stomach. While they slowly worked on wriggling free from their bonds, they pretended to struggle, to keep him talking while they formulated a plan.

"Why are you doing this, Adam?" Frey cried, tears forming in their eyes as the fear began to creep in. "Please, you don't have to do this."

They didn't want to die. If they died here, they wouldn't be able to finish their degree, finally take that trip to Tokyo they always wanted to, or most important, witness how their favorite author's latest series was going to end. They were odd thoughts for a person who was about to die but they saw value in their life, even if Adam thought their desires trivial.

"That's what they all fucking say, isn't it? Initially, I wasn't going to kill you. I only sought to steal parts from those who killed her. However, when I looked into those eyes— Oh, Frey, *when I looked into your eyes,*" Adam repeated with sickening perversion. He leaned in close to delicately whisper into their ear, "I love your eyes, for they are ones my lover should have. And well, Frey, I never meant you."

Horror dawned across Frey's face as the pieces of Adam's puzzle fell into place. He was going to take *their eyes* and give them to the hollow, rotting woman in the fridge.

"Adam, why her?" Frey asked, staring at the woman.

Adam shot Frey a look of icy disdain, like they had committed the greatest offence. Then, as if praising a revered deity, Adam began to explain, "She is my everything: Penelope, the one who showed me all the world could offer. And she was taken away from me, her pure light snuffed out. It was a tragic traffic accident—there were so many people who could've saved her, and yet they chose to save themselves. And that night, by divine proclamation, my mind cleared: I would bring her back; I would give her life again."

"You're fucking with me. She is literally a rotting corpse inside of that fridge."

"Don't be so rude about her looks! She is beautiful; she is eternal." Adam smiled as he kissed the glass of the fridge. "Love drives us to do the impossible, and I'm almost there. I've devoted my entire education to bringing her back, and not even God will stop me from doing so."

"Oh, so you're not just insane. You're also a necrophiliac, great!"

"Petty words will do nothing. There's nowhere for you to run now." Adam returned to Frey, placing a tender hand on their cheek while his gaze bore into their eyes. "She had always wanted brown eyes. Soon, she will see the world with the innocence you hold, and you will be dead. Finally."

As the modern Pygmalion cackled, Frey stifled their own grin. Adam really thought he'd succeeded in playing them for a fool, huh?

Good, they thought. It was time for the real charade to fall and their final act to begin.

"You never asked about my parents, or what they looked like," Frey coolly said as they twisted their wrists and let the rope go free. "You never asked about their murder, but you knew they could never find who killed them."

Adam shrugged, continuing to stare at Penelope and whispering small things to her as he prepared to kill Frey. The electricity hummed in the walls, and the anger brewed inside Frey. They continued to breathe deeply, feeling their mother's presence with them.

"Oh, dear Adam, you know what they say: keep your enemies close."

Adam froze, then turned slowly toward Frey. For the first time, they saw real fear in his eyes. As they stared at one another, the iciness of Adam's gaze met the fiery blaze of Frey's anger, the two caught in a battle that seemed to last an eternity yet occurred in a single second.

"That's impossible." Adam uttered, "You couldn't have possibly known—"

"That night my parents died," Frey began, "our eyes met as you left their hospital room, don't you remember? Their fingers were in your possession."

Adam paced back and forth, his breath becoming unsteady, shaking his hands fervently. "I remember now. I . . . I was on a work trip."

"Yeah, you say that, but do you really? Remember, I mean. Because to me, a year later, it appeared you had forgotten all about it. I didn't believe it at first, how something so traumatic for me was so meager to you. But you had the privilege of erasing a minor detail. You loved my eyes and yet forgot them in an instant. However, your eyes became the source of my nightmares, your face a permanent memory."

"How did you even find me?"

"Oh, my love, did you *ever* pay attention to my research? My mum once lost her wedding ring, and it was so devastating to her. And so, when my father gifted her with a new one on their anniversary, I ensured she could never lose it again: real-time location tracking, coded into a small object. I found you because you stole the greatest symbol of their love, you fucking prick.

"So when we met again that fateful day, like I had planned, I knew you and your life. I played house, like I was unaware of your scheming and plotting, and all the while you couldn't possibly believe I would develop a game of my own. All for you, my dearest love, my deepest pain."

"Shut up, Frey! Shut the fuck up right now. Or I'll *make* you shut up." Adam drew closer toward Frey, but he came too near, too close. Frey's hand flung to Adam's throat, digging their fingernails deep into his skin. Frey stared into his eyes.

"I love your eyes, Adam. They reminded me every day that on this day, I would get to fulfil my vow to avenge my parents, my vow to drag your fucking soul down to the depths of HELL ITSELF!"

Frey screamed. After three years of pretending, three years of suppressing every single urge, they were able to let it all go. This was the moment they would finally kill him. Though it wasn't exactly the way they had imagined it—killing Adam in the middle of the woods and leaving his body exposed for nature to consume—this would still be oh so glorious.

Frey dropped Adam to the floor, who attempted to stagger away as they searched the room. With no weapon of their own, Frey reached for the bottles of lamp oil that lined the shelves along the wall, unscrewing and launching them directly at Adam. The pain in Frey's wrists from being bound made it difficult to throw far, and Adam managed to avoid each one.

So they attempted a more direct approach. They ran at Adam, tackling him to the ground. Adam grunted as he fell, and Frey's grip pinned him to the floor. Frey grinned as their fist connected with Adam's face. A distinctive crack sounded with the impact and Adam's now-crooked nose bloodied once again. Frey had to admit: they were *enjoying* this, finally being able to toy with him openly. But Adam needed to suffer more, and for that, he needed to bleed.

The basement became a maelstrom of chaos, and the refrigerator hum seemed to grow louder as the two fought. Adam kicked Frey off him and returned with a series of punches to Frey's face and chest. Frey stumbled backward with every hit. And with every hit, Frey could *feel* him—feel his rage of being misled, feel his fear of being caught. Frey *reveled* in it and vowed to show him their own pain, their own suffering. Their own rage.

Frey delivered a vicious kick to his groin. Adam screamed as he took hold of Frey's foot and dragged them down, smashing one of the ceramic lamps buried underneath a pile of junk. Scrambling back to their feet, Frey snatched a shard of ceramic. They felt its icy grip cut their own hand and growled in anticipation.

Frey attempted a second tackle, but they stumbled as Adam charged towards Frey. Their heads smashed together, the room spinning as they both winced, each rushing to be the first to refocus.

In their haze, Frey decided this was the moment. Like he was a ritualistic sacrifice, Frey attempted to bring the shard down into Adam's heart, but Adam pushed upward just in time. Still, Frey delighted in his screams as the shard plunged deep into Adam's leg.

Adam would feel every day of their pain, every moment of the suffering Frey had endured. Breaking his body would not be enough; they needed to break his mind.

Frey walked toward the refrigerator, placed their hand on the glass, and whispered, "So, this is her, huh?"

Adam clung to his bleeding leg, which seeped dark and wet on his trousers. His gaze met Frey's, eyes widening as he realized where Frey was. "PLEASE FREY!" he shrieked. "Do not touch her. Let me bring her back; she's done nothing wrong. If you ever loved me, you'll let me do this."

Frey gazed at Penelope, the woman Adam loved, at the patchworked creation he had turned her into. There were not only the fingers he had stolen from their parents but also everything he had stolen from others: lips and ears, a bicep and a leg, half a foot. Each of them had someone who loved them, each of them had people to love, and each of them had that stolen away by Adam. It was only fair that Frey returned the favor.

"That's the thing, Adam. Maybe I did love you once, but I loved the thought of killing you more. And that was enough." Frey smiled manically as they withdrew the gold lighter from their pocket, their grin growing ever wider as Adam questioned the lighter. They watched him try to piece it all together

"Be reasonable, Frey." Adam crawled closer, clutching their leg tightly. "Please . . ."

"I am simply revenging my injuries, for in killing my parents, you fashioned your own death." Frey turned, held up their father's golden lighter. They felt the weight of having carried this lighter, this memory for so long. It was finally time. This was always going to be its destiny, the final thing their father would give them. "Love corrupts us, turns us into these awful monsters. And you made me into your monster, Adam, and I don't want to be that anymore. And I won't be, once your soul is mine."

Frey smirked, then turned back toward the refrigerator. "You see, Adam, you always miss out on the details, the smaller things. This was why your plan would've never succeeded, why you never caught onto *my* grand deception, why you will never bring this fucking rotting corpse back from the dead. She's dead, Adam. She. Is. Fucking. Dead."

Frey paused a second and let Adam's sobs fill the air as they reveled in the sound of his tears. "I had to think quickly, but y'know? I had so many wonderful choices for weapons in this basement: the toolbox, the armchair, the shards of glass. But why, why did I choose the oil?"

"Wh— No," Adam uttered breathlessly as Frey struck the lighter. He moved backward as they stepped over him, avoiding his pathetic attempts at grasping onto their leg.

"Fire is the ultimate form of cleansing, purification, and destruction. With this fire, I cleanse the world of you and your creation, Adam, and I cauterize my pain. Get fucked and have an awful afterlife."

Frey dropped the golden lighter behind them as they began to ascend the stairs, the fire catching, spreading across the basement floor toward the refrigerator.

Adam screamed and crawled toward the burning refrigerator, his hand clambering toward the body of his beloved—his Eve, his most intricate art, rivaled only by that of God. As he pulled himself up, he placed a hand on the glass, and Frey saw the realization dawn on his face of how awful and rotten the body had become. His cries of suffering became a sweet melody that Frey would dance to for the rest of their life.

"I'm so sorry I failed you," Adam sobbed. "My love, I thought I could do it. I thought I could cheat Death and bring you back to me." Adam opened the refrigerator, desperately clutching the body of the person he loved. But she was locked in a state of decay, liquifying by the minute, a rejection of Adam's invitation of resurrection. "I love you."

Frey smelled the burning flesh and rot and watched the intricate stitches that had taken so many hours to weave melt away. The hours dedicated to the worship of his beloved were fading, the tithes he had collected from his victims falling away. His work was coming undone, and with it, so was Adam.

Frey was curious to see who Adam would ultimately choose when faced with the undoing of Penelope. Was this experiment truly about love? Was it truly an honest wish to see the love of his life return to living flesh and bone? Or was it an act of self-indulgence, an egotistical move to prove that not even Death could stop him? Frey waited until Adam inevitably made the choice Frey realized they knew he would make: the wrong one.

"Frey, help me, please!" Adam screamed. "Save me from this! It's only you who I love. I *love* you. You love me too, right?"

Frey, however, slowly turned their back to him. After so many years of giving into Adam, tasting his French onion soup, and internalizing their pain, it felt good to reject him for the first and final time.

Frey took a deep breath as they turned and closed the basement door, locking it tight and sealing Adam to his fate. After collecting their phone, they opened the front door one last time. They felt the manor get warmer and heard the fire below cracking and splintering the wooden foundations. And so it was only when Frey closed the door on Adam's life that they finally answered his question.

"I cannot love a monster."

And then, everything burned.

The Consumption of Vienna Montrose

by

Joelle Wellington

The name on the deed does not change when she inherits the crumbling home in the empty cul-de-sac of Magnolia Lane.

All the rest of the homes are gone, carcasses that had been emptied and worn away to their underpinnings before the city cleared them away. It's all empty, overgrown lots now. They had wanted to do the same to this house, Vienna Montrose's house. But Vienna Montrose, one of many, had not allowed it.

VIENNA MONTROSE, the piece of yellowing paper declares. It is signed in a hand that is not hers, but Vienna recognizes the curl of the *s* and the looping curlicue at the end of the *e*. These are notes of script that she's inherited from her namesake, just as she did the shape of her mouth and the slope of her nose.

This is Vienna Montrose's home. Hers, at all of eighteen years and nine months.

She repeats this out loud. "This is Vienna Montrose's home. *Mine.*" She clings to the keys, wraps the lanyard around her wrist twice, and knots it so it doesn't come loose if she starts swinging her arm—she never realizes when she does that.

Vienna should be sad—the dirt over her grandmother's grave is still fresh. She can still smell Nana's perfume, layers and layers of cloying florals that clash with a lasting vanilla and patchouli. But then, Vienna remembers: *Stand straight, arms out. When I was your age, I had already been an accomplished young woman.* Vienna blinks her way through the not-grief and decides that she does not feel sad at all. She does not mourn a bitter old woman, and she won't. Her mother does enough mourning for the both of them.

It was not very often that Vienna came to this house—this is not the house her grandmother lived in, in her old age, but it is the one Vienna's mother grew up in. Vienna's memories of this place are paper thin and wobbling, like a house of cards.

The rich blue that she remembers has faded to a watery gray by way of storm. The paint on the door had started peeling when Vienna was just a girl, and then she had spent time peeling it away with child finger-nails until her nailbeds bled. There is still the faintest color of rust there, around the doorknob, and she cannot tell if it is her own blood or the blood of the house or the blood of age.

Vienna does not recognize the scent of the house at all.

Vienna smells the mothballs and old water. She smells rot, but not the kind that hints at dead things. Though there are still plenty of dead things. Dead leaves, dead mice, dead people. And so the memories fade until there are only shadows and this house. This cracked up house.

But the bones are good. The bones are beautiful. Vienna runs her fin-ger over the hand-carved banister, her skin coming away coated in dust as the dark wood is revealed. She presses her hands to the paneling on the wall and looks up at the tile work on the ceilings. It's all so lovely, so beautiful. Yes, the bones are good.

Her phone buzzes every three minutes as she walks through the house. The parlor could be pretty if the colorless wallpaper was stripped out. A fresh coat of green over the walls would contrast nicely against the mahogany trim. There are pocket doors. There is something living in the fireplace—Vienna can hear skittering paws and soft squeaks. There are torn remnants of McDonald's bags where the old ash sits. She ignores it, leaving it for another time, and walks through the dining room, through the butler's pantry, to the kitchen, which was updated in the sixties and never again. Vienna goes up the servants' stairs.

She is not careful, her foot sinking into soft wood, which cracks loud like a gunshot. She can make that comparison because she knows the sound of a gun well, knows the way it booms and rattles in her teeth. Her ex-boyfriend used to shoot skeet. Her never-brother—almost stepbrother before her mother and never-father broke up—hunts. She knows the weight of gunmetal in her hands, and again, she hears her grandmother's words: *It is not ladylike to shoot, to know how to skin a deer, to know how to salt and prepare venison. Look at you, you've sweated out your hair.*

Vienna would say in her own mind, *There is nothing more ladylike than blood play.*

But only in her mind.

She does not keep it to herself now, when the only other sound—real sound—is her own breath and the buzzing of her phone every three minutes. "There is nothing more ladylike than blood play. Than knowing how to heat a hearth or cook over a stove. Than keeping a home. I will keep yours," Vienna says to Nana, to the air, as she walks the corridor toward the front stairs.

There's another flight up to the tower. Vienna doesn't take it because even from the outside, she can see how it leans. She won't be her own Rapunzel.

It is cold. The old injury in her ankles aches up through her shortened Achilles, up the straight rod of her spine. Vienna will come back another day with contractors and repairmen and an inspector or two. She'll bring friends to clean and evict the vermin roommates, and then she will make a place to sleep so that she can work when chooses to.

Vienna passes through the front hall again, leaning her shoulder into the long stretch of wall that is seemingly uninterrupted. She drags her fingers over each divot and curlicue, until her fingernails catch on a seam and she feels a draft. When she wrenches the seam open, a rush of cold air soothes her feverish skin, and she sighs, hearing the sound of her own breath echoing back at her from the swallow of blackness.

She has never been afraid of the dark. Vienna goes down the stairs.

"The water is turned off. Power too," her uncle said to her when he handed over the keys. But Vienna hears the whine of a boiler. She thinks she hears the screech of it.

She can't see past her own nose; the dark is so exact. Reaching blindly, her hand sinks into something furry that does not move. Vienna strokes it slowly and then reaches again, flicking at a light switch. A light does not come on.

"It's warm," she notes, in contrast to the cool air that had greeted her like a blow of breath when she'd first opened the door.

She rocks back and forth on the concrete ground and sneezes once. Then she goes back up the stairs.

In the foyer, she just breathes, and for a moment, she thinks someone is breathing right next to her. It is still so warm, warmer than it has any right to be. And then, there is a groan, the type that comes from an empty stomach burbling with gas—the sound of steel clashing. Something is hungry. She is hungry, and that unsettled feeling is like a fist in her throat, one she cannot breathe around until she stumbles out the front door and locks it tight.

When Vienna leaves her house—1320 Magnolia Lane—she finally checks her phone. Twenty missed messages from Mama and more than a hundred text messages in the family group chat.

She does not answer a single one.

I remember you. We remember you.

You used to come every weekend when you were young. You and the other girl. You in flower patchwork jeans and an oversized T-shirt. They dressed you like you were made for softer things. Your mother used to pretend she was made for softer things too. You both liked to play pretend.

You liked cherries. You picked the cherries from the tree that sits next to your father's grave. You did not know that's your father's grave. You did not care that's your father's grave. It's everyone's grave. Your grave. The mausoleum was a dollhouse to you.

"You broke her. You broke the one that looks like me," you wept when you were young. You are in your patchwork jeans after a Saturday the ballet studio two towns over, where you lived with your mother.

"You shoved me."

"I didn't," you wept; I remember the taste of mucus and salt. It was sweet on the floorboards. You melted, sinking to your knees, cheeks pressed to the wide planks. You were so warm. I remember you. "I didn't shove you."

"You did*. You* did*. Look I'm bleeding. My mom says it's gonna scar. You did that."*

You do not cry anymore.

You have discarded softer things.

You are beautiful now. With giving, brown hands and a voice that echoes. You speak about the hearth. About the heart of this place, how it is yours. Yes, I think, yours*. Yours.*

You descend into the belly, the furnace. You do not shy from the darkness. You notice—it's warm. I am warm for you.

I miss mucus and salt. But sweat and blood taste good too. You will taste good. You are beautiful. We could love you.

We remember all of you. I remember all of you.

Do you remember me too?

When you leave, your hand lingers on the doorknob.

Yes, we think you do.

Vienna doesn't have any friends her own age. She has friends her never-brother's age, all entering that late stage of their twenties when they start thinking of longevity and stable careers and all that shit. Cassiopeia, his long-term partner, is of that age, but she seems content in her position as sous-chef of her parents' lauded soul food restaurant. She turns her nose up at the idea of any permanence beyond that. She turns her nose up to Vienna now even as she opens her and Samuel's home up to her; Vienna is nearly an in-law and that's repugnant.

"Are you okay?" Samuel asks Cassiopeia as he digs into his food. He and Cassiopeia are having Vienna over for brunch.

It is a brunch of champions: fluffy carbohydrates and the fresh meat that her never-brother has butchered. Cassiopeia cooks everything to perfection; Vienna's grandmother would think this means she is well suited to enter the next stage of life as a wife. Vienna's grandmother would be wrong.

Cassiopeia's arrogance is a stench that nearly overpowers the scent of powdered sugar as she places her latest creation on the table. Vienna is usually her semiwilling guinea pig, submitting herself as judge, jury, and executioner of this new addition to Cassiopeia's menu. Not today.

"Do you think it's good enough for Sunday brunch?" she asks immediately after Vienna's first bite of lemon ricotta pancakes.

"I think it's good. Is there syrup?" Vienna asks.

Cassiopeia scowls. "No, there's no fucking syrup. Jesus Christ."

"Come on, Cass. None of that at the table," Samuel warns.

"Not you so concerned over the Second Coming. Whatever," Cassiopeia says, and she leans forward, gaze flitting over Vienna. "Where are you staying? You're not staying at your mother's, are you?"

"I'm staying at the house," Vienna says. "I got the water running. Power too. I found a work crew to fix up what needs fixing."

"I'm sure." Cassiopeia sneers her way through disapproval. "It's going to cost *so* much money."

"Nana thought of that," Vienna says. She does not eat, instead dragging the curve of her spoon over the rim of her half-empty teacup. She's already eaten, having shoved half of a cream cheese bagel down her gullet.

Soon, she'll make the clear signs that she can't possibly consume more, and then this shit will end. "I won't have to worry about that."

"You really want all those people in your house?" Cassiopeia asks.

"I can help you out, Vi. I've got you," Samuel says immediately. "I just promoted my apprentice. He can watch the shop. You don't have to have all of those people—"

"What people? Who are all of 'those people'?" Vienna snarls, and then she bites her tongue.

Cassiopeia looks at her like she's *stupid*. "Those construction people, all of them. They'll just be in your *house*," Cassiopeia says with a dramatic shudder.

Vienna sips her tea because she doesn't know what to say.

"There's already people in my house," Vienna says.

They live in the walls. They live in her dreams. Even when she is not there, she sees the ghost of them and hears the whispers of old conversations. It is meant to unnerve. Instead, Vienna lives in the gray of it all.

Cassiopeia snorts. "Yeah, I'm sure your psycho family is always there." She ignores Samuel's wince and leans forward, her plate scraped clean. She glances at Vienna's. "You're not going to eat that, are you?"

Vienna takes the fatty slab of duck bacon and then shoves the plate toward Cassiopeia with only her index finger. She ignores the way the limb buckles and cracks, pain shooting down to her wrist. She watches Cassiopeia devour.

"Fucking syrup," Cassiopeia hisses. "This is terrific."

Vienna's mouth twitches, and she gets ready to make her excuses, one of six she always has prepared in the soft palate of her mouth.

"You want pie?" Samuel asks. "Your mom made cherry pie last time we went over for dinner. Cass loved it to so much she's been trying to recreate it ever since. You're close, aren't you, babe?" Cassiopeia is barely listening, too busy weighing notes of flavor on her tongue.

It doesn't matter—Vienna is sick of her mother's pie. "I'm allergic to cherries. Remember?" This is a lie.

Her never-brother's brow furrows. "Oh, I forgot, I'm sorry," he says, contrite and sincere in a way that seems to devastate him. That devastates her.

He's older than her by some years, but Vienna feels old looking at him.

"It's okay. I don't like pie anyways."

"The young madam of the House is sleeping upstairs. Saw her mattress on the ground. She swept the master bedroom clean, and she's living out of a suitcase. Don't reckon she's got anywhere else to go," the electrician says, swiping a red hand over his pale, sweat-dotted forehead. He slams his hat back down over his straw hair and scratches himself through the boilersuit.

Inelegant. His sweat tastes like shit.

"She's a looker. I knew her auntie when we were young. Pretty enough. Uppity. The girl with her mamaw's name looks a hell of a sight better than the mother." The foreman squats by the heart-h, mayo spraying from his lips onto the delicate tile work he's just laid down.

It is disgusting, the sourness of him lingering too long in a hollow, hallowed place where he does not belong. They do not belong. Not like you.

"What about the mother? You knew her too?"

Your mother liked cherries. So did you. You tasted like them. Even now—cherries.

"By sight is all. All I remember is she wasn't all there. A bit excitable. With too much teeth and a big eye," the foreman says.

"What does that mean? What does that mean?"

The foreman taps the youngblood on the top of the head and shakes his head. His eyes are roving. He moves like a man without a worry, but he avoids the basement door. He'd rather brave the cold. "Do you remember this house? Growing up?" the foreman asks.

"I do. A little." A pause. The electrician clears his throat. "My grandmother warned me away."

"What's wrong with this house?" Youngblood asks.

"There's nothing wrong with the house," the foreman says. "It's the woman living here."

"Problem?" you ask.

You startle them. Your steps do not echo. Not in me. You are one with me. You move like our shadow. You peer down at them, imperious and curious. They do not like the light of your eyes. They do not like how you are so above them, wrapped in old wool, mended and expensive, with inherited gold dripping from your ears. You are misplaced in time—you are forever—

and this startles them to distraction, like the way your mouth curves into a smile that you believe is kind.

There is no kindness in that mouth, just rows of teeth.

"No. Just taking a lunch break."

"Oh. Would you like rabbit stew?" you ask. It is in earnest. They do not trust it anyway. You remind them of warnings. You are a warning. "Or braised rabbit? I have the meat."

"No, thank you, ma'am."

You leave them alone. They do not make eye contact again.

When you have rounded the corner, you laugh, delighted by your own wickedness.

Vienna is an only child in every way except for the ways that she is not. She has her never-brother. She has two godsiblings, by way of her dead father's God. And then there is her cousin, Florence. Her cousin was born second to Vienna, and so she does not have the name Vienna, though Vienna knows she wishes that she did.

Florence is a sister that Vienna does not want. Vienna and Florence are inseparable. They were enraged in their early teens. Vienna does not know where her own body ends and Florence's begins—the seams of their fusion are messy that way. They starved for the world and ate each other when hungry, until they were pulled apart and Nana asked, "Who will you have when I am dead?" And so, they were meant to learn to eat other things, to do things other than self-cannibalize. Vienna learned.

But Florence had developed a taste, and she is invariable. She will never stop cutting her teeth on family flesh and her own bones.

She stands in the foyer of Vienna's house not because she is invited but because she is hungry.

"It smells in here," she says.

"That's the fresh drywall," Vienna says. "And the sawdust. And the paint."

Florence steps into the foyer, by the built-in seat without a cushion yet. She peels off her sneakers, letting her feet bare. Vienna doesn't warn her that not even she walks around barefoot yet. There are nails and old wood and dangerous things. Maybe Vienna is hungry too and wouldn't mind blood on her floorboards.

"Let me get a look at her," Florence says, shoving past Vienna to swan about her entrance hall.

"The house is not a 'her,'" Vienna says, arms folded as she leans against the door, the back of her head pressed against the cool, warped glass window set in the center of her door. It will be the last thing painted. She thinks she wants to paint it the same orange-brown that it used to be, before it had been faded by time and the pain of being discarded.

"What is it then?" Florence retorts lazily. Vienna doesn't answer. Florence meanders through. She stops in the parlor, the only finished room, decorated with reupholstered rococo furniture from storage and secondhand bookshelves shoved up against the wall. "It looks better than I remember. Remember the dollhouse you used to have? The one that looked like the house?"

Vienna squints at her. "You remember this place?"

Florence rolls up her left sleeve, brandishing her tattooed arm. She keeps the ink mostly covered now, like she regrets getting it now that Nana isn't here for her to rebel against. Florence is a being of spite in the face of judgment. She taps her finger against a black-and-white watercolor flower, and in the space between two spindly lavender tattoos is a stark white gash of a scar, a blinding sign among the brown of her skin.

"You shoved me here, and I fell against the nail in the wall. Tore my arm open. It scarred. I told you it would scar."

Vienna swallows hard. "I don't recall."

"You've always had a bad memory," Florence says dismissively. She walks through the set of pocket doors into the dining room. There's a tarp over the unfinished floors and a ladder in the middle of the room. Florence passes underneath it without superstition. "It looks better—different. None of Nana's god-awful flower pressings or the rabbit skins she used to hang on the wall. You can open the curtains, you know. Get some light in here."

Florence marches toward the window and suddenly, for a moment, she looks like Nana. In her sheath dress, with an Hermès scarf wrapped around her hair, curls hanging out underneath. If it weren't for her tattoos, twisted roots and crooked foliage creeping over her skin, Florence would look just like Nana—but also not at all.

Maybe Vienna did shove her. Maybe she did watch a nail tear through skin. Maybe she licked that jagged nail clean. She thinks now all about Nana, and maybe she didn't like Florence for other reasons.

"*Don't.*"

Florence freezes, just shy of the curtain. She breathes slowly and then looks over her shoulder, her eyes hard. "Don't speak to me that way," she warns.

"What way?" Vienna asks.

"You know the way you do," Florence warns.

Vienna doesn't. Florence scoffs and stalks past her, through the butler's pantry and to the kitchen. Vienna's kitchen.

Vienna tries to shove her way past, but Florence is taller and stronger. She takes measured steps into the kitchen and looks around. She doesn't react as Vienna expects her to. She sniffs once and smells copper pennies and wood polish and ammonia.

"Samuel brought you meat?" Florence asks.

"I can butcher my own meat," Vienna says. She leans against the island, drumming her fingers against the butcher-block wood. "Are you hungry?"

"I could eat."

Florence is the first person who has come to Vienna's home to eat. Florence is always starving in her presence. Vienna is never hungry. She eats only enough that it takes up space inside of her. This is the only way she will expand enough to let the oxygen in. She always has extra food. On the fine white china, with the pretty silverware, Vienna serves rabbit stew.

Florence takes one bite before she raises an eyebrow. "Rabbit?"

"There are fluffles of them in the backyard. They eat everything in sight. It isn't helpful for landscaping," Vienna says severely. She watches Florence eat carefully, watches the way her face shifts. "Does it taste like Nana's?"

"You didn't get everything from Nana," Florence says.

Vienna purses her lips. "Are you still mad about the—"

"We're adults now," Florence says swiftly. Florence had only just turned eighteen last month. Vienna didn't go to her birthday party.

Vienna feels young and old, all at once.

"Your mother asked about you," Florence says.

Vienna laughs quietly. "I'm sure she did."

"You should pick up the phone."

Her mother is not a bad woman. She's not even a bad mother. It's just that Vienna can't breathe around her. It's different from how she couldn't breathe around Nana. Nana made her feel bad for breathing wrong. She is not the firstborn grandchild—there is a dead one somewhere. But she is the one with Nana's name. So, things were exacting with Nana. Everything had to be measured or Vienna was *incorrect*. Unworthy.

But for Vienna's mother, Vienna could do no wrong. So, no, she wasn't a bad mother. It was just that her love smothered.

"I'll have her over when the house is finished. It nearly is. Just the dining room left. The guest bedroom too," Vienna says.

Florence hums and taps her throat. "Water?"

Vienna rolls her eyes and goes to get a glass. She thinks it's cowardly of Florence to ask her "Have you been in the basement?" when Vienna's back is turned.

"Only once," Vienna says.

A beat of silence.

"Do you remember?" Florence asks.

"I thought we'd established you had the better memory," Vienna retorts, setting the glass of water down too heavy, spilling it over the edge.

"You used to say you saw your mother's ghost in the basement. But it looked like you—but it looked like your mother. I don't know. You said a lot of weirdo shit when you were a kid. Nana beat you once for talking mess. Saying that you were trying to speak your mama's death into being or something. I don't know." Florence shakes her head, sipping her water. She blinks and shivers. "You got anything stronger?"

"Why?"

"It's cold up here. Aren't you cold?" Florence demands.

Sometimes.

Florence doesn't say anything else as she eats. She takes her time, and Vienna watches her from across the kitchen island, drumming her fingers in a rhythm that mirrors the hummingbird in her ribcage.

Something echoes back. Something drums with her, and it is a twofold sound. Florence moves just off beat as she eats, not in sync. Not belonging. It itches at Vienna's skin, how long Florence sits there gorging, not in sync. Not in *line*.

Florence scrapes the last of the red-wine sauce onto the tines of her fork and sucks it off before she pushes her plate away.

"I've got to go." Florence stands and reaches across, grabbing Vienna's hands. "Thank you for feeding me."

Before Florence leaves, she lingers in the doorway and says, "Nana really loved you."

"I think it was easier not to change the deed over," Vienna says, thoughtlessly.

It makes it worse. Florence wants her name. Florence wants to feast. Her pretty hazel eyes—these are not their grandmother's eyes but rather Florence's mother's eyes—glint in the setting sun.

"Call your mother," Florence says. "She misses you."

It is easy to lie and say, "I miss her too."

Florence hugs her, pulling Vienna's head into the curve of her neck. Against Vienna's curls, she whispers, "Once, you tricked me into the basement too. We were playing hide-and-seek, and you locked me down there for hours. Nana didn't beat you for that one though. I don't know if I ever told."

"You should've told."

"Should I have?" Florence asks. Her hug tightens. "This house isn't good for you."

"What do you mean?" Vienna whispers.

"It rubs you raw. You'll start peeling, and I do not think you'll like the new skin."

Florence disappears into their grandmother's old Rolls-Royce and drives down the long, long hill. When she is gone, Vienna rests easy. She sinks to the porch of the house and lies on her back, staring at the underbelly of the roof, a mouth closing over her.

I think I was haunted as a child, Vienna thinks. *There was a monster when I was a child.*

Your sister-cousin-soul does not understand the reverence you show to this palace of mine. You barely understand it yourself; but you understand this: when you cook at my hearth, it should be with the warmth and carefulness with which a priest approaches his pulpit. You keep the curtains closed to keep the sun out, to keep the cold in, to keep the world out, to keep us in.

Your mother calls. The shrill ring startles you from sleep. You do not get to bed again, shivering in the nest that you have made for yourself in the master bedroom, so far from the heart-h of me. So far from the stomach where I would keep you warm.

Your mother calls. You do not pick up. You listen to her voicemails though. I know the twitch of every expression.

"Vienna, darling, pick up. Pick up for me please. Your nana is gone. Everyone is gone. I cannot lose— We cannot lose each other. Vienna, darling, pick up. I would do anything for you to pick up."

You do not smile when you hear her mourning your absence, begging you to take the communion of grief together. You do not understand the way she wails, the way she offers you cherry pies that you say that you cannot eat.

Your mother calls. Your phone no longer rings. Instead, you pickle the fallen fruit from the magnolia trees in the back and stay clear of the mausoleum and the cherries. You catch the fluffles of rabbits until there are few and skin them. You cook them in your nana's red wine and fashion scarves from their skin.

The woman whose name you've stolen does not belong here. There is only you. Everywhere you step, the ghost of her body disappears until there is only you. Only us. And you are lovely, staring in the glass mirror, only relaxed when it is us, and all the water is running in the master bath. You are lovely when you cry so hard that you start to scream and the only reason you don't shatter your fist in your own reflection is because you spit pink into the porcelain basin, your throat raw.

You stop. You dry your face. You continue your work of making me beautiful, you beautiful. Your sweat is in my foundations.

Sometimes, I think you can hear me. See me. Feel me. When you pass the door to the stomach, when you ignore the stairs up to the tower—the one that's no longer leaning, not after the foreman and Youngblood and the messy rest straightened my spine. I won't call out for you. That's gauche, humiliating. I show my love in other ways.

There are no nightmares in this house, except the ones that come from the throat. There is no fear, not the kind you live with constantly, until you step past your driveway, where I cannot reach you. I let those heathens—the ones who walked my halls—visit. Even your sister-cousin-soul. All so I don't have to miss you when you're gone.

You still sleepwalk—not very far, just out of the nest. You stand at the window and look down sightlessly at the driveway, down the empty cul-de-sac. And then, there—a car that you recognize. You close the curtains.

You will make a cage of my body.

You will paint it green and gold and live in it. And I will lock it shut and keep you there. In here. In me.

The House is alive.

Vienna has always known this subconsciously. She knows the throb of this place like the one in her chest, like the throbbing between her legs, but she only lets it form when she is ready.

She is ready, she realizes one night when she is laying in her bed— now with added bedframe, an old, heavy wooden behemoth that she found at a flea market one town over. At the flea market, the patrons and sellers alike had stared at her like she was this alien presence, and Vienna supposed she was. It was the kind of town that people rarely came to and people rarely left.

But that is beside the point.

The House is alive.

Vienna thinks she has always known, ever since she'd found herself here again—from the moment she'd heard the boiler in the basement when nothing should have been turned on. There is comfort in knowing. It means she is not crazy.

She is not crazy when she screams in the mirror with the water running, because there is something under her skin that she cannot see but only feel, when she is only sated if she is wicked or eats rabbit. When she is pleased with herself when someone is grieving. Any other time, she is hollow. And she finds very little to get pleasure from, not even when she touches herself.

Vienna does not mourn her namesake, nor does she have much from her but her nose and mouth and a house that she has reshaped, but she remembers her vividly. *It is not ladylike—*

"She did not love me. She couldn't have," Vienna realizes.

Because Nana knew her.

Vienna wants to know her too. The way Nana knew her and could not stand her. The way this House knows her and loves her for it. Vienna leaves the master bedroom, her bonnet slipping off her head and landing behind her as she walks down the long corridor. She staggers with each step, wearing only a dressing gown, her nipples peaking from the cold. It's so cold.

Vienna doesn't come this way. It's colder up there. She can tell by the draft. She hates the cold. But she still goes up there. Up the stairs. Up the tower. Maybe she is Rapunzel. Maybe she's Mother Gothel too. Maybe she's neither and fairytales are foolish.

The wood spirals up in its steps. The tower is different. Though it still creaks, even when everything is new-old. There is nothing up here, not really. Nothing but the dollhouse that Florence talked about, the dollhouse that Vienna doesn't remember.

It doesn't look like the new house. It doesn't look like Vienna's green behemoth with its orange-brown door and brown roofing. It does not have the pretty Tiffany glass in the door window or the gleaming sanded porch.

The old house was blue on the outside with faded orange roofing and ugly shutters placed on the top floor where they needn't be. That is what the dollhouse reflects here.

"I made you beautiful," Vienna murmurs.

She feels the House shudder its agreement. Vienna sits on the banister and looks down into the abyss. "And you find me beautiful too. You keep me warm, when you can," Vienna acknowledges as she brings her leg over to straddle and plants one foot on the floor to keep her steady so that she doesn't tumble down to the second floor below. "Did you like the other occupants of this place as much as me?"

The House says nothing for a minute. And then it groans, just like the day that Vienna first arrived. It is not a greeting this time but a call. It is *hungry*. It knows what it is to want. It used to love another too. That's okay. Vienna doesn't believe in soulmates. She grinds down once and gasps, feeling wood between her bare thighs.

"You don't mind, do you?" she asks. "I feel as if you have only seen the ugly."

Vienna feels the House again. She gets the impression that it finds no part of her, even the cracked parts, ugly.

"I think I used to come here a lot. But . . . we stopped. When Nana moved out. I think I loved this house and it loved me," Vienna says. "In the right kind of way. The infinite way."

She moves faster and grunts softly. This feels right. She is taking. She is always taking, and it's only when she is that she feels whole and normal. When she indulges in her hedonism.

"House," Vienna rasps as she chases pleasure, one thigh hooked over the banister edge, heat burning her nose, her cheeks, her chest. "I was the monster under the bed. I was the haunting of this home."

Her confession is met with benediction, and she cries as she shakes apart at the seams. She can taste pink in the rawness of her throat and slides off the banister, leaving it glossy. Curled up on the steps, limbs crooked each way, she feels a bit like the doll that Florence had accused her of breaking in their youth. She could slide her way down the spiral staircase, back into bed. She doesn't.

Instead, she stands on colt legs and wobbles toward the wide windows of wavy glass.

Vienna looks at the empty driveway, at the empty cul-de-sac. Except for one car. There is always a car. Her mother's car.

Her cell phone rings. Vienna very slowly—just this once—picks up. She breathes.

"Vienna? Vienna, I can hear you!" Her mother's panic is raw and fluttering. Vienna cannot see her, but if she closes her eyes, she can picture the thin brown skin of her mother's neck, frail and weak with age and grief. She can imagine the trembling of her fingers. "Vienna, are you all right? Is everything all right?"

"Sure," Vienna says. She is steady. She feels at home.

"Please . . . come outside."

"What's outside?" Vienna asks quietly.

"Florence. *Me.* I don't like it. You all alone in there. You're hurting, I know. Hurt with me. Let me hurt for you. That house is not right. It can't do anything for you," her mother says. She is begging. It is beneath them both. It is *typical.*

Her mother's love, her worry, smothers. Or maybe, it doesn't smother. Maybe her mother tries to feed her because Vienna is hungry. Vienna would devour her. And Florence. And Never-Brother too. All the rabbits and all the memories. This is a kindness.

Hanging up would be a kindness. She does one more than that and grants mercy too.

"I'm not hurt. I'm cold," Vienna says firmly. She places her phone on the windowsill and backs away until her mother's voice comes through tinny.

Vienna is so cold.

She presses her face against the glass window. She thinks about what it would be like to throw herself from the tower of this place, and then she brings herself low to stare at its perfect replica, with a doll that looks like her and Florence. Florence's doll doesn't have a head. Vienna's doll is nowhere to be seen. But she knows.

She is so tired she trips down the stairs. It's too cold to be up here. That's what her Nana always said. That's what she always says.

She finds the notch in the wall. The lights still don't work in the basement.

She is so tired.

This time she can see. The entirety of the basement is empty, except for bottles of red wine nestled in thick brown fur, a soft fur that wraps the walls and covers the floors, except for the seams where floorboards peek through. The only concrete down here is the small patch she stands on.

It smells like animal, like warmth. Vienna sinks to her knees and crawls. Her fingers dig for something—anything. They press into something soft that gives and Vienna slips through.

I think I love you, Vienna thinks. *I think you are uncomplicated and easy and warm. I think I'll keep you. I'd like you to keep me.*

She closes her eyes, nested under the rabbit fur, under the floorboards, that night and every night after.

The Landscape of
Broken Things

by

Brent Lambert

I hate coming to this cramped, smelly torture chamber they try to pass off as a hospital. I've been walking down the Silent Eye Institute's tiny halls, with their too-bright pastel floor tiles, for the past two years. Dr. Greystone and his goons want to create some facade of bright happiness, but every clairvoyant locked up in here knows with certainty their futures are bleak.

Nothing is going to keep me from seeing my mom though. Not Dad, not his new boyfriend, not my nosy-ass aunties, and definitely not the Silent Eye Institute. Mom could see the future so that made her a "monster," but there's a chance I might see it one day too. Will they throw me in a cage and shove pills down my throat too? I need her to guide me, to show me how to not end up trapped.

The closer I get to the private visiting rooms, the more the rhetoric against clairvoyance ratchets up. Gold posters with bold, black letters line the hallways like marching orders for all the patients in residence. The letters are jagged and harsh like the broken glass of so many of their minds.

CLOSE YOUR EYES. REFUSE VISIONS.

THE FUTURE BELONGS TO NO ONE.

THE EYES LIE. TRUST ONLY THE NOW.

A SILENT EYE IS A STEADY SOUL.

Each message makes me walk a bit faster. They're not as bad as the T-shirts, the hateful rallies, or the raucous commercials, but I'm just not in the mood today. The world spends every waking moment telling me that my mother and everyone like her deserves punishment, that their powers failing was justice for their corruption.

I can't lie. I haven't been feeling so pure lately.

My head stays down as I walk. There's a big-ass clock coming up ahead, and I'm doing my best to avoid looking at it. Clocks are where all my current troubles started. About a month ago, I started to see them in every reflective surface, in my dreams each night, in every glass of water. And they're looking at me. The Roman numerals are eyes drilling right into me, and I know exactly how wild that sounds.

Trouble, like I said.

Trouble my mom might be able to help me with if she wasn't stuck here getting dangerous medicines forced upon her day and night. The rest of my family can't be bothered to care about that part as long as it keeps my mom and her powers away from them. My dad came to this room a few times in the beginning. He stopped around the fifth or sixth visit. I yelled at him pretty bad once I realized he wasn't coming anymore. He told me, "It's too much to see Alyssa like that."

Too much?! That asshole was the one who'd called the Silent Eye Institute in the first place. She wouldn't be here if it wasn't for him, and he couldn't be bothered to see her anymore?

"It's for the best, Julian." Dad being a damn simp in front of his new dude.

My aunties never even tried to come, and they spent a good bit of time assuring me I was better off not being here too.

"She can get the help she needs there." The aunt who knows it's wrong but needs somewhere to stay so keeps her mouth shut.

"Chile, you know what she has ain't right." The aunt who I just plain don't like. She had no problem with her sister's abilities when it came time to decide on a house, car, or trip destination. Everyone secretly loves a clairvoyant until they can't control their power anymore.

If my mom isn't right, then neither am I. That's what I want to scream at Aunt Nina—who really needs to worry more about holding down a job than what should happen to my mom, but that's a nuke I'm not quite ready to launch yet. Mom ended up there because the family convinced themselves they love her. There are worse places than the Silent Eye, and I don't want to think about where they would send someone they were angry with. I hated my family for giving up on her. They put a knife in my heart and a dagger in her back, and I don't plan on forgiving a single one of them for it.

I'm almost past the clock. Just don't look at it. This is the last place I need to see it. Some of the rumors passed around by the Unseen, a rebel group of clairvoyants in hiding, say the guy who ran the Silent Eye, Dr. Greystone, could sense whenever clairvoyance was activated. The Unseen say a lot of outrageous things. They claim time is breaking and clairvoyants are just a step ahead of where everyone else will soon be. Everything I read on the subject made that and Dr. Greystone's ability pretty unlikely, but I'm not chancing it.

There are too many people who'd be happy to see me end up here.

"You sure you just guessed that?" An obnoxious question Dad's boyfriend never seems to get enough of.

"You aren't that good!" More than one cousin in response to me beating them at a video game.

"You ever thought about a different city for college, honey?" I would have preferred my aunt to be blunt and just tell me they'd be happier with me gone.

Focus. One Converse in front of the other. I'll be past the clock soon. The tiles are too bright in here. I can see the clock's reflection in them, and I feel everything around me start to slow. Even the dust mites in the air come to a standstill.

Shit.

My body isn't mine anymore. The power inside me compels me to look straight ahead. Clairvoyancy is a thing that grips you, Mom always said. The vision takes you and you can't look away from it, no matter how hard you try. Sometimes, if you are skilled enough, you can decide where in the future the vision would at least focus, but no one can ever shut it off. The hallway is no longer bright but blanketed by shadows. I hear the shambling of the creature coming down it. It is from the future—what kind of future I have no clue, but it wouldn't be able to enrapture me so completely if it weren't.

It's never harmed me before, but I never know if this nightmare is the one that makes it happen.

Clairvoyants tell stories about this creature. Mom said no one ever gave it a name because doing so might call the creature to come collect them. It is thought of as the thing that takes all clairvoyants to the end of time, where they might find paradise or damnation. I took to calling it Clockface, and I've wondered ever since if that's why the thing won't leave me alone.

Its face is a gigantic clock with Roman numerals composed of desiccated fingers. The brown, withered flesh stands out starkly against the white surface on which it tells time. No mouth, no nose, no eyes. Only dim yellow light flickering behind the surface and a loud, persistent, mournful *tick, tock*. It shambles forward on too-thin legs and arms, but it is much heavier than it looks. The ground cracks and breaks beneath Clockface with every step.

I'm struck by a nightmare of this beast whenever I see the time. I can't even unlock my phone anymore without having to look away. I constantly ask my phone to tell me the time. I'm late to school a lot and afterschool detention is practically a second home, which isn't so much of a problem when your father is trying his best to pretend you're not there anyway. My friends give me shit for getting online late to play games. I'm managing so far, but I can't keep it up forever. I slip, and when I do, there it is.

Those fingers stare at me. I feel it right in my chest, like they're burrowing into me. One of those long, unnatural fingers reaches out toward me. I want to look away. I'm nearly breaking my neck trying, but its clairvoyancy: you see what you're going to see, and all you can do is lean back. If that finger touches me, I don't know what it's going to do.

"Please," I barely whisper. "Please go away."

Despite not having a face, the creature does have a voice, and what it always repeats makes my stomach roll. It feels like a cold hand around my throat.

"The end of time calls. Answer it and save us all." It drones this over and over, like the ticking of a clock, until a nurse's voice calling out a medical code on the intercom system brings me out of the nightmare and into the present again.

I look around and take a deep breath as I run my sweaty hands down the front of my pants. Rubbing the back of my neck, I massage it as a point of focus until my heart stops racing. I've been through this before. No time has passed at all. No one probably even noticed me pause for that brief moment. The head of the Silent Institute definitely couldn't have felt the power of that nightmare here . . . Could he?

Nope, I refuse to consider it.

But the visions have never happened here before. The Silent Eye Institute, in a horribly ironic way, felt like a safe place from them. If they are happening here now . . . it means I am getting stronger. Mom had been among the strongest. She, like many clairvoyants before the power went toxic, worked as a politician. They could see into the future, so it only made sense they were allowed to guide the policy decisions of the world. Mom could see further and clearer than most. It made her downfall all the worse.

That won't be me, though. I refuse. After seeing Clockface, the refusal to accept fate feels like an accusation. With all her power, why couldn't Mom see the breaking of her mind coming? We could have run away—maybe joined the Unseen. Now angry at the world for taking her away and terrified of the day I'll be forced to join her, I'm stuck coming to this sterile prison trying to pass itself off as a hospital. The concoction of feelings makes my stomach turn.

The private visiting room is the same one they always assign me whenever I come to see her: room 96. It must make it easier for them to keep track if they just corral us into the same spaces every time.

Room 96 is cold and drab, and the metal seats suck. As cold as it is, you'd think the space would smell a little less like sour milk. The wallpaper is white with a pattern of eyes *x*-ed out as a reminder of the power this place seeks to "cure." They probably thought it was quirky, but all I want to do is rip it down. The single steel table here is off balance, and the chair I sit in stings my skin. Might as well stick an ice block up my ass, but the dull lights are better than the yellow of Clockface.

Waiting here for Mom in this small chunk of discomfort puts my nerves at ease. She knows things about clairvoyance that no one else will tell me, and although discussing them might get us in trouble because of dumbass institute regulations, I think it's time I ask her about what's been plaguing me. Before it lands me in here too.

I really hope she's in a good place today. The meds they have clairvoyants on in this place are rough. My Dad would have been livid if he knew the amount of clairvoyant research I pored through, so I just pretended to drown myself in video games. That was a reaction he could live with. I studied all the theories about why clairvoyancy went rancid, all the chemical concoctions people had devised to suppress that power. They called it helping, but the side effects of most of these drugs were terrible.

Mom had sudden bruises, momentary bouts of blindness, skin that blistered and would take weeks to heal. I documented everything I saw on her when I came to visit. Not that I thought people would care—my own family couldn't be bothered to—but I wanted a record for when I finally decided to do something. I just wasn't old enough yet. I needed her to hold on a few more years until I could move out, find the Unseen, and fight to get her and everyone else out of here. The Unseen hasn't turned to violence yet, but all their literature made it clear direct confrontation wasn't off the table if things didn't change soon. I'm sick of them holding back. I'll find a way to convince them to fight.

That's if these nightmares don't find me in a room right next to her . . .

The door to the room creaks open, and I sit up with a start. I've been through this a million times, so getting the shit scared out of me now is stupid. I take a deep breath and smile as my mom shuffles into the room. She is wearing a red bandana that holds her long locs back and a blue gown, not as elegant as her campaign days, but far better matching her personality than the standard fare. At least they are allowing her some color in her wardrobe now, some style. For the first year, she was stuck with light-ass gray sweats. It made me unreasonably angry when I first saw it. One, she hates sweats, and two, she hates gray. Everything else had already been taken from her; couldn't she at least get to wear something she liked?

Her smile for me as she enters is tight, and before I can ask why, I see the man standing behind her.

Dr. Patton Greystone is an exceptionally thin man, with an aura that screams arrogance. His clothes are a patchwork of expensive name brands, and he walks with a cane he must not need, because not a thing about the object looks functional: There's nowhere on it to get a good grip as running up and down it are black glass eyeballs, the symbol of those who believe clairvoyancy corrupt. The cane's ferrule is a clock made to look wavy and distorted, another emblem against the people who were once so loved for their power. I grit my teeth at the sight of it. I've done enough reading to know exactly what it means.

This world *owes* clairvoyants. They have saved cities from natural disasters. Prevented murders. Stopped epidemics. And now when clairvoyants need help, they are called corrupt and locked away, all because there are some, like Dr. Greystone, who saw a chance at making themselves powerful. The Unseen talk about how much money flows into the pockets of institutes keeping clairvoyants captive.

So why is he here? Others at the facility would make sure Mom was up on all her medications, have me sign a waiver and give us a few minutes alone. But Dr. Greystone just stands there, smug and judgmental. My throat feels like it's about to close shut, and my palms are sweaty. I just want him to *go*.

"Julian, am I correct?" Greystone's voice is silky smooth and carries an easy air of authority to it.

"That's me. You're—"

"But of course I am. No one else but me should escort Silent Eye's star patient. Your mother raves about you, so I took this as an opportunity to come and meet you."

I can tell Mom doesn't exactly feel the same about Greystone. He's a prick, so not surprising there. But her eyes are darting up and down. She does that when she's nervous. And her ears are redder than normal; she's scared. What the heck is happening here? The guy running the whole operation popping up during a private visit is a red flag anyway. Gotta keep my cool here, even if my legs are telling me to get up and run.

"How's your medication going, Mom?" Innocent enough question. One that doesn't make Greystone perk up at all. What loved one wouldn't ask about it?

Mom smiles at me, but she quickly moves a finger to her lips in a gesture of pain. They're blistered. I tried not to notice at first. "I'm doing fine, baby. Just a few side effects, but the clairvoyance is gone."

The "for now" is implicit in there. Mom's powers have always been off the charts, and they just keep growing. They've had to up her medication three times since she's been in the Silent Eye. It makes the prospect of my waking visions even more terrifying.

"The new medications are marvelous," Greystone smirks from behind her. He looks so satisfied with himself, a bird preening. "You should take her hand. Let her know her son is here for her every step of the way."

Mom's ears might as well be glaring stop signs. What is going on here? I swallow hard and look Greystone right in the eye, trying to project confidence. "Touch isn't allowed here."

"If there's anyone who can allow a rule to be broken at Silent Eye, it's me."

"Thank you, but I don't want to break the rules. Mom and I are happy as is."

"Of course." He smiles hard, and I can feel the sweat beading on my forehead. "But if I could be allowed an indulgence?"

The walls of the room feel like they're closing in on me. There's no way I can tell Dr. Greystone no to whatever he's asking, not if there's any chance to tell Mom what I've been seeing. I look at her, hoping she can see the love I have for her, because no one else does. If I could, I'd kick this doctor's ass and run Mom right out of here. But I'm just her son; I'm always going to be her baby, and it's hard to expect a baby to protect you from a wolf. I plan on doing it all the same.

"Sure. Of course, Dr. Greystone."

But then he rushes forward, and before I can even yell to stop him, his fingers grip my chin, viselike—I can't move. *Why* can't I move? Mom begins to cry.

The room falls away to complete darkness. I think I'm screaming, but I can't hear anything. It's so cold. I think I'm shaking, but I can't see my body. It's a vision, one I'm hardly here for. The darkness gives way to dozens of faces, each familiar but too blurry to precisely recognize. Recognition sets in fast as the faces solidify in detail. These faces are mine: One is covered with tattoos. Another has white locs. Another wears diamond ear gauges. Each face is a twist on my own.

They all scream in terrifying unison.

"The end of time calls. Answer it and save us all."

Rushed back to the real, I fling backward, almost falling out of my chair, but I'm caught by Dr. Greystone. Fuck, fuck, fuck. Mom looks at me like I'm wrapped up in a coffin: eyes sad, horrified, grieving. I push Dr. Greystone off me and stand up, all thoughts of restraint gone. I point an angry finger right between Greystone's eyes. "What the fuck! You knew that'd happen!"

Greystone shakes his head and tsks like the outburst is a minor inconvenience, and it pisses me off even more. But Mom's slackened jaw and wide eyes root me in place. Greystone gives her a pat on the cheek. "Looks like she was right about you. You're full of power . . . and danger. I should have known they'd be after you soon."

"Mom?"

She just shakes her head and mumbles something, but I can't make it out at all. This was what it was like the day they took her away. All tears and mumbles, me shouting at dad to *do* something. I swore then I'd fight for my Mom no matter what. But now? She didn't fight for me. She is supposed to protect me, and she sold me out. How long has she known? Did she see Clockface torturing me too? I can feel a roar wanting to rise up from my gut as I take slow, deliberate steps toward her and the doctor, an unasked question on the tip of my tongue: *Why?*

"Don't blame her," Dr. Greystone said, his voice slow and patronizing. "As I'm sure you know, prophecy has a way of dominating the mouth, making it speak what it'd rather not." Each of his words feel like dark slime oozing down my arms. "She said you had power. This wasn't a task for anyone else but me. They want to claim you, and I can't have that."

"Shut up. Nothing's claiming me!" I can't take anymore. The roar comes out in one great burst, and I shove Greystone away from Mom.

He hits the door but makes no move to retaliate. He massages the bridge of his nose, looks at the floor, and sighs. "It's better you work with me, before things get out of hand. You will get *so many* people killed if you don't."

Mom whimpers. "He doesn't know."

Greystone's nostrils flare as he grips my mom's shoulder. She won't look at me. "The Silent Eye works to cure this illness, this . . . ability to see what shouldn't be seen. The future is supposed to stay unknown. By studying you at the burgeoning of your powers, I can stop the others. That would bring your mother back. Isn't that what you want?"

Mom starts to moan and says, "It won't work."

She grips the side of her head. Her words come out in rapid fire. "Time is too heavy and will collapse. The eye goes blind in the end. A choice is made. Certain fates cannot be changed. The end of time calls. Answer it and save us all."

Those. Words. How did she—

Then the room goes dark. I can't see anything, not even my fingers in front of me. The floor suddenly feels like I'm on the first drop of a roller coaster. My stomach climbs into my throat, and I scream for my mom, hoping she's okay.

My only answer is Greystone's wail. The darkness and the roller coaster fall and continue right along with the scream. I bend down, hoping I can touch the floor, but I never reach anything. I can feel myself. My feet are planted, but nothing else around me has form. It's an ocean of darkness, and we're countless leagues away from any spark of light. When the shadows fade and a floor is beneath me again, one mindfuck is traded for another. Greystone is in the grips of the clock-faced demon. My mom is nowhere . . .

Fear keeps me rooted. With Greystone's every punch at the demon, age spots appear on his fists while his knuckles become gnarled. Gray hair quickly overtakes his head and face while his eyes become rheumy. A strange yellow light emanates from Clockface, beams down on Greystone, and accelerates the process. I do the only thing my body allows me to at this moment.

"MOM!"

Clockface fades away, and an old, withered Greystone is left behind. Collapsing to his knees, he reaches for me. I resist the urge to back away, remembering how often that creature's fingers reached out for me, how that could have been me! I go to him, and with trembling hands, I help him sit where Mom once was, in a chair colder than ice. I run my hands down my face and breathe, methodical and slow. On the third breath, I realize Greystone's dying gasps are in rhythm to my frightened ones.

I need to find Mom. "Did he take her? Do you know where?"

"The end of time calls. Answer it and save us all."

"People keep saying that, but what does it mean?" I'm sick of being haunted by words with no definition I can hold on to.

"We're all the same. We're all each other," he mumbles as drool slides down the side of his face. He looks up at the ceiling, grimacing. "In time. We all are—"

Then he's gone. I can tell by the stillness. The vomit comes all on its own. The vertigo before this, the sight of Dr. Greystone dead, the sudden bowel release of a fresh corpse—it's all too much, and my body lets me know it. The tears come on their own too. I curl into ball on the floor too close to my vomit, but I can't bring myself to care. None of this makes sense, and the only person who can help me is gone.

But losing my shit isn't going to help Mom. She needs me. For all I know, Clockface attacked her first, and she's suffering. That's enough to get me wobbling to my feet.

Staggering out into the hallway, I call for Mom again. Call and call, but I stop after the third shout. The building around me is different. The same, yes, but just like Greystone, it looks older.

The paint on the walls is gone. The building is all concrete, and the windows let in a strange red light. The tiles on the floor are riddled with cracks and fissures. My chest tightens. This isn't right. I want to move fast and find my mom, but my legs won't obey. Each step is slow, like wading through molasses, as I approach the window.

The sight, the source of the red light, is the landscape itself, one I can only think of as broken. The ground is littered with burnt-out cars, smashed toys, chunks of buildings. It's all things that used to be part of something whole. I look up and see pieces of houses, carnival rides, and ships floating by in a long stream that stretches beyond what I can see. Some are covered in ice, others are aflame, and many are just translucent, like they're about to fade away into nothing. Echoes I can't quite make out sound from the distance over and over, a litany of what seems like people trying to be heard. Where am I? Is Mom lost out there somewhere? I take a breath.

"Get it together, Julian." I look at the ground and clench my fists, trying to bring some sense of calm over myself. What would Mom tell me? In the good days, she would always say that the future could either be a river you drowned in or one you let carry you to a safe shore. Either I can let wherever this is make me useless or I can try to find my own shore.

Fuck it, I can do this.

A few deep breaths, and Mom's advice makes the world more solidified, like it's not falling out from under me anymore.

I need to make sure I completely comb this building. If I leave, I don't even know if I'll be able to get back. Why didn't I tell someone sooner about my visions? Dad's a jerk, but maybe he could have done something, stopped me from bringing a monster right to Mom. And Greystone . . . is that my fault too? Would the monster even have—

No! Focus, Julian! You have to focus!

I call out for Mom the whole way back to the front desk, having no idea if it's safe or not. I just know there are screens for the cameras at the front, and I might be able to find her on one of them. And if not, it could maybe be a focal point. Mom taught me that clairvoyants could sometimes use objects to help guide their visions. I don't know if I'm capable of it, but I can't think of a better way to see what lies ahead for this whole place than there.

Greystone became old and died. Everything outside this building is broken and decaying. The air smells like raw chicken juice left in the trash too long. The floor is coated with dust to the point that I'm leaving footprints. Wires hang loose from the ceiling. I'm starting to think this entire place is a much older version of the Silent Eye. But if that's true . . . No, not another spiral of thoughts. Get to the front desk. Look for the screens. Start there and figure it out.

I get to the front desk and stand behind it. All the camera screens are shattered, one so badly it has a large weblike burst at the center. I bite my bottom lip to keep from letting loose a long string of expletives. The broken screens aren't a problem for what I plan to do. Mom said that to bring forth a vision using a focal point you need to be in contact with the object. Then, she said, to close your eyes and imagine the future, any future. A plume of dust shoots up when I put a hand on top of a screen. I choose to see Mom and me in some underground hovel with members of the Unseen.

Finally free.

My body feels light, and there's a smell of rust in the air. Mom said that scent was the best indication a vision had been invoked. Please just show me something I can use to help her—

Clockface is there. It's all I see. I can't scream, but it doesn't try to reach out for me this time. It's face just shatters, and I'm pulled back to this dark and shattered future.

A thick manila folder is on the reception desk in front of me where it hadn't been previously. A large 96 is plastered on the front of it with the ink still dripping. The folder is too clean against this dusty and cobwebbed place.

I gotta pick this up, don't I? I don't want to. I really, really don't want to. But Mom is out there somewhere, and if something is fucking with me, playing its game might be the only way to find her. I swallow down the lump in my throat and grab the folder like I'm sticking my hand into a pot of hot oil.

Okay, it didn't do anything to me. I don't feel weird. No rashes. My vision's fine. Okay, okay. I'm okay.

I crack open one eye and see it's just a patient file. Nothing but white boxes, black text, and some badly taken headshots. My sigh of relief echoes across the empty front lobby. Still, someone left this here, so there must be something in it I'm supposed to see.

I flip through the file, and at first, it's all stuff I know. The file starts by detailing the day Mom started screaming in the middle of the mall about how time was going to collapse, grabbing any stranger she could and telling them how we were all going to die. She had turned to me and told me how I had to keep it together, her last lucid moment before the Silent Eye Institute came and took her. I've been trying to keep it together ever since.

The paperwork moves into how the first few rounds of drugs did nothing to stop her visions and her powers kept growing. But it starts to veer into things that I don't know. Things that I couldn't possibly know because . . . they haven't happened yet. Greystone decides to stop medicating Mom for a while and allows her to use her abilities to help him map out exactly when clairvoyancy will break. They spend a couple of years trying to figure it out to no real result. The dates on the file are years into the future, and slowly they start to creep into decades. One failed treatment after another until Mom has a catastrophically bad reaction to a medication and ends up with complete loss of self.

She's never the same. She dies alone.

I shake my head vigorously and close the file. It crumbles to ash and falls between my fingers the instant I do. Mom's not going to go out like that. I don't give a damn what I have to do. Why did Clockface even want to show me this? It had to be Clockface. He was the only constant in all of this.

An unexpected *ticktock* resounds throughout the lobby, and I let out a quick yelp. It comes with that same rhythm of speech, with its same proclamation: "The end of time calls. Answer it and save us all." This time though . . . it sounds just like Greystone. What's happening?

"Fuck you!" I shout into the air. "Where's my mom?"

There's no answer.

I can't crumble here though. This thing has my mom. I know it does. I need to figure this out. Why show me her file? It must want me to take something from it. Try to think, Julian. Think! That file had "96" written in ink on it, but 96 isn't Mom's room number. They wouldn't keep a file with a visitation room number on it for her. Room numbers aren't kept on any of the files. The Unseen are known to be infiltrators, and they could do damage with patient records. Now I know where I need to go next! Back to where this started.

I run.

The rooms fly by me, all of them with clocks nailed to the center of their doors. Their ticks and tocks are like a path guiding me to room 96.

When I near, I slow to a stop. The door is closed. Standing in front of it saps all my courage out of me. Every time I come here, all the fraught possibilities of what lies behind it stop me. I think of my mom, bruised and bleeding from medicine forced on her, and I envision myself right behind this door with her. But the future I want isn't going to happen by standing still.

"Okay, Mom. This is for you." I grab the door and step inside.

It's not her room. It's a giant chamber, and looking down on me, like a row of judges, are a half dozen Clockfaces. My legs are screaming at me to back out and take my chances with the landscape of broken things. But I swallow another lump and step forward.

"I want my mom." I would like to imagine I sound brave, but every word has a tremor in it. "Give her back."

The *ticktock* starts again. It grows louder and louder until I'm forced to cover my ears. But the noise keeps growing, and I fall to my knees in pain. *Tick! Tock! Tick! Tock!*

"I just want my mom!" The noise stops, and I can hear myself think again beyond the never-ending signal of time marching forward.

"Our mother is safe."

I look up, confused and angry at the possessive. "What are you talking about? Give her back!"

"Time is broken." It's a Clockface to the side of me. I quickly back away, but it makes no move to follow. "If your wish is to save her, then you have to help us fix it."

I laugh, an incredulous sound that comes out of me unbidden. "So, you do all this . . . to ask for my help?"

"You had to believe. We are stubborn. Mom always said that." The voices sound like me. I can't deny it, and I think back to my vision: all my altered faces screaming at me. Was this connected?

"Mom says a lot," I respond.

"There's no point in holding back anymore," another Clockface says.

I couldn't agree more, and I'm not sure if that should scare me or not. "Tell me where she is! Tell me where *this* is! NOW!"

"The end of time."

Not the answer I was expecting, yet somehow, it makes sense. All the broken things. Mom's file stretching into the future. Greystone dying like an old man. I can't forget that. The end of time . . . shit.

"There is no future where we get to be with our mother," a Clockface says. "Believe me, we tried and so did Greystone. We failed a dozen times to save her, and time just kept growing."

"Greystone? What does he have to do with any of this?"

A ball of light springs up in front of me. It's composed of millions of tiny pricks of blue light. The ball expands as the Clockfaces explain its presence. I step back, wide eyed, and am struck by a sudden happiness. Something about this light feels like home.

"A simple construct of time. Each light represents a timeline and the connections between them where the points of divergence occur. Creation started as only one light and quickly expanded from there. Every second, every moment, yields new lights. Clairvoyants like us can tap into this grand construct and understand its connections, see the way time might flow. But it has grown too large, and the immensity of it has turned what was once a gift into a curse. If it keeps growing, time will collapse under its own weight, and everything that has ever been will be snuffed out."

"Dr. Greystone was trying to do something about this?"

"He *is* us, Julian. He thought he could fix time by fixing clairvoyants. His work took him to dark places."

I take that in like a blow to the stomach, burying my face in my hands with slow deep breaths. The chamber feels a lot smaller, like it's closing in on me. I did all this? In a different timeline? "And you're me too?"

"Yes. The Time Judges were all us once. They brought me here to fix time, and I did not succeed. Now we come to you, hoping that you can do what Greystone and I could not."

This is way too much to digest. And I'm not even sure how I'm supposed to believe any of it beyond what I've seen with my own eyes. I want to find a way to claim that this is all total bullshit, but I'm not sure how. "Why me? Or . . . us, I guess."

Another Time Judge takes it upon themselves to answer. "You are a lynchpin, Julian. You exist in all timelines. You can walk through all its wonders and all its horrors."

An angry red light appears in the center of the time construct, and I shield my eyes to adjust to the change. "Lynchpin? I don't understand."

"Our only real success was creating this place to serve as a commonality for all timelines to end at. But it can only hold the weight of an ever-growing variety of creations for so long."

The red light snuffs out in a flash, and the entire construct explodes in a cascade of light. I gulp, knowing what that signifies for me and everyone here.

"The only way to save time is to safely break it apart. Instead of one singular construct, you must create many. Allow them to grow and prune again. It will be an endless task, but one that would keep creation safe. But to do this without destroying oneself means only those who exist everywhere can do it."

The Clockface's finger finally touches me, caressing my chin with a degree of concern. "The work . . . changes you. We survived—learned we can alter aspects of reality—but none of us have ever successfully served a piece of time."

"You don't have to do this, son."

It's the sweetest voice in the whole world. At the end of time, maybe more so. I turn, see my mom, and rush right into her arms. "You're here!"

"They looked after me. No matter how you look, I will always love my boys, and my boys will always love me."

She feels . . . better. Lucid. They altered her. Brought her back. I can't explain it, but it's like she was before the Silent Eye . . . before some twisted version of myself . . . took her. I bury my face into her shoulder. "I'm sorry. I'm sorry I did that to you."

Mom strokes the back of my head, and it feels like home. "It wasn't you. Not the one I know. These other versions of you protected me. Stubborn like always, they wouldn't let me go to you. Rules and all that nonsense."

A few chuckles resound over the ticking noise. In the end, all these things really were me.

Seeing Mom healthy again helps me to make the decision. I pull back from her, give her the most genuinely happy smile I've mustered up in a long time, and turn to the Time Judges. "I'll do it. As long as she stays like this, I'll do it."

"She will return to her timeline and be safe, but she will have never been a clairvoyant. And she will have no memory of you. Our alterations do not come without cost. We have to cut you out of time to do the work that needs to be done."

"No!" Mom shouts. "You can't do that!"

A Time Judge speaks. "If there was another way, Mom, I'd do it. But Julian wants you safe as much as we all do. It has to be this way."

"Everything," I say to her imploringly, "literally everything, is on the line. I have to try."

I have to fix this. For her.

She puts my face in her hands, like she always did when I made her sad. Tears well in my eyes despite my best attempt to hold them back. She kisses my forehead, and my tears run free. "I don't care what any version of you says. I'll never forget you, baby."

"I know, Mom. I love you."

And then she's gone.

"What didn't you want to tell her?" I turn into the Time Judges and take in their immensity really for the first time since arriving here.

"We've gone through a thousand other Julians, and the only ones to survive the work have been us and Greystone. Time is a place full of . . . darkness. We will teach you what we know and help you navigate it, but some things can only be experienced."

I nod. She's worth facing whatever is out there.

"Show me."

The faces of the Time Judges all *ticktock* in unison, and they say in the same manner, "Very well."

The floor opens beneath me, showing the brokenness of time, the calamities across a thousand versions of reality, and all the death it brings. The *ticktocks* around me grow louder and louder, as do the voices of myself in unison.

"Answer the call. Save us all."

I dive in, finally ready to embrace my fate. And the loss of everything I've ever known.

Mother, Daughter, and the Devil

by

Donyae Coles

hen the witnesses testified, they said they heard a gunshot. They knew a gun when they heard it. Anyone who hears a gunshot knows it when they hear it. Weren't no engine backfire that rumbled in the soul like that. Only violence echoes all in your ears and down your chest. Only thing them men knew that could sound like that was a gun, so a gun it was. The county residents were used to the cracking roar of a weapon. And when they saw the Good Doctor all sprawled out on the floor, well, there was no doubt.

They never found a gun. Or a bullet, not in that whole mess of guts and blood that used to be the Good Doctor, but even so, it had to be a gun. There weren't nothing else it could be.

And Lily must have been the one that shot the gun. Not that anyone could seem to find it when it was time for finding.

They said later at the trial that there was a panic, evidence was lost—it's a small town, small police department, but how you lose an entire *gun*? Don't make no sense 'cept for the fact that there never was no gun, but Lily did kill the Good Doctor.

No one saw it but she did it.

Weren't no witnesses to what happened. Not a one. They came later, saw later, and if they had any sort of mind, they would have known that what their eyes were seeing and what their brains were saying weren't in line with each other, and when that happens you need to trust your eyes. Your brain is going to try and rationalize, make sense, like them witnesses tried to make sense, but your eyes, well, the eyes just see what they see.

But you can't really blame them, because what they saw, well, it's not a thing fit for seeing.

The Good Doctor sprawled on the floor of his examination room, green linoleum beneath him turning into a fire-engine red puddle that spread like wings across the floor and soaked into the white of his coat, turning it past red into black. His torso weren't no body no more, just a mess, and everything that weren't pink was red, but his face was white as his coat used to be. And there was Lily, her back against the examination table, a wide smile on her pretty Black face. Her hair all a mess, and she looked like a little girl. Sixteen but a little girl.

She was wearing a yellow summer dress and an old peach-colored shawl, and there was blood on all that too. Her hands were covered in white dust, her arms ripped and torn, blood covered and sticky, full of something. Something dark and violent that squirmed and twisted in her grasp, and they, the men who said they were there but really didn't come until after, said it was a gun.

Even though it was moving, they said it was a gun.

Sometimes they say it was still smoking, that it was big and a darker black than Lily's own Black hands, and that was true. It was too big for her and slippery, that dark thing. Young like Lily was young but already dying. But it was hot too. Burned through Lily's whole body, and each breath it took was Lily's own heartbeat. It weren't no gun—it was moving, and guns don't move, and those men who came later, who came running, they said they saw it, but they didn't know what they were looking at.

Here's the truth though.

The sound they heard was not a shot being fired.

It was the crack of an egg.

And the thing in her arms, that twisted black thing she held, that's what came out of it.

But no one could make sense of that, so it was a gun, and the truth didn't matter because the Good Doctor was dead all the same. And Lily, who stood over his body, was glad of it.

In that moment, after that crack, after all that blood and heat but before the Good Doctor's wife came screaming and the men came yelling, it was just Lily and the Good Doctor and the thing between them in a room that smelled not as it should.

For that moment, bloodstained, Lily holding the dark thing that had made a pile of guts of the Good Doctor, the world was silent, and the curse she had carried so long was over, and whatever would happen after that didn't matter none, because right then, that end was all she wanted.

At the trial, no one could understand why Lily had killed the Good Doctor. She wasn't one of his patients—no one knew what she was doing there, in that house, looking a mess. Must be a poor child who had been taken with a sudden case of vapors that drove her across the woods and marsh, seeing red. But it wasn't vapors, and it wasn't sudden. It'd been brewing for near seventeen years.

Lily was always gonna walk through them woods. Was always gonna be the end of the Good Doctor. A curse is a promise. And Lily's people, they good about them deals.

But you can't tell men who are looking for a bullet from a gun that doesn't exist anything about curses. Everyone thinks they know about curses, but what they know is mostly wrong. Lily weren't born with a twisted body or a hand that turned everything to dust or something fanciful. It wasn't a fairy tale. No, Lily stank.

She smelled like a chicken coop left to rot, like a mouse died in the walls, like a thousand awful everyday bits of filth and death all rolled up into one and put on her body. She was beautiful, which made people stop, stare, but that smell! That awful, curdled, rotting smell that leaked from her every pore was too much.

When Lily thought about it, the smell, which was often, more often than she'd admit, because admitting it meant she would have to be true about how much time she had to think about it. Had to be true about how lonely she was, and she couldn't do that. Admitting it would be unbearable, so she didn't, and that worked some. Not a whole lot—that loneliness still made a hollow place in her chest, settled in, and took root—but it worked some. But when Lily thought of it, she thought what a cruel, sorry joke it was to be named for a flower and smell like dung.

She couldn't smell it herself. She heard about it, the funk that wrinkled noses if they were polite and dragged out gaging and dry heaving when they mamas didn't train them as well as Lily's own mama had trained her, but she didn't smell nothing on herself. When she sniffed her arms and pits, it was just sweat and salt like any skin. But everyone else could smell it, so it didn't matter what she did or didn't smell.

It started the night she was born. Lily, that's her mother's name too, the Lily Before Lily, was only a little older than young Lily was when she killed the Good Doctor. Her mother, Before Lily, was seventeen when she felt the first pangs of labor. She didn't go to no hospital. Before Lily didn't have no hospital to go to, and that was part of the trouble if you want to get right down to it. She had who everybody else had who couldn't get into no hospital, who couldn't see no Good Doctor. She had Mrs. Nettie.

The difference was that's all she had. Everybody else had they aunties, cousins, three-generations-back mawmaws, neighbors, and who have you, but all Before Lily had was Mrs. Nettie and her own mama.

Just three women, and not even that, because, truthfully, Before Lily was just a girl, scared and in pain.

Mrs. Nettie said that baby Lily was the most beautiful baby she'd ever seen and she didn't care what nobody else said about them, the Lilys. She had hope in her heart for all God's children, great and small, and even though she had been there and knew that there was something wrong in Lily's house, knew that what drove Lily to kill the Good Doctor started there, she still said that Lily was the most beautiful baby. Whatever else, she was a beautiful baby.

Before Lily lived with her mama in a house on a good, flat plot of land. There was an old weeping willow behind it, but most of it'd been cleared for crops, then left to weed because Before Lily's mama didn't know nothing about farming. The building was all of one floor, straight through from front door to back door, one long hall to catch the wind that was lined by three bedrooms, a kitchen, a living room, and a dining room. It was space for a bigger family than had been there for a long time, and now it was just three, and in short time, just two. Before Lily and Lily.

All that land, but they only kept a few chickens. They didn't grow anything but babies, and there weren't many of them neither. So Before Lily popping up pregnant weren't really a surprise any more than when her mama popped up pregnant with her. And the whispers all over town said the only reason Lily didn't swell up right around the same time her mama did was because of that smell. Hard to get close to a girl smelling like she smelled, no matter how pretty she was. This might have been a different story if she had gotten pregnant. No daddies in that house either, just them women. Last man to live there was Before Lily's grandpa, and he passed on years before. As it was, near everybody had their suspicions about who Before Lily's daddy was.

Some said the Pastor and that's why Before Lily's mama stopped coming to church on Sunday. Another favorite was that he was Mr. Made It Big in Music, Mr. Left and Never Came Back to where he was a nobody like everybody else. They said that's why she didn't have no TV in her house, so she never saw him rocking and rolling on *The Late Show*, never caught him smooched up on someone who weren't her. There was talk about neighbors, about an out of towner, as if anybody ever came through that little nowhere place. Lots of talk, always good for a slow day.

Before Lily's mama never said though. When Before Lily asked, all her mama said was, "I swallowed a pumpkin seed, and there you were nine months later, garden fresh." Lily never asked Before Lily who her daddy was. Didn't need to.

Everybody knew who Lily's daddy was.

Before Lily moaned and screamed like she was dying when that baby was coming. Her mama buzzed around like a fly, useless. She tried her best, to be motherly, to be attentive, but she weren't really one for that life, which is how she ended up with Before Lily and how Before Lily ended up with her own Lily. But this ain't her story. This is about Lily.

Before Lily, who pushed and groaned, hated the world. Hated her mother for not being better. Hated herself for being so weak as to get herself into the mess she was into. Tried not to hate the baby that weren't even there yet—weren't the baby's fault what happened, what her mother was going through—and she tried and tried not to be angry at it, but Before Lily was only human. Only seventeen and scared.

The land turned to woods and marsh past what Lily's people owned. Wet, reedy land in some places, where spirits would take you off the path, plunge you into the muck, and keep you. A tiny little town swimming in the middle of it, little nowhere town that people came from but nobody went to. You'd never know how close other living bodies was. Standing on the porch, you'da thought there was nothing else in the world, but go a coupla miles down that road and find another house, a collection of buildings, a real farm. Those two to three miles between Lily and everything might as well have been a thousand for all it mattered.

You could hear a scream. Her neighbors, in name only, sure heard Before Lily's that night. A shot could carry clear across the county; a scream could too. Wouldn't be nothing to pop on over and have a quick look-see, but the world was funny in the dark. All those wet places were wider, wilder when the sun went down, and no one was going to cross them for Lily. No one 'cept for Nettie, who would come to any woman birthing. The whole county heard Before Lily's screams that night—had to, nothing carries sound like the dark—but no one came to check in on the girl but Mrs. Nettie, the Granny Midwife.

Everyone knew who Before Lily had been with. And no one blamed him of course—what was the point? He weren't there no more; Before Lily was, and she should of known better. Everybody said it, so it had to be true.

That didn't matter to Nettie. She was there to catch a baby, and the who and how it happened weren't important to her—weren't part of her business, and she only minded her business. Might as well have been another pumpkin seed for all it mattered to her. When she got the call to come out because Before Lily was having the baby, she came. She didn't regret it, but it was the last birth she ever went to.

She couldn't use those hands to catch babies after what she held that night. Couldn't risk that whatever came into that house was following her around, waiting to jump on some other poor little baby. Call it superstition, but those old stories come from somewhere, and Mrs. Nettie had her fill of being in one—didn't want to pass it along to someone else.

Before Lily waited to ask her mother to call the midwife. Didn't want it to be time, but it was time, and there was nothing Before Lily could do about it. So, scared and in pain, she told her mama to call, but she waited as long as she could. Which was mighty long because Before Lily knew how to hold in pain, how to roll and live with it, but she couldn't hold in a baby.

The birth came quick when it came, mostly because Before Lily had waited so long. Nettie would have missed it if she'd left just five minutes later, but as it was, she got there just in time to catch the squawking baby in a blanket. To clean her off and weigh her and press her to her mama's breast.

"Beautiful baby. Prettiest baby I've ever seen, like a doll! Give her a good biblical name," Mrs. Nettie said, all coos and soothing and sweet things.

"She's mine. God didn't push her out, so I'm not going to give her a name for Him." Before Lily's voice was already hard, a mind-made-up voice. "I'm going to call her same as me. Her name is Lily." And Lily, at seventeen, became Ms. Lily to everyone but Lily, who called her—when she was old enough to call her anything—Mama.

"That's bad luck," Nettie warned. "Carry her mother's name, carry her mother's pain." Girls ain't like boys, Nettie knew that and wanted to warn Before Lily. She had a good heart. Girls don't get legacy. Girls get blood and debt and trouble. Girls get that regardless, no reason to make it worse.

"Can't be worse than the luck she already got, me as a mama, and her daddy—well, can't be worse," Lily's mama said, and Nettie had to agree. She didn't believe what they said about Lily, not then, not in that sweet moment when she was watching a girl too young a mother hold her little doll of a baby and trying her best.

No, not this Lily. This Lily couldn't have run with the Devil.

But that Lily, that sweet girl, she *had* run with the Devil. It weren't her fault though.

It was her teeth.

Lily had real bad teeth, so bad she couldn't eat and would just cry and cry. Kind of teeth that start rotting out the mouth soon as they grow in. And she tried. Lily tried so hard to keep 'em up. Brushing and rinsing and avoiding sodas and candies, but it weren't enough. They were bad from the start, and when they ached and she couldn't do nothing else, she went to Willie. He could always be counted on to steal a few sips of his daddy's hooch for her when it got too bad. To tell the truth, he was sweet on her—everyone was a little bit, back before. She wasn't as beautiful as her daughter would be, but she *was* beautiful, with a mouth full of teeth that screamed and kicked right there in her jaw.

What the girl needed was a dentist, but weren't no dentists for girls named Lily any more than there were hospitals for them to have a baby. No, only thing they had was a Granny Midwife. Nettie didn't deal in teeth, but she knew a little bit about a lot of things: "Rub some clove oil on your gums. Rinse with saltwater." And that weren't near enough to heal Lily's pain. Didn't even get close to the root of it.

Lily tried to dance and laugh it off. She tried to smile and be, but the pain—oh that pain was deep down all through her. From her teeth to her head and all in her chest, straight down through her belly to her toes. It hurt and nothing she did to try to take care made it better. She was desperate, so she drank the hooch that Willie slipped her, and that helped for a little until she was all messed up all the time. Her mama called her wild. All over town they talked—gossip's good for any day and Lily was always good for gossip. She was sixteen and she just wanted the pain to stop.

It got so bad that one night she begged for someone to come and take her life just so the pain would end, and who would appear but the Devil. The Devil is always listening, waiting for someone to call on him. You don't have to say his name for the Devil to come to you; you just gotta call. He's always willing to help the pitiful, the forgotten, the pained. And Lily had called because she needed someone to help. She was the pitiful, the pained. She wanted to smile unburdened or be nothing at all.

Lily was a girl, like any girl. She wanted things that she couldn't have in her small life. Like maybe her own mama wanted. She wanted to dance and travel and be somewhere, someone, without the whispers and looks of a whole town. She wanted a life. She held that desire deep in her, the same place that would be all hollow in her own daughter later on. She held it all swallowed up because the only thing her aching mouth allowed her to sing was pain. The only thing a body carrying that much pain could do was serve it, serve the pain.

Lily didn't tell the Devil any of this, but he understood it, and there he was, dressed in white with the kindest smile, looking just like the angel he used to be.

He tapped his cheek. "I know why you called me. I can hear you all the way downstairs. I can fix that tooth right up for you. Fix them all up for you. I just need a little something in return."

And Lily, she was ready to give him anything to not feel that crush of pain, but she asked first anyway because her mama didn't raise her a fool, even if all that pain had made her foolish enough to trust the Devil. "What do you want?" The words came out funny. She couldn't move her jaw right, but the Devil understood. The Devil always understands.

"Your dreams. I'll gobble them right up; nothing tastes better. You won't miss a thing, and you'll make more every night."

And she agreed. No second thoughts about it. Not because she was a fool—Lily was clever and quick—but it's hard to be anything at all when you're in pain, and she was in terrible pain. The kind of pain that turns the world red, that makes you want to end everything.

It was a good deal too, because who cared about those half-remembered things? Those hazy moving pictures and nonsense prophecies? They were all near forgotten by morning anyway. Let 'im have 'em. But one word can mean two things sometimes, and Lily wasn't thinking about that. Pain makes you foolish.

The Devil pulled up a fog, and she expected it to smell like sulfur, like burning or like shit and rot, but it didn't. It smelled sweet, as sweet as he was charming. She relaxed, and it felt like falling into a bed of feathers. She didn't even know she had been asleep till she woke up. She felt a little funny, but the tooth pain was all gone.

And she could smile. She could eat all the good, hard food she wanted. She could laugh and talk and sing without all that pain getting in the way. And she was still a mess, for sure, that sixteen-year-old Lily, but she was smiling and dancing and *happy*. There was *joy*, and who could speak against that? Her mother watched, didn't want to say anything because her daughter was happy and she wasn't a little girl anymore, so who was she to say something? And Lily wouldn't have taken to anything her mother said anyway, because it was her mother's fault she was in pain. Same as it would be that her Lily, when she had her, would be in pain.

See, her mama weren't no saint either, and maybe that's why she didn't see that her Lily was still just a little girl. Maybe she was too tired from being out all night. Maybe the world was just too blurry through the bottom of a glass to see that her child was still a child. Maybe Lily's mama didn't really understand all that.

And there were reasons, sure—everybody got *reasons*, and Lily's mawmaw's was probably that nobody ever saw *her* as a little girl. That's why the chicken coop was behind the house instead of good crop from the dirt in the first place.

Way back when they called her by a name instead of just what she was to other people. Before she lost her name to being someone's Mama, to being you-know-who-from-that-house. Back before all this mess, her people put that chicken coop on the land because chickens was easier to keep than working the fields. So easy a child could do it when they ma and pa woke up smelling like something last night drug in.

And she did, like a good girl. Collected eggs, talked to them birds like they was friends, cried when they turned to dinner. Till she didn't have no more tears to cry, living that way with night hauling in your pa and ma more mornings than not. Well there's a story there—there's always a story—but it ain't Lily's, not fully, so all that really needs understood is this: that house with its little chicken coop had a lot of pain in it, and everybody been staying away from Them People, Lily's people, for a long time.

Blood, pain, debt, carried down the line mother to daughter to mother to daughter.

Lily weren't the first girl with problems from Them People, but she had the worst teeth of 'em. Soon enough, another one went. It's like that with teeth: one thing after another or all at once. She waited and waited until finally she couldn't wait anymore because the smiling and eating just hurt too bad—and she didn't want to call on Willie, didn't want to be all wobbly and weak from drink. But she didn't want to be in pain. So she called the Devil.

He came just like before: All in white. Kind smile. An angel. He asked for the same price, and she agreed because it had worked. The sweet fog came again, and then later she woke. Feeling a little funny but no pain.

Now people were talking—seeing her smile and laugh, seeing her walk down the road with no pain and dancing with Willie. They couldn't be bothered to help, but they could always talk. They said that her musician daddy started sending money, sending promises of a different life, so she was getting high and mighty off that. They said she crossed the woods between the town and everywhere else, took up with one of them boys from over there in secret behind poor Willie's back. They said she made a deal with the boo hags and was one of them now. They talked just like they would after her Lily would come creeping down they streets smelling like the hottest part of summer at the dump. No help but a lot of people who had something to say, and Lily heard them.

She heard when they said that she was getting all high and mighty, that she was thinking she was something she weren't, something other than a girl from a little house on all that wasted land with its little chicken coop and nothing else. Something other than a poor Black girl with a wasted mama and disappeared daddy.

But she didn't think that she were better than that little town. She just wanted what everyone else had, didn't she? Wasn't that the dream? She heard them, and she thought, and then she knew something was wrong, wrong, wrong.

Lily weren't no fool, so pain-free and laughing, she thought, *Isn't this too much of a good thing? Isn't this too much of a good thing* from the Devil? And sure, she needed that help badly; sure, she needed to be free from the pain and he had made that happen. The Devil had helped her, sure, but he was the Devil. The price he tells you ain't never the price you pay. She wondered then, after all the dancing and laughing and singing, what he was really taking.

Couldn't be her dreams. She still had them, every night.

And maybe that's why she listened when her mama, who tried not to say too much, said something over breakfast one day. With Lily at her softest and most open, her mama began to ask questions—maybe the questions Lily should have asked herself, but the older woman understood why she hadn't. Wasn't it too good of a deal? Wasn't there too much goodness in it for the Devil? And that got Lily to thinking. So, she came up with a plan for the next time, because there was always going to be a next time. And sure enough, one of her teeth began to ache.

There's lots of ways to protect yourself from the Devil. There's oils and bags you can buy, roots and herbs, but Lily and her mama didn't know Lady Estelle then. All they had was Mrs. Nettie, who hung an ash branch in her house, so that's what Lily did too.

It weren't nothing too big. Lily was strong in the way that girls who live in places where it's more field than road tend to be, but the branch was really just a little thing, nothing more than a switch. But it's what she had. She slipped the ash branch under her bed this time and called again. There he was. All in white, beautiful. But when the fog came, she held her breath, just breathed in a bit of it, so her body felt heavy but her mind stayed awake. She let herself pretend to be asleep and waited.

He called her name a few times, and when she didn't respond he got to work.

The Devil looked in her mouth first, and it seemed like he was going to keep up his end of the bargain, do right by her. She could feel his fingers poking around for that bad tooth, but they didn't feel like the fingers of a man. No, they felt thick and wet, like a fish slipping and sliding all over her tongue. Now and then they would poke at the right tooth, but then they would move on, in search of something else. Lily stayed still, but she was scared—scared that she had made a mistake, that this was all too much—but she was too far in to back out now. The fear seeped into her, red and hot. The Devil pulled his fingers out her mouth, leaving the tooth there.

Lily held her body still when he climbed over it, rationalizing that he needed to take position to get to the tooth, needed that leverage to pull it out in one go, but he was crushing her breath and soul right out of her body. Like a stone sitting on her chest. She could hardly move under his weight, but the red of her fear turned to anger. He lied to her, as the Devil does, and while Lily slept, he took something she had never agreed to.

Lily remembered then that she wanted something else, something more from life. That she had *dreams*, and not just the kind that play pictures on the back of your eyelids. Future dreams, big dreams to be something other than Lily of Them People. They all felt so far away, almost forgotten altogether, and she was angry for it because she knew—she *knew* now—what he was taking.

All that anger burned through the little bit of fog in her blood, and she pushed him off. He wasn't expecting it—the Devil never expects to be crossed—so when she bucked under him, he jumped off like someone hit him with holy water. She didn't remember reaching for the ash branch. Maybe it jumped up into her hand itself; stranger things have happened for sure. But she beat the smile off his face, smacked him all about the head and back.

The Devil was furious, his anger even hotter and redder than Lily's by the look on his face, but no one's anger was stronger than Lily's. It burned his pretty face clear off, and underneath that was another. Still beautiful he was an angel once, you know—but this beauty was something else. He howled things in languages she couldn't understand, curses probably but other things too. He looked like he would hit her, beat the teeth out of her face, so she kept whacking at him with that branch, and he jumped away from it as if the twigs were claws.

He had been beat fair, caught in his lies. She wouldn't call him again; he couldn't get what he wanted from her no more. The Devil isn't one to take a loss though, and he is, more than anything, a gentleman. He tried to be charming and asked her to stop hitting him and just listen. "Lily, Lily, we're friends, aren't we? I helped you when your mama just let you suffer. I've done more for you than Willie with his little bit of stolen liquor, didn't I? Because of me, you could dance! You could be happy! And I didn't hurt you, did I? And you've already given me some of your soul. Why not agree to let me have the rest, honest and open now? Oh Lily, you're so special to me. Don't make things ugly between us now."

And Lord help her, she thought about it. The tooth was still aching in her jaw, and when the fog faded, it would be kicking and screaming at her. There would be no more dancing or singing or smiles—just pain, because the Devil was the only one who could help her. And what did it matter? He'd already taken from her and nothing had changed; things even got a little bit better, if she was telling the truth. But.

It was different knowing he'd lied and that he weren't no true friend, like she had made herself believe. He was being honest with her now—mostly, close enough to truth that it was all right—and maybe if he had lied some more, she would have said yes, but she couldn't agree to what he was asking. Couldn't do it because of what he *wasn't* saying. That she would stay there, stay Lily of Them People, hoping that the Devil loving her in secret was enough. So she gathered all her courage and strength and swept that branch across his beautiful face.

That should have been it, but the Devil is petty. Anyone will tell you that. Because she had beat him and rejected him, he yelled that she was cheating him, that he would make her pay for breaking their deal, never mind that he had lied and tricked her. He called her all manner of things outside her name. She chased him out and only ever saw him one other time.

That next day she went to Willie. Told him to steal a jar of his daddy's hooch and she'd give him whatever he wanted. He was sweet on her, so he did it and traded it for a kiss that Lily gave to him, because let nobody but the Devil say she didn't keep her bargains. But that was the last kiss that was ever between them two. There's a story about what coulda been, but the real story is just about what was.

Lily went home, full jar of hooch in one hand, and slid into the chicken coop where her mama used to cry, where she kept the little flock, and drank the entire jar down in one go. It burned the whole way to her belly.

Feeling fuzzy and funny, her fingers numb and the clucks and bucks of her chickens a dull racket she prayed would cover any sounds she made, she took a pair of pliers and ripped every single tooth out of her mouth so she would never, ever be tempted to call the Devil again.

And that part of her where she kept her dreams, her real true dreams, hollowed out, emptied faster than the Devil coulda swallowed them.

She spit blood for a week, and by the time she realized that she hadn't seen any blood from anywhere else, it was too late. There was no pulling that out. It was a little less than nine months before she bled again but long enough for her to turn seventeen.

The night Lily pushed her little girl out, every single bird within a mile started singing. Middle of the night, they woke up like the sun was high in the sky, tweeting and hooting and cawing.

The whip-poor-will started it, and then the owl came, but these were night birds and not so unusual, 'cept that they sang together. Then Lily's chickens, the ones that had watched her yank her teeth out and pecked at the little pearls she had dropped in their bedding all bloody, they all started clucking and calling like they did that day nine months before. The rooster started up, his cock-a-doodle doing like he was welcoming the morning, but weren't nowhere near dawn. Finally, the songbirds and crows joined in. No one could even hear the baby crying over all of it.

It stopped all sudden like: Not even the night birds sang. The wind didn't whistle through the leaves. Nothing but the high cry of new life.

Lily held the baby to her chest, the fussy small thing wrapped in a peach blanket from her grandmother, and held her breath. A knock came at the door.

Lily knew, she weren't no stupid girl no matter what her mama said when she was upset about what happened. Of course he knocked, because the Devil is polite.

Another knock. Polite but insisting.

"Must be a neighbor. You screamed to wake the Devil, girl! Someone is probably coming to check on you, welcome your little one," Nettie offered bright and sweet. It made her a good midwife that she could be hard and soft. It made her a fool in that moment though.

Lily reached out a shaky hand and gripped the midwife. "Don't open the door. Please, Nettie."

"I'll tell them to come back later," Nettie said, and she'd regret it.

The knock came again as she walked down the hall to the door. When she opened it, there was nothing there but night, the expanse of tall grass too wild to be a yard, the road a still river after that, and another field past that. Nothing moved, nothing sang. Nothing at all really and still as the grave.

Lily sat on the bed, shushing her little girl. She held her breath, waited. A nervous, sick feeling came in her belly, twisted her guts, and rolled through her body. The kind of fear that comes when you know you did whatever it is that you've done and the reckoning is coming due.

Lily dealt with the Devil and he had cursed her, and now he was coming back with his night chorus because he couldn't just let things be. Down the hall, Lily heard the creaking sound of Nettie closing the door, and then, just as she wasn't surprised when the Devil showed up, she wasn't surprised when the door didn't close. Lily would know the Devil anywhere, even when he came like the wind. That false wind picked up fierce and angry. It swept past Nettie, swirled and whirled into the house, and brought with it the song of a thousand birds and a sweet candy smell.

Lily wrapped herself around her baby while her Mama pounded on the air, her fist hitting it like glass. A solid, invisible thing.

The house dipped and shook around them, the floor moved like water, but Lily stood up, weak from birthing, baby still held to her chest, and that little branch, all dry and brittle now, was in her hand again. Didn't matter though, still fit to do what it do. "Out! Out!" she shouted chasing the wind, chasing *him* all back through the house. He roared and slammed the shutters and doors. The birds sang, and under that all, Lily could hear him, charming and smooth but the Devil all the same.

"It'll be different. I'll be good to you, be good for you, you'll see. Come on, Lily," he begged and promised.

And Lily wanted to believe him. Wanted to take all his sweet promises and believe that they would be true, that she could smile and dance and be happy with him, but they were lies. Everything the Devil says is a lie. And 'sides, Lily wasn't Lily anymore. She was Before Lily now, Lily's mama now, and that's why what happened happened.

She screamed and beat at him until he left and took his terrible bird-song and the sweet smell of his lies with him. But the Devil is good on his promises too. He said he was going to curse Lily, and he did. He took all the sweetness from their lives, made sure they wouldn't have any, not so long as he could have a say, and the Devil always has a say. Made sure everyone would know right away that Lily was his so no one else would have her. But there was more than one Lily now, and when the Devil gets angry, he lets details slide.

"He won't come back here no more," Before Lily said, rocking the baby in her arms, and she was right, because he had done his work.

And that baby looked up with the biggest, prettiest eyes and so locked in that gaze that the three women hardly noticed the smell.

Before Lily smelled it first because she was holding the baby, started faint but it grew. The smell of shit, bird shit, a coop that hadn't been cleaned in a long time. Dry and awful, it rose from the baby and made the women gag.

Before Lily lifted her baby who took her name, took on her history, to her breast and kissed her little head. She swallowed down her sick feeling and started singing a lullaby. She was a mother now. The only mother that baby was gonna get.

Nettie left right then. Let Before Lily's own mama put the fresh mother to bed. Sent notes for her aftercare and refused to step foot in that house. She prayed though. Always prayed for Lily and Lily. That's all you can do sometimes.

She talked too. Later when Willie became Mr. Willie and was running that little bar, Nettie'd get in her cups and tell everyone who listened about the night she caught the prettiest little baby she'd ever seen and the Devil came straight from Hell to meet her.

Before Lily didn't blame Willie for not keeping after her. She couldn't blame nobody for not volunteering to be shackled to the mess of her, mess of her family.

Lily was the last of them, the very last baby Mrs. Nettie ever caught. She said it was to keep from spreading whatever terrible thing chased them that night, but it weren't, not really. It was cause she was shamed by a seventeen-year-old girl. She shoulda helped. She shoulda fought off whatever came through, shoulda listened and not opened the door at all. But when the Devil came, she couldn't do nothing but cover her own head and cry while a girl, still bleeding, chased him out. After Lily, Nettie was too ashamed, so everyone else went to the Good Doctor when it was time to give birth.

The morning after the birth, Before Lily went out and butchered every single chicken in that coop, every single one that sang her misfortune. All 'cept the rooster. Couldn't find him nowhere. She did find a big ol' tom cat, all black with yellow eyes and named him Bones. He stayed in her yard mostly, but people talked about seeing him miles away. He was so big and dark, everyone knew Bones when they saw him. Weren't going to be no more birdsong in them fields, but they'd already sang they curse, and you couldn't stop what was already done. That old cat was a good hunter though. He caught all those whip-poor-wills and swallows. Even brought home an owl one time when Lily was five. Sat it at her feet like a gift.

He didn't care that she stank.

Maybe everyone would have forgot about it, Before Lily and the Devil, because Lily was so pretty and a pretty child will make a lot of people forget a lot of things, let bygones be bygones, let gossip die out. Then she could be just that beautiful girl from Them People, such a shame to be born in that house. But the Devil wouldn't let the Lilys have anything good. Nobody, no matter how good they poker face was, could pretend they didn't notice Lily's curse. People tried to be polite, and when she was little little it didn't matter so much, but Lily grew and grew beautiful, and the stench of Hell grew with her. All bird shit and swamp gas and dirty festering things. Poor girl paid for her mother's sin.

And Before Lily paid the price too. Because here's the thing about the Devil: the Devil is a liar, but he always tells the truth. He told Lily that he'd take her dreams, and he did, because there was nothing that she could do with her life after she became a mother. Nothing that seventeen-year-old

Lily ever wanted would come to pass because every morning she woke up a mother. She would forever and ever be one of Them People, never go nowhere because that town, that place, would never let her go now. They loved their gossip, and Lily was good for a story. Dealing with the Devil always ends bad, 'cept for some especially clever men. Before Lily was clever, but she weren't no man.

She took another lead from Mrs. Nettie and prayed. Prayed and prayed, but there was no lifting the curse, no turning back what the Devil had done anymore than she could make the teeth grow back in her mouth.

She prayed to God, the angels, and every saint she could think of, which weren't that many because the girl hadn't been to church ever. They didn't answer. It's not like with the Devil. They too high up to listen to everything, to hardly ever answer. But she prayed anyway, because if the Devil answered, maybe God would hear her too.

Before Lily tried not to let her daughter see her grimace at her stench. It weren't the child's fault. Weren't nobody's fault but the Devil and bad luck.

Say what you want about Them People, but them girls were clever, and Lily the daughter weren't no different from her mama or her mama before, all the way back longer than anyone could rightfully remember straight. Best believe she knew, knew long before her mama and maw-maw caught on that she knew.

Lily went to school some, not much. Weren't fair to the other kids really. She got her letters and numbers, but she couldn't stay in that school building. The other parents hounded her mama to pull her out—the smell.

The other kids were never nice about it. They stayed away, complained about being near her. Nobody came round the house asking to go play, no can-you-come-overs. Even if there wasn't the smell, their parents wouldn't have had her, not the child from that house. There was a little mercy in that, the smell, having a *reason*, because at least Lily could understand why no one wanted to play with her.

"I don't smell anything," she said to her mawmaw one day before the woman passed.

"Skunks don't smell theyself either," the woman replied, and that explained it. They were skunks, she more than everyone else, and that meant she weren't no good for being around anyone but other skunks.

Sometimes, when she was real low and lonely, she thought she could smell it though. It crept into her nose, all manner of foul things, reminding her of her misfortune, of her mama's misfortune—which was all one and the same when you get right down to it.

She grew up pretty and she grew up alone, but at least she knew *why*. There was something wrong with her, wrong with all of them. She was one of Them People, and Them People ain't fit for everyone else.

She wasn't like her mother though, maybe because her mark was worse. Before Lily just carried that taint of a rough house, but Lily was cursed for real, so she didn't even dream of being free or leaving. Weren't nowhere she could go where she wouldn't be herself. She wanted people to know her for herself, wanted the world give her a chance even if she were damned from birth because her mama committed the terrible sin of needing help like her mama before her. Like Lily did.

Her mother tried to keep her from the knowing. It was impossible as Lily got older: She couldn't go to school; she couldn't go to church; everyone knew. No friends, no people to call on, 'cept for those stragglers like Willie and even old Mrs. Nettie who took pity on Before Lily so they pitied the daughter too, and pity was better than nothing at all.

But Lily, Lily weren't no quitter, and though she may not have had much school, she was smart enough. Smart enough to know she couldn't lick this thing on her own. Smart enough to know she couldn't trust the Devil and wise enough to catch on that God wasn't answering. Or maybe she'd learnt that you couldn't count on any man to solve your problems, so she didn't go to no man. No Preacher, no Good Doctor, though he was in practice just 'cross them woods from her little house. Lily didn't have the type of problem a man could solve. But her mama was so wrapped in her own pain and guilt there was no asking her. So instead, she went to Lady Estelle, the Conjure Woman.

Lady Estelle did business at Willie's, had been doing her business there since long before Lily and probably would stay long after Willie stopped doing business, or the next Willie took his place. They called it a bar, but it weren't even properly that, just a few tables, some wood stacked on top of different wood to make a place to sling the shine that Willie's daddy taught him to make. The same recipe that he gave to Before Lily the day she pulled her teeth out.

Now under normal circumstances, if Lily had been the kind of girl who lived under normal circumstances, she wouldn't have been in no bar, but her mother sent her to Lady Estelle once a week to buy a candle, and the only place that Lady Estelle did business was at Willie's. So to the bar Lily went.

The Conjure Woman sat in the back at her own table, which had a velvet cloth thrown over it. Lily loved her. Night-dark skin with her hair all pulled up under a scarf that wrapped around her skull and reached toward the heavens. Always in an evening dress even if it was daytime. She sipped on a jar of Willie's hooch all day but never got drunk. Rows of beads with all manner of charms hung from her neck and arms and jingled with every sip. And she never made a face or pulled away when Lily came.

She sold all types of candles: trouble with money, trouble with the law, trouble with love. Whatever shape, color, dressed thing you needed she always had at that velvet table. No matter if you came weekly or if you'd never stepped foot in the little bar a day in your life. This weren't Lily's first trip though. She was a returning customer, Lady Estelle's favorite kind.

Lily always came for the same candles—tall, white ones in glass that Lady Estelle poured oils on and dusted with herbs before handing over. Lily's mother lit them and prayed over her daughter every night, the candles burning down little by little. They smelled like beeswax.

Her mother recited from memory, "Yea, the sparrow hath found a house, and the swallow a nest for herself, where she may lay her young, even thine altars, O lord of hosts, my King, and my God." Lily knelt next to her, knees hurting while Bones, old but still sharp, licked the blood of the birds he had caught off his paws.

Lady Estelle smelled like her candles, the warm, sweet smell of melting wax and herbs. The smell of a church but without all the judgement. Smelled like coming home. The air felt different near her, more alive and fuller, than it did anywhere else. Lily loved it, loved getting her mama's candle if it meant she could have a minute wrapped in that warm homecoming where she could pretend she was just like anybody else.

Every Sunday she went, the only church that would have her, cursed as she was. A few folded bills and an empty glass jar in exchange for a full one dressed with rosemary and sage, adorned with lilac and marigold flowers. A beautiful thing meant to burn.

Lily didn't have no money to buy any of her work, but she paid attention. She watched from the door when the Lady was with another customer and tried to listen in to what they said. Had to be something in that. Wasn't much ever, but it was something. Something to let her know that there was another power in the world 'sides the Devil.

Let her know that there was someway that her burden could be eased.

"You want your palm read, girl?" Lady Estelle asked one day. The leaves had already changed from their summer's best to fall shrouds, but it was hot. Burning, sticky hot, and the world was dying all around them. So hot that sweat ran down Lily's face, and the wax was soft in the candle glass that Lady Estelle handed her. But the Conjure Woman's face was dry and smooth.

Full of envy at the Conjure Woman's effortless comfort and with that sharp, tight feeling of wanting something you can't have, Lily shook her head. "I ain't got no money. Just enough for the candle."

The woman smiled and held out her own palm, beckoned her forward. "Didn't ask for no money."

Lily, quick as a cat, put her hand in the woman's. She knew she should be careful, ask questions, but she wanted and Lady Estelle was offering, and she was her mama's child after all.

"Eager?" she laughed her gap-toothed laugh.

"No, no ma'am. I'm—" she tried, embarrassed at her eagerness, at her youth.

"I know what you are." Lady Estelle gripped her hand up tight, kept her from pulling away, from thinking about it more. Maybe the Conjure Woman wasn't the Devil, but everything has a cost. Lady Estelle's hand was hot and dry under Lily's sweaty knuckles, but if the woman minded any more than she minded the smell, she didn't speak on it. She bent real close, and Lily was sure that the woman could smell her, smell the dried chicken shit and curdled milk awfulness that leaked from every inch of her. Humming and huffing as she moved this way and that way, Lady Estelle took one long, dark finger and traced the lines on Lily's hand, clucking her tongue to herself.

"Strong life line, strong heart line," she chirped, feeling along the palm, tracing lines that Lily had never noticed in her sixteen years of life. "All right, girl, you see here?" she tapped the pad under her pointer finger. "See how these lines make that little box? That's your trouble."

Lily wanted to be smarter than her mama who had fallen for the Devil, but she was a girl just like her mama had been a girl. A girl who needed help. And 'sides, Lady Estelle was not the Devil. "How can I fix it?"

The Conjure Woman smiled wide and slow like a summer's day, all her beads and charms ringing and chirping like birdsong. She was clever too, and people paid for that. She knew how to do things in the old ways, secret ways passed down through blood and whispers. But even she couldn't make something out of nothing, and she needed something from Lily that day. She drank the last of the hooch and slammed the jar back on the table. "I need your mama's teeth."

Lily had never seen her mama's teeth. Not once had she smiled down at the girl and showed anything in her mouth but her hard, pink gums. "I don't—"

"Everything's right where she left it. You know the story."

She did; everyone did—the story of how Lily climbed into her chicken coop and snatched her own teeth out her mouth. "What you need them for, what—"

Lady Estelle sucked her teeth. "None of your business what I need 'em for. Your business is getting 'em and bringing 'em to me tonight. That's all you need to think about."

"And what if I don't?" she said turning the idea over, already trying to convince herself to go 'head and do it. What's the harm? But her people were a people that knew harm, and she wasn't stupid.

"What if? The only what if you need to worry about is what if you don't do this. What if you just take your little candle and walk away? You want that fortune, it'll cost you." The Conjure Woman had that look on her face like she was hearing something far away, like she saw it all, front to back. It made Lily feel small and ignorant. "But then again, I guess you'll pay either way."

"But my mama. What'll you do to my mama?" Lily asked. You could do things with pieces of people, with fingernails and strands of hair. These were her mama's teeth though, not made to be discarded, supposed to be settled into her mouth good and true, and her mama tore them out, left them for the chickens and whatever else waited in that old coop. Left them sitting so anyone could scoop 'em up, do whatever wrong to her they wanted.

"Your mama?" Lady Estelle laughed big and loud. "Nothing! Why would I do anything to her? She's had enough. If that's what you're worried about, then you can go on ahead and let that go. Your mama got nothing to worry about from Lady Estelle."

Lily picked up that little jar, drops of hooch still ringing the bottom, and held it to her chest. "All right," she said, and just like that, the deal was made. Lily should have asked more questions, but she was her mama's daughter. And when you need help, you need help—ain't no use in asking questions when the answer won't change a thing. And Lily was tired of stinking. Tired of walking around the edges of life because of some old dealings between the Devil and her mama. Sixteen and just so, so tired.

Lady Estelle slipped a long chain with a bit of metal stamped with a winged foot hanging from it over Lily's head, settling it on the center of her chest. "For safe travels. Come by my place tonight with that jar full if you want my help. You come by, you bring what I asked for, and I'll have what you need. You don't come, that's fine! We don't speak of this again. Up to you. You know where at?"

At the very edge of town, just at the space that the world went from familiar to woods, where the shadows shifted and more than just the Devil lurked—worse than the Devil. A soul could get lost day or night out there. Body that eventually shambled out, clothes all ripped, eyes all wild, wouldn't be nobody *in* that body. It was *that* kind of place. She knew not to go past the Conjure Woman's house, better not to even go near it.

Lily walked home slowly, the candle that couldn't help her held in one hand and the usual bag from Willie in the other. He always caught her on the way out with "a little something" for her mama. She thought he felt bad about not marrying her, but everyone knew that Lily weren't his. When she was little, she used to wonder what it woulda been like if she was his, or at least if he had been there when she was born. Maybe the Devil wouldn't have come up at all. But that was all dreams. She put the empty jar with the full ones.

"I'm home, mama!" she called when she came into the house. The tom cat, Bones, looked up at her, eyes still sharp, darting back and forth, watching something move around her head that only he could see. He wrapped his long body around her legs when she came in. Animals don't care nothing about the Devil.

"I got your candle," she said.

Now Them People never went to church, but that don't mean they didn't believe. Don't mean they didn't have a proper place for their prayers. The altar was fitted with a photo of her mawmaw and prayer cards for different saints that her mother collected and displayed. A cross hung over it on the wall, the wood all soot darkened from sixteen years of praying over oil-rubbed candles.

"That's my sweet girl," her mother crooned, taking it like a holy object and placing it in the only clear spot on the table. All above and around it, the stain of the smoke framed it like a promise.

Her mama took the bag from her fingers without a word and went to the kitchen with it. Lily made a deal with whoever was listening then: let fate decide—as if everyone hadn't had enough of fate already. If her mama asked about the empty jar, she wouldn't go. Would leave things as they were. She took a deep breath, made a deal with the Spirit, and counted to ten.

When she walked into the kitchen, her mama was over the sink. "I'll start dinner in a minute, baby," she said, her words already wet, half drowning. Bones stared at Lily from where he sat on the counter, a witness. Like the cat knew what she promised, ensuring she would see it through. The jar sat on the table. Her mama sat it aside, but she didn't say a single thing about it.

Before Lily asked even less than her own mama had. She thought praying was enough.

Lily took the empty jar from the table and left the full ones.

She waited until after her mama was done praying for the night in front of the useless candle, waited until they were in bed all nice and proper, her mama in her room, Lily in her own. The house all creaky quiet around her, Lily slipped out. Still wearing the same summer dress she'd worn earlier that day, she made her way outside to the moon-soaked ground.

Insects sang in the grass, a choir of buzzing, sawing noise to meet her in the darkness. They'd all be dead soon, but they lived a good life with no birds to hunt them. The night sucked the heat of the sun right up, leaving the air cool and heavy. She didn't have a jacket; it was still in the closet, smelling of moth balls. She wrapped the peach shawl that had once been a blanket around her shoulders and looked into that night dark for some last sign.

Two yellow eyes stared back at her from an old tree stump that used to be a weeping willow. Bones jumped down, looking sleek in the darkness, like he was cut from it. Not old and rickety no more, he moved in his element like water down a stream.

Lily followed him to that old coop.

Weren't no chickens since her mama'd killed them all. Those same chickens that looked over her and pecked at the bloody teeth she'd dropped in the hay, the daughters and granddaughters of the chickens that Before Lily's mama had cried to. Murdered and left to rot. Nothing but bones and feathers and memory now. Been years since anything bigger than bugs been in there, but it still smelled like livestock and rotting. It hit Lily as soon as she came close, because there weren't no chickens—but it wasn't empty.

A squat little building, just enough space for a girl to crawl into, but she'd be on her hands and knees, which was just fine for what Lily needed to do. Bones jumped up on it, sunk his claws in old wood, and climbed, wood splitting and splintering under his weight, but he made it, settled hisself on the roof like a king, and waited.

Lily went down on her knees and crawled inside.

There are a lot of places that aren't the places they seem on the outside. Lot of places that look like one thing and are a complete 'nother when you crawl inside. The coop was one of them places. Outside, it looked like a rickety old shed, full of holes, barely standing, but inside—oh, inside was another matter entirely.

Night is dark, but night don't mean without light. That place, that chicken coop—that was a place without light. Not a single moonbeam or bit of starshine came through that roof. It was by feel that Lily made her way through, one hand clutching that little jar, the other feeling for nest boxes and fallen beams.

All the heat from the day was hiding in that small space, and the smell! Her eyes watered from it. It burned her nostrils, made her gag, but that just flooded her mouth with the taste of it. A sharp piss smell and the meaty rot smell of blood left too long.

For the first time, she really knew what everyone smelled on her, without a doubt, and she understood why her mama kept her away from the coop. Kept her away from the truth that Lily reeked of filth and pain—just like all Them People did, but Lily had the bad luck for it to be a smell for the nose and not for the heart. But she needed those teeth and understood what she had to do. Understood that the truth was there was something not right in her, something that her mama had passed down to her because she couldn't live with her own pain and it was on her to sort it out. A sad, angry truth that things could have been different but they weren't.

Her fingers slipped over something heavy and metal. Shaking, she felt out the shape of the pliers, blood still sticky. She didn't question it—she didn't have much school, but she knew enough to know that she was in one of them impossible places. Like when you wander too far into the woods. One of the right-on-the-edge spaces, a space where past and present collide and mix into one. Where old pain waited to be poked at, like a bad tooth.

Feathers ruffled, and clucking sounds joined her breathing.

Lily froze. Pigeons she told herself. Never mind that old Bones hadn't let a bird roost closer than a mile to the house in over sixteen years. Above her Bones shifted, making the roof creak, and just below that something moved again, unsettled. Watching.

Her fingers found the first tooth, and she rolled it over the floor. It was hard like a little pebble but with a sharp end. Still sticky. It rang and jingled in the jar like one of the Conjure Woman's charms. The ruffling of feathers again. Her fingers went back to the floor, and she found the bones.

Everything was just where Before Lily had left it: the pliers, her teeth, and her chickens. No reason to come home to roost because those birds never left.

A hard beak, a sharp claw. Sweat dripped down her face like it had earlier that day at Willie's, ran all down her arms and chest, and made her as sticky as the pliers, as the teeth. *Ping*, another in the jar. Dried bird crap turned to powder in her fingers and made chalk of her hands. Another pebble for her jar. More shifting above. Close, because that was the only thing to be in that broken down bird house. It clucked and shuffled, and Lily tried to say it was a pigeon, or a possum even, but she weren't no good at lying. The hay that hadn't fallen to dirt pierced the skin of her hands as she dragged them around the floor. Hands slow, to not miss anything, but her heart beat for running. Another pebble, another *plink* in the glass.

Darkness like the dark of the coop was different than the dark of outside. There weren't no air in there, not like outside air. No, it was all the air of blood and waste and pain. Lily choked and gagged on it, knew it's what she smelled like, and let all that heat and dark and foulness press her forward.

Hollow bones crushed under her palms and mixed with the leavings and feathers and whatever other filth had come to reside in that old coop that used to house a flock of fat, egg-laying birds, who never had a thing to fear in their life until Lily's mama came in with a pair of pliers.

The wooden walls remembered that something had happened there. The bones remembered. Lily could feel it in her own teeth, in her belly. She held both tight to keep them from moving, grinding. She couldn't stop. The thing in the rafters was moving, more chatter, low and slow and hard.

Another tooth. Into the jar.

The thing in the rafters remembered.

The bones moved, lifted, sluggish and slow. She could feel them against her thighs and arms.

The first was a soft poke.

The second was a hard nip against her hand, and she snatched it away. She looked into the darkness but couldn't see anything. Could only feel it—feel them, those old, angry chickens. She went back to searching, but they were up now.

They pecked at her, all in her hair, old bones tangling up in her curls, her thighs and hands. What Before Lily had left, they didn't want Lily now to take. It was theirs and they meant to keep it. Meant to hold it till the roof fell in. Didn't matter that it didn't do them no good. Didn't matter that it was what killed them.

Covered in sweat, tasting fear like acid in her throat, she bent over and kept searching. Couldn't leave—she'd never go back, she knew it, and they knew it too. That thing that waited above them all knew it. Another tooth, another chime, and they rose those old bones and pecked and scratched harder, fiercer, pulled at clothes, went for her eyes.

Crying, growling, swallowing her scream and the filth she breathed, she reached blindly for anything and found the pliers, still sticky. She swung them and bashed those fragile, sad things into dust. But they weren't what she needed worry over.

The thing above shifted, let out a legion of birdsong, and landed on Lily's back, heavy and foul. It stank of all the worst things, its beak beat and pounded at her head. Still, she searched—she couldn't stop—and the thing pounded against her.

Fear wasn't the right word for what Lily felt running through her—it was crushing, a hot, sticky feeling. She couldn't name it, but it grew with every stab of that thing's beak, the ripping of its claws. It boiled in her chest where the hollow, lonely feeling lived. New, it drove her forward, made her stronger.

Lily wasn't counting, but something about the sound of the tooth hitting the glass let her know that was it. The job was done, and she needed to get out of there before that creature tore into her for good, made it through skin and muscle and bone, pounded straight through her back and got her heart.

She bucked back, wild, and fell through the front wall of that coop. The air flooded with night and the smell of grass and cricket song. The thing on her back startled, released, and tumbled off. Jar of teeth went wild too, but she didn't have no time to think about it.

Hands free, she could fight. She swallowed her scream because, in drink or not, she didn't want to wake her mama, but there weren't no need for flailing and kicking. Bones stared yellow eyed at her from across the field, a chicken—if you could call it a chicken—caught in his teeth. Quicker than he had any right to be at his age, him and the thing that Lily's mama had left in the coop were gone into the woods.

It weren't over though, not for Lily anyway. She found her little jar of teeth, felt the weight of them, and held them to her chest. The coop was all fallen in now, broken to bits and pieces, and her hands around the glass were white as snow.

But it weren't over.

She followed Bones into the woods. The cat was gone, but she knew the way. She cut through their wasted fields and then the neighbor's, bare for the season, taking a ragged route to the house just at the edge of the woods.

She saw things, night things, Devil things—lost girls floating blue in the air singing sweet songs, big-eyed creatures, and small, crooked things—but she walked on. Further out there were men carrying lanterns, coming home from work, but weren't no work that way, not anymore. No homes the way they were going neither.

She walked past them, didn't stop when they called her name. Didn't stop for any promises or offers to rest. Didn't stop when they called her pretty. They tried to come to her, reach out to her, but then when they got too close, their lips curled, and they backed away. She couldn't say if they smelled her, accursed things like themselves or if her person just offended the dead too. But they left her be and let her pass. She held her jar and kept her eyes forward until she made it to the Conjure Woman's house.

The door swung open as she arrived, and Lady Estelle pulled her inside, whistling and humming. The room smelled like the wax from her candles, because a bunch of them were burning all over. Lady Estelle kept the tools for her work right where everybody could see 'em, no shame to be found. Every wall was top to bottom covered in shelves, and every shelf was front to back, side to side, full up with jars and candles and curios and all manner of strange. Skulls, herbs, figures of women and men—sometimes together, sometimes apart. Jars with strange fleshy bits floating in a clear liquid, old coins, bones, and bundles of plants tied and hung to dry all around.

"It got you good in that hen house, huh? But you did it, girl! I knew you was brave!" Lady Estelle laughed good and rich sitting Lily down. "Now what you got for me?"

Lily's hands were dusted white, but the jar didn't hold the pearls she had thought them in the dark. In good candlelight, them teeth were stained and brown, rotten as anything left to rot. "What you asked for."

They still sang when she moved. They jingled and jangled as she passed on the jar to Lady Estelle, who turned them in the light. "And the charm?"

She'd forgotten all about the charm truthfully but reached in her top and fished it out. The little winged foot was turning green, slick with sweat.

Lady Estelle sucked her teeth. "Keep it."

"It didn't work. That thing in the coop, was that the Devil?" Lily asked, the scratches and cuts all coming alive now that she was sitting in a living room, strange as it was.

"That? No. You'll know the Devil when you see him. That was your mama's rooster. Wait here," she said all matter of fact, like it was everyday a rooster that shoulda been dead sixteen years just hops on your back. But maybe for the Conjure Woman it was.

Anyhow, when she came back, she had a little wooden cage, and inside a rooster. Still pitch black and off in that way that night things are off, but a rooster it was for sure.

"Where'd you get that? How'd you get it?" Lily asked, the questions rolling stupid off her tongue. Pain makes you stupid, but she had seen what happened. Bones finally caught the one bird that her mama had missed.

"Not none of your business how I do business. Got what you need though." The Conjure Woman put the cage on the table, stuck her hand under that bird that really weren't no bird, and pulled out an egg. The shell the same light brown color as Lily's skin. "Freshly laid, but it's been a long time coming. A nasty little thing waiting to be born." Lady Estelle moved closer to Lily before slipping the egg right between the girl's breasts, nesting it against her skin.

The shell was all smooth and warm and perfect.

Lady Estelle took Lily's face in her hand and pointed her chin up. "Now you listen good. Spirit told me to get this cock, get that egg to you. Spirit told me to help you so I done that, and now I'm done. You keep that egg good and safe right where I put it. That egg's gonna burn, but it's going to take you where you need to go. This night ain't over."

"And if I do, the smell?"

Lady Estelle smiled, her teeth like stars in her midnight face, and Lily had never seen anything more beautiful. "Sure will," she confirmed.

Her mama had told her about deals, deals that were bad, but more than that—deals that were too good. "If this works, then we won't need your candles. Why you helping me?"

The Conjure Woman waved her hand, laughter trickling from her lips like water. "You'll always need my candles. Getting rid of one problem just makes room for another. Tell your mama to start learning Psalm 89. Spirit says she'll need it."

Lily stood up. She was tired, beat up, and the egg were sitting against her skin like an itch. She could feel it, whatever was in it, still warm, twisting and turning. Waiting. And because Lily weren't no quitter, she kept going.

Her feet had a mind all they own, and back out into that night she went, alone this time. Cold now, freezing, she wrapped that shawl around her shoulders tight. But the egg burned at her chest like a little fire.

Lily walked but not home. What she needed weren't there no more, and so she let her burning passenger guide her feet, the egg twitching and shuddering with the first signs of life that wants out, a second heart against her chest.

Like a girl possessed, she went into them woods, and all the strange things caught between the here and the there of the world watched but stayed away because she reeked of curse and they didn't need no more troubles.

The woods thinned and became a road and field she'd never been to before, where night things and spirit things didn't go no more because the people forgot they were real. She walked until her legs ached. Walked through creeks, walked the mud off her feet, walked until the bottom of her summer dress turned brown-gray with dirt. She walked until the sky turned from black to blue to orange. The egg shuddered and shook, burning like a brand against her skin.

The egg grew hotter and hotter with every step.

The smooth shell burned against her. She thought, *It's happening*, but she didn't know—couldn't know—what. Had no idea what was in that egg other than that it was hers to deal with, just like her curse. She didn't really understand it, but it was hers to deal with, so she was. The Conjure Woman coulda told her a little more, could have taken a little more time, but that was done now, and Lily just had to believe. Sometimes believing is enough, believing is all there is.

But Lily was tired. Deep down, beat up tired. Her feet were all swollen. Her back all tore up from the rooster and arms from chickens and branches. Doubt came like a snake slithering all through her. Even though she'd seen all she'd seen, she thought, *What if?* What if it were all a lie? What if there was no way to help her?

Silently, she cried for help, because she was just a scared girl who didn't want to be in pain anymore. And someone is always listening.

Out of the dawn, a house.

A big house with a careful lawn in the front. Walls made from beautiful red brick with fresh white shutters on the windows. Nothing like the rundown shotgun house she lived in, nothing like the gone-to-seed fields that surrounded it. This was a real house for real people. The egg jumped against her, rocked and rolled over her chest bone.

It didn't look like a place where a curse could be broken, not like Lady Estelle's. It looked like a house, with money but no magic. She didn't have time to think on it. Her legs were pulling her up the front steps, and then her arm was knocking on the door. She saw her bone-and-chicken-scat covered hands. Saw the holes and tears in her that the skeleton chickens and demon rooster had left on her arms. The stains on her dress.

A pretty white woman opened the door, still in her dressing gown and curlers. She took one look and stepped back, all wide eyed at the sight of her. "You poor thing!" she exclaimed in a sweet voice, but then her face wrinkled and crumbled. The smell.

"Lady Estelle sent me." Lily couldn't think of anything else to say, and it seemed better than saying that the egg had led her there. That Spirit had pulled her across the county to this woman's doorstep wouldn't do. She wouldn't understand.

"Oh! Of course, what happened to you?" the woman gasped waving her inside. "It must be bad; she never sends anyone to us! Just keeps trying that voodoo or whatever. She should have called; she knows my husband would have come for you. We got a lot of girls after Nettie retired. Do you know Nettie? But then that woman came, and they started going to her instead. You poor things!" She yelled into the house, "Honey! There's a girl! That Lady Estelle sent her! I'm taking her to the clinic!"

The woman led her through the house, still talking a mile a minute, but Lily weren't listening. She was staring at the wallpapered walls and plush furniture, and that thing that she had felt in the coop, the hot not-fear thing was building in her—but she didn't know why. And the egg was jumping and rocking fit to roll out her dress and crack itself open.

The white woman led her into a more sterile, colder room. All tile and smooth seats and glass. Lily'd never seen a doctor's office before. Jars of cotton balls, wooden tongue depressors. Cabinets that probably held bandages. A green floor to match the green walls. The woman patted the table for her to sit but didn't once touch her. When the white woman presented the thermometer, Lily opened her mouth for it, pretty as you please.

"You're burning up! Poor thing. Don't worry, we'll get you all cleaned up. My husband will get you some care, and then we can take you somewhere safe. How does that sound?"

Lily nodded, didn't know what to do. The egg was twitching and jumping against her skin. The white woman slowly covered her nose, still smiling. Polite. "You just sit there," she said, passing through the door. "I'll bring back some water and a rag in a few minutes."

Lily touched the egg, a hot coal against her fingers.

"Now what do we have here? That witch woman sent you over?" A man's voice, yawning, sleepy. Just woke up.

He was the most beautiful man. His white coat almost looked like wings in the dawn light. "Why, you look just like Lily!" he said before he could stop himself from the saying of it. So surprised because she *did* look like her mother. But she was beautiful. Just like her father.

"I am Lily." The egg, which was rocking so hard now she thought it would jump right out and under that the seething, sick pressure she'd felt in the coop, pushed at her chest, filled that place in her that was so hollow and empty so often.

The Good Doctor stared, mouth hanging open all silly. Lily'd given him such a shock! He looked like he'd seen a ghost, but Lily had seen a bunch that night and could say she weren't no ghost. "How old are you?" His voice was all shaky and soft, weren't no charm in it because he couldn't gather hisself enough to be charming.

"Sixteen," she said easy as you please, and he knew what that meant.

The Good Doctor went all sweaty, and that shake from his voice traveled all through him, and he didn't know what to do with his hands at all. He was shaking and wiping his forehead, and you'd think he'd never seen a cursed little Black girl before in his life. "Listen."

But what he meant to do next, what he meant to say to her, no one will ever know.

Just at that moment the egg cracked, and what the cock had laid burst forth from the shell all black and wet. It came into the world loud, all wrong. Like a rooster on top but a lizard with too many legs and a sharp tail on the bottom. A cursed thing, not quite right but there all the same.

Cock-a-doodle-dooing and hissing and roaring and screaming, it ripped through that dress that was barely holding on. It made the most horrible sound Lily had ever heard, before or since. And the Good Doctor couldn't stop it.

Hungry and wild and determined to eat in the way that brand-new things are, it burrowed into the Devil's chest and returned the curse he had meant to lay on Before Lily but had laid on Lily instead. Hollowed the Devil right out, ate its fill of him. The Devil screamed and screamed until he didn't anymore. That thing ate and ate till it couldn't eat no more.

Done, full, it hopped right back up into Lily's arms, almost too big to hold and covered in the blood of the Devil. It was hers, her rage and loneliness and anger. Her mama's rage and loneliness and anger. And her mama before then, all the way back. Mother to daughter to mother to daughter. It'd come back to her sated and full and finally done. Lily stared at the thing that she held in her arms and smiled big and wide. The thing settled down, started to die and disappear in the way that those things do, like hail on a summer's day, loud, violent, but not meant to last. A candle all dressed up, burning to nothing.

She coulda held on to it, but Lily didn't mean to keep it.

Lily was done being cursed.

The pretty white woman came running, and that's what she, the only real witness, found. She called the men, her neighbors, who came and lied on Lily after that. But what she saw was Lily standing over her dead husband, hands all bloody and holding something black. She was the one that said it had been a gun, and with the sound, everyone believed it. No matter what anyone says, she was the only one there, that pretty white woman. Her and Lily, who never said a thing about what happened one way or another. And the Good Doctor—Devil, Daddy, whatever you wanted to call him—he was dead, dead, dead, as far as that town was concerned, and couldn't say nothing ever again.

When the police came, the creature from her egg was gone. Just Lily standing there, all covered in blood. They called her a murderer, and maybe she was in the strictest sense, but it weren't really her fault. All that pain had to go somewhere. And he was her daddy after all, might as well do some right by her.

Lily went on trial and went to jail, because she was for sure a murderer as far as the law was concerned. But from that day she smelled sweet like candy. Like candles. And lots of people talk about how Lily killed the Good Doctor, but mostly they talk about how she beat the Devil.

Papa Pearlie

by

Ryan Douglass

When I wake up with a toothache, I imagine my grandfather playing in the mouth of a porcelain doll—poking at its gums with a tartar scraper, squeezing a molar with forceps.

The pain follows me from class to class, worsening with each passing hour.

Mom calls me in the late afternoon when I'm heading back to my dorm. "Just wanted to remind you that your grandfather's one hundredth is coming up," she says. "Papa would want you to be there."

I'm not sure Papa Pearlie knows the difference between me and my sister. And this campus, with its blooming dogwoods and wide sidewalks, will always feel safer than his lonely house in Alabama.

"Probably can't make it," I tell her as I move through my dorm's revolving door. "I have a lot of work to finish."

"It's one weekend, Zeke. I'll pay for your ticket. Can you do it for me?"

———⁂———

Two years ago, I traveled up from Alabama to New Jersey to leave my conservative upbringing behind, but whenever there's a family gathering, my fading sense of loyalty compels me to return.

Family gatherings are important to the Moulins. When I was a kid, our Thanksgiving dinner brought dozens of cousins, second cousins, and family friends from all over the world. But over the years, that crowd has dwindled. Some family moved and cut contact with the rest of us. Some died.

I wonder if I want to join my runaway relatives in that no man's land, free from obligation to these events. I'm a religion major, but in all my studies on prophetism, mysticism, and the holy gospel, I haven't found much that speaks to my family's faith.

My family's faith is based not in a deity but a man: Papa Pearlie. Most of what I've learned about him has been from my mother. He wakes up at dawn, takes his coffee with toast and jam, and then tends to the cattle on his twenty-acre farm. From dusk and into the night, he makes dolls in his attic. Dolls of all sorts. Ones that mirror supermodels or cartoon characters. And some of the dolls, the ones he holds most dear, look exactly like us.

Mom says Papa makes them and remakes them as we grow up, ripping the baby stuffing out and replacing it with harder materials like foam and plastic by the time we hit puberty.

On occasion, Mom has commented on how strange it is, but she says it's his way of "keeping track of us when we're not around."

Now I find myself in Papa's folk-Victorian home for his birthday, and it's like something bigger than me has pulled me there—bigger than obligation, loyalty, or curiosity. It's as if invisible wires traveling through time and space folded the clothes into my suitcase and boarded the plane on my behalf. Those of us who stay attached to Papa Pearlie aren't here for the man himself as much as we're here for the value of family.

Papa's house is too isolated to belong to a well-adjusted man. It sits on a hill in a sea of weeds and grass, like a slipshod mansion blown here in a tornado from Kansas. Eight long windows grace the wraparound porch; the windows are square on the second level, and round on the third. From one round window you can see a doll's face, brown, dead eyes staring into space, its surrounding obscured by shadows, so it appears as a floating head.

In the entryway, you see the pictures: Of Papa, toasting with his friends from sixty years ago. Of my aunts when they were younger adults, posing by the signs of their Ivy League alma maters. Of my mother as a little girl, next to a doll that looks like her twin. That one freaks me out the most.

She does not look happy.

Not at all.

———— ∞ ————

My Aunt Lauren asks me how school is. Mom asks me if I'm unresponsive to her texts because I'm busy or if I'm just ignoring her. The questions are always the same. And ten minutes in, I regret even coming.

Mom pulls mac and cheese out of the oven. Aunt Lauren stirs greens on the stove. My sister, Brandy, stacks presents *Tetris*-style in the living room: big ones vertical, small ones horizontal. Here, at Papa's house, a stiffness sets into Brandy's disposition. She keeps her eyes cast down.

There is a robotic rhythm to everybody's movements—they are in sync even as they do different things. Mom and Brandy are very much alike. Same hairstyle, flat ironed and side parted, but Mom's stops at the shoulders and Brandy's at the forearms. And Aunt Lauren—well, you can only ever see half of her at a time. She wears a silk head wrap and sunglasses and gloves, both indoors and out. It doesn't occur to her to take any of it off until someone comments on it.

Aunt Lauren's daughter is my cousin Jada, who always has her shoulders and arms exposed, in direct opposition to her mom. I spot her vaping on the balcony. She flinches when I open the door and then relaxes when she sees it's me.

"I'm ready to go," she says as I rest my elbows on the wooden railing beside her.

"Before dinner?"

"I don't fuck with anybody here."

"Not even me?" I try to laugh, but nothing comes out. "Yeah, no . . . I get it."

Jada looks at me like she can't say what she's thinking, like I'm too young to know what she knows, even though I'm technically older.

She's street smart. She skipped college to sell glassblowing art and she's doing just fine. The thought of being an entrepreneur straight out of high school didn't even occur to me—I'm always in need of guidance, and maybe that's why I've never had the guts to take a stand for anything.

Jada takes a puff from the vape and looks away from me.

She's not supposed to be smoking.

Her mom tried to get her to stop doing it at family events, because Papa hated it. But Jada ignored the advice. She liked that Papa hated it. After Jada smoked at the last gathering, Lauren had an acne outbreak, which Jada swore was brought on by Papa, who controls her mother and everyone in this family.

"I'm sorry, but I think he's certifiably insane," Jada says. "And needs a straitjacket."

"Who?"

"You know who. All of us in this family would be cool if it weren't for him."

"You can't say that."

"I know. He'll *get* me, right?"

"Well . . . he'll get *someone.*"

Papa doesn't often punish the youngins as badly as he does the "grown-ups." But Jada and I are getting to be grown-ups.

"I can't have him getting you," I tell her. "We're the only queers here. If you go, I go."

Jada chuckles. "No guarantees."

My brave cousin has four tats and a buzz cut. Her presence changes the room when she enters it, forcing you to look and admire the mannish way she carries her weight and spreads herself out. She would have the balls to free us, if she'd heard what my dad said about Papa on his hospital bed before his heart monitor flattened. But I was the one who heard it, the story of what he found when he broke into Papa's attic after Grammy died. And like a coward, I've held that secret close to the vest ever since.

Someone knocks on the glass behind us. My sister is waving us inside.

Papa hides in the attic as the dinner is prepared. Papa comes downstairs when we're all waiting at the table. He's been wearing those same faded over-alls for his whole hundred years, and they've absorbed every milk stain from infancy, every pee stain from elderhood. He is too old to be so young, but he's outlived the gap in which you'd expect a normal human to kick the bucket and has seemingly done so at no cost to his lucidity or range of motion.

Conversation quiets as he waddles through the kitchen, observes the stove, and meets us at the table. He sits at the head, before the plate set for him, and tucks a napkin in his shirt like a bib.

"Good evening, Papa," Mom says.

He doesn't respond. He lays his big palms up on the table, spurring us to join hands. "Father, bless this food, for the comfort that we are about to receive, for the nourishment of our bodies. Bless this twenty acres."

I close my eyes and then open them. I want to observe Papa when he can't look back. But only one of his eyes is closed. One eye is some sort of enhancement that never closes. It moves like a roving marble of milky glass and watches me as he issues the final line of prayer.

"Bless the prosperity of our family name and our future generations. In Jesus's name, amen."

When we break hands, Papa looks pointedly at Jada. "Jada, who let you put that rod through your nose?" He's referring to her nose piercing. She's got them in her ear, lip, and eyebrow too.

"It's just a nose ring, Papa," Aunt Lauren says in defense of her daughter.

"It's ugly."

"Good thing it's not for you," Jada snaps.

"Who's it for then? Satan?"

My sister laughs, and Papa pulls his shoulders back with pride at having said something funny. But I'm almost certain the laugh was one of discomfort. Mom and Aunt Lauren are stiff as scarecrows, and I can tell they're hoping this doesn't spiral into an argument.

"It's literally just a piercing?" Jada says. "Can I express myself? Damn."

"And who told you you could cuss at my table? That's what I don't like about your generation. We never did that when I was coming up."

"Different time," I mutter.

No one hears me though, and Papa keeps going. "The talented tenth is rolling in its grave seeing you mutilate your pretty face like that."

Jada rolls her eyes. "Imagine I don't give a shit about the talented tenth." Something thumps under the table. Jada flinches, and so do I, which makes Brandy flinch too.

"Jada . . ." Aunt Lauren's tone is a warning. Her long neck stiffens, her lips tense. She slices her chicken until her knife scrapes the plate.

"Mom, I don't believe in that." Jada's voice is a whisper at first. And then she raises it. "I just want to be a regular person. I wanna get piercings. I wanna cuss. I wanna smoke weed and sell my fucking art. I want to be me. Does that make me a bad person? Or does it just make me a person?"

She's right. But I'd never say it out loud, and I'm scared for her now.

Mom is watching Papa. There's hope in her eyes. Too much hope for a man she's afraid of.

Papa's not eating anymore. "You shouldn't have come here if you intended to break the rules of my house," he tells Jada.

"No, I shouldn't have." Jada stands up, chair scraping the floor. "Did it for the tradition, but I'm truly getting too old for this. Happy birthday, I guess." She looks at me. "You coming, Zeke?"

I've found some motivation to pull my sad, skinny body out of bed every morning for the last nineteen years, but suddenly I've forgotten how to move.

Jada pulls her face back with defeat and blinks. "Typical. Can't trust any of you." With an ironic chuckle, Jada slings a tote bag over her shoulder. There are two pins on it—ACAB and Protect Trans Kids—two pins you'd not catch anyone else in here wearing.

Papa leaves the table as calmly as if he were fetching a new napkin, and Jada crosses the dining room, going the opposite way.

I should stop her. I should be better than this—less embarrassed to exist in that space between independent and "raised by" . . . What does my upbringing know about me, anyway? Why can't I be a rebel like Jada? Why am I so quiet? When I'm in school, I can walk around without a shirt on and not explain why I have a lotus flower tattooed on my chest. It's a part of me—not a desecration of my temple or whatever Papa would say. In college I can join like-minded individuals to theorize all day about civilizations, without worrying about Papa asking me his favorite question—*What are you going to do with a religion degree?* Sometimes study is for curiosity or exploration.

A noise stops Jada. Something mechanical, like a robot booting up.

Blinds made of hard plastic, or . . . steel . . . fall over the windows by the balcony and living room. Under other circumstances, I could chalk it up to a modern renovation, a screen to keep the sun out for daytime napping. But we're eating, not napping. And those shades feel specifically designed to stop anyone from seeing in. Or out.

I'm hoping that my anxiety has conjured a hallucination before my very eyes because there is no way Papa is trapping us here. There's no way this could be happening again.

"What . . . the hell?" Jada whispers.

Aunt Lauren's hand is shaking so badly she drops her fork. Mom is shaking too.

Jada breaks for the balcony door. The lights go out, leading us into pitch-black darkness.

Three heavy footsteps and then—*THUD!*

"JADA?" someone shrieks, in a panic. "*JADA? NO!*"

There's silence before the lights come on. Jada is lying on her back, eyes wide open.

Someone is screaming—it must be Aunt Lauren—but I can't see past the foam trail seeping out of Jada's mouth. My family runs to check on her, but Papa, with great calm, holds a hand out to them before bending to check her pulse himself.

"We need to bury her," he says. "In the backyard."

———⚬⚬⚬———

This is not the first time something like this has happened. My family is rattled but not as shaken as they were the first time, when Grammy faced the same fate—dead, suddenly, in the middle of a family event. It was his ninety-fifth birthday. She'd been challenging Papa for a while then. She wanted to sell the house and move into a senior living community. They'd be closer to other people and could plug into social events. Papa said that the history of the house was sacred and that everything they needed was right here.

The coroner said my grandmother passed of a heart attack. I don't know if that is true, but I have to accept it as a coincidence, even if the timing was weird. If Papa ever loved at least one person in this family, it would have been her.

"Look away," Papa instructs us. "I can't have you all seeing such tragedy." He removes Jada from the room. I can't stand to be still or to walk, so I divide my time between both. Aunt Lauren is screaming somewhere, and Mom is calming her down.

I escape to the bathroom, and by the cold window, I surrender myself to tears, clutching my shirt in my fist to remember I'm still here. If I'd never come to this dinner, would she still be here? She thought she had a friend in me, a fellow rebel, someone who'd go out with her, but all she had was a coward. There's no reason I shouldn't be buried with her.

Someone knocks at the door. "Zeke?"

It's Brandy.

Reluctantly, I open it, and my sister hugs me in that little space. I hold on to her sweet, floral scent to remind myself that life exists beyond the steel shades of this place.

"It was him," I whisper into her shoulder. "Papa did it."

"It was a freak accident," Brandy whispers back.

"It wasn't. It's him. He's been doing this to us our whole lives. He did it to Dad too. Killed him."

Brandy pulls back and blinks at me in her innocent way. "What are you saying?"

"Dad warned us. Did he never tell you?"

Brandy is sixteen now—so maybe Dad thought she was too young to know. I'm not sure I want to puncture her innocence myself. Brandy grew up dancing ballet and pointing out the beauty of butterflies and sunny days. When we're at home, she's featherlight, spinning sometimes for no reason, hitting a pirouette when golden hour hits the windows just right.

But I just don't feel right holding in what I know.

"We can't escape," I tell her. "Not since what Papa Pearlie's father did."

"What he did?"

"Dad found the pact in the attic. It was an agreement with a witch— that she would set Papa Sr. free from his slavers and kill them on his behalf if he handed over his firstborn son."

"Zeke, what?"

"You never liked coming here before. You said Papa was weird. And now you don't even question it."

"Well, he might be weird," she says, looking up at the wall like she may find the rest of her sentence there. "But . . . he's family."

"This is just what Mom's trained you to say."

Brandy looks at me, and her eyes open so wide I can see the red veins around the whites—like cracks crawling to the center of a plate. "I-I can't let anyone get hurt." Her voice trembles like an earthquake. "After Dylan . . ."

"Who?"

"Nobody. It wasn't Papa's fault."

"Who is Dylan, Brandy?"

"He was my boyfriend. But then Papa found out I was dating . . . and then . . ." She stops, like the memory is too painful. "It was too early for me to date, anyway—that was the issue. If I just would've waited like he said."

"You never told me you had a boyfriend."

"I never told anyone! I can't tell anyone anything I do. Everything I do has to be some big secret all the time because I don't know if he'll approve!" She puts her hands on her head, breathing hysterically.

I pull her in and hold her. "I know. It's happening to me too."

Brandy pulls away. She looks past me to smile in the mirror, but it only looks staged and helpless. "Once the party is over, we can go home and never come back, okay?" Her words sing like a birdsong as a tear slides slowly down her face, barely perceptible. "But tonight, we're still here. He's still listening. *Move. Carefully.*"

She leaves me in the bathroom, and I slap my hand over my mouth. What little I ate is threatening to come up again.

Everyone either adjusts to his power, falls off the map, or just gives up. I don't want to have to ghost my entire background just to feel free. Someone has to do something to stop it. What if all of us face the same fate, one by one, and Papa is the last Moulin standing?

I throw up in the toilet and hug the toilet bowl with my chest.

⁂

I must be perfect.

Perfect as the family pictures in this home. Silent as the house when I leave the bathroom.

It feels empty. Everyone's retreated to separate corners to be alone. Aunt Lauren is wrapped in a blanket by the fireplace. She's moved on from crying to a stage of numbness. And Brandy is still organizing the gifts.

I sit on the floor by the staircase for a while, pounding my knee with the side of my fist, observing how my leg jumps as a result. Maybe none of this body ever belonged to me. My heart was always made of fake material—every motion outside of my control.

Mom comes to sit beside me and wraps her arm around me. "I just want you to be safe," she whispers. It's clear by the fear in her eyes that she also needs comforting. She's been trapped in this cycle far longer than me, desperate to protect her children the only way she knows how. I've seen Mom age decades in the course of three years since my father's death. Depression has settled in her shoulders, slowed her pace when she walks. Grief has dulled her vocal range. And yet, she comes back to Papa, as if latching on tight enough will wipe away the truth.

And Aunt Lauren's been divorced twice now. Every time it happens it draws her back to Papa, the loss of trust in her husbands seeming to only strengthen her trust in Papa. He's got his rules he doles out about the men she must pursue—men with college degrees and traditional family values. No deadbeats. No journalists who go around snooping where they don't belong.

"Is the story Dad told me true?" I ask Mom. "Of the doll that started showing up on the porch of Papa Sr.'s home?" Mom has often denied this story. Her lips tremble as if she wants to deny it again, but she doesn't this time. "It carried the soul of Papa Pearlie's lost older brother, didn't it? That mistake—that curse of betraying his son—never stopped haunting him. The doll spoke to him. Asked him 'Why did you give me away?' The doll of that boy, the son Pearlie Sr. betrayed."

"He couldn't get rid of it," Mom says, staring at a spot on the floor. "It kept coming back. Pearlie Sr. had no choice but to keep it. To make peace with the doll. It's been this way forever."

"So, you've known."

"I know that something was corrupted in our lineage when my grandfather sacrificed his son so that he could enjoy his own freedom in this country. I know that it's something we can't fix now, so we ought not even play with it. If your father hadn't defied him," Mom says, tears welling in her eyes, "he'd be here today." The tears start to fall, pain erupting from her in subdued sobs that I can hardly bear to see. I hold her tightly. Maybe my father died for standing up to Papa Pearlie. But if it weren't for him, I'd never know the truth.

In the next few minutes, Mom and Brandy grow eager to leave, to go somewhere less teeming with dread. And while I want nothing more than to drive off this farm and never come back, I wander upstairs instead, to the long wooden hallway that reflects through ancient mirrors. There are family photos—so many photos—but the photos of my late grandmother are missing. I want to assume their absence is because it's hard to have reminders of her everywhere.

Was she killed? Would he take it that far? Papa hasn't cried for any of us in the way we've cried for each other—maybe it's just what he learned from his father.

His sandals and church shoes line the walls. At one time, Grammy's were here too: turquoise green with sequins, black platform shoes, beige lace up heels. I tried them on when I liked what I saw. Grammy would cheer for me, but Papa, when he saw me, looked on with disgust.

Some mornings I would wake up screaming because my ankle dislocated in my sleep.

I was thirteen in my room, passing a ball between myself and the ceiling, when I pieced together that Papa may not want me kissing boys. But he liked that I played basketball—good, masculine athleticism would compensate for the softness. I was an athlete, a hero to the public eye.

One pair of my grandmother's shoes are left in the hallway, just under the string to the attic. Blood-red pumps that my feet have grown too big for. I try them on anyway. And the string—I pull it so the door comes down, and with it a ladder and spool of light.

The circumstances of Grammy's death were too mysterious for the investigative journalist in my father to accept. He found a pact Papa's father, my great-grandfather, made with a white witch—one that would bind the family forever in its curse. Papa would go free. His son would not.

—ᙏᙏᙏ—

My father passed away minutes after he revealed these things to me, growing tired as he spoke, his heart seeming to attack him in real time as the words came out. That's when Papa loses control of you—when you free yourself from him. When you choose your own destiny, that's when you risk dying at his hands.

What is my life worth if it isn't mine?

Details of sound become apparent—carnival music, deep horns and drums, playing over a scratchy record player. And moaning. Painful moaning.

I walk up the ladder, and with each step, my toes squeeze tighter toward the nose of the shoes. At the top of the ladder, I can see Papa at a desk across the room. He looks like Santa in his workshop, firm as a pillar, tinkering away. There's something so whimsical about the way he spends his time: playing with toys. How do you explain something like this to the authorities? That a dollmaker could be a madman?

This overrun, musty space has seen such a long life that the lights dangling like uvulas from the ceiling flicker as feeble candles do. Moths spasm around the bulbs.

Did he hear me clicking up the steps?

There are books on shelves, ancient names and unfamiliar languages collecting dust on their spines.

Does he hear me clicking toward him now?

There are dollhouses—all of them with open walls. All of them are different: Plantation houses with kitchens, and in those kitchens smiling figurines. A modern house with a ventriloquist doll who looks suspiciously like Jada's ex-boyfriend. He's wearing a suit, lying in this leather bed, clutching chocolate and roses, and by the slant in his eyebrows I can tell he's lonely. The doll is uncannily expressive, like a clown at a children's birthday party.

Every second I take this attic in makes me sweat a little harder. My stomach turns, the truth squirming beneath my skin like a parasite.

There is another dollhouse, long and painted white, with a red cross above the door—a hospital. There is my doll dad, on a bed, his face fashioned into a frown.

I like to remember my dad as the writer, explorer, and free spirit who spent entire days awake, putting his heart into his stories and paintings . . . not the man who lost his life to a cantankerous father-in-law, who saw no value in his career.

Had Papa Pearlie made Dad's doll before my parents married? Was he at their wedding, charting the moment he'd take the hammer to my father's chest?

I meet Papa at his desk, where he's shoveling soil from a bucket into a tiny wooden coffin. Tools are splayed out on a slab of fabric. Little hammers and scalpels, little marbles and tweezers. "You make these dolls and deposit lives into them that are reflections of what you want us to be, regardless of what we want.

"Did you kill her?" I ask.

He grunts, driving the spade into the wet earth, which I can see now is teeming with maggots and worms. "All because you wanted her to be different?"

"Hmm." Papa doesn't look at me. He's tossing dirt into the coffin onto the shiny plastic face of my doll cousin. Jada's doll is still smiling, as if she wants this.

"Why do you do this?" I ask.

No answer.

"Please answer me. *Why do you do this to us?*"

His glassy, white eyeball spins to place me diagonally behind him. "This is how our family works. You should know, shouldn't you? As much as you and your father go snooping around."

"I don't know. He was trying to tell me, but then he died."

"My father felt guilty for giving up his son," Papa says quietly, like he's afraid I'll hear him, even though he's talking to me "So, he gave the doll his son's name, Marcel, and built him a dollhouse. 'Here, this is your home, my son,' he said. 'Here you will have clothes, a bed, and books to read. Here you can live your life as if it was never taken from you, as freely as I live mine.'

Papa takes his hands off the table and rests them on his thighs, looking straight ahead into the shadows at the far end of the attic. "My father thought he could move past the mistake. He married, became a farmer, and had another son—me, Pearlie Jr. But Marcel became jealous of PJ. I would wake up with an incision in my face, or a piece of my ear missing, and I would find it clutched in the hard hand of Marcel. 'What's happening to me, Papa?' I asked my father, the tip of my ear like a cigarette butt! 'Marcel,' he told me! Marcel thought it only right that Pearlie Sr. do away with his second-born son the way he'd done his first. Marcel had no brain, or heart. He couldn't be predicted. He couldn't be controlled.

"My father scrambled to appease the doll. Built a new doll from scratch, made it identical to me, and called it Marcel's brother. He told his doll son, 'He is a part of me, see—just as you are.' But Marcel was not buying it. *If he is just like me*, the doll rationalized—in silence, because he had no voice—*then he must be made of bisque, cloth, leather, and wood. If he is my brother, I must have human flesh too.*"

Papa stands up abruptly and invades my space, so that I fall over on the shaky wooden floor. "I got my body ripped apart by an object!" Papa shouts. "Who replaced my bone marrow with sawdust and pumped glue into my blood when our father wasn't looking! How much of me was real after that?"

He falls back into his chair, calmly. "I don't know. I was being punished. And so, when I became half-doll, my children, too, became tethered to the dolls. There is no way out but to play by the game that Marcel started."

I turn my attention to the chests against the walls, overflowing with hands and toes, tongues and tonsils, bones and silicone butt cheeks. I sit between Papa and this treasure of parts, and I begin piecing something together. With some thin fishing line I make a wig of gray hair.

"So now you do it yourself," I say. "You build the dolls to look like us and control us the way you see fit."

"I can assure you he'd do much worse if he got a hold of you," he says. "No one would be human if he had anything to do with it. We'd all be dolls."

A rattling explodes from a corner of the attic. A locked chest begins to slide across the floor, as if someone is desperate to break out.

If Papa's half-human, half-parts, maybe there's some lapse in his brain that's preventing him from realizing he doesn't have to do this anymore. What did Marcel remove from his skull in his effort to dominate this family? And how did Papa gain control of this master operation?

"Now punishment has to loom over us for every mistake, just because your father betrayed his son?" I ask him.

"Punishment looms over all of us," he answers. "Punishment is constant. The only thing that can be controlled is the punisher."

So if I carved out the iris of one squishy eye and glued it to a plastic skull, would I be the puppet master then?

I build a smooth torso that feels mysteriously like human skin and slather it in a coat of light brown paint, like Papa's face.

"Cut it out."

His voice cuts a gash through my knuckles. Blood spills forward and backward across one hand, rendering it unusable. I hiss through my teeth and put my fist in my mouth. It must work in all directions, the magic. There must be a way to end Papa's reign by playing his own game. That's what he did to Marcel, isn't it?

"Don't be bold, grandson," Papa says. "This fight is too big for you." The doll that Papa holds looks like me. And the knuckles are cut, the plastic coming off in shavings that mirror my blood. My doll has beautiful red heels. Aunt Lauren's wears a pantsuit, and the hair is long and flowing. Its face is full of tiny holes as if stabbed by a needle.

I can hear words whisking through the air now—muffled voices, like prisoners trapped behind crawl-space doors. But we're the only ones up here . . . at least the only humans.

Is my dad in here, between the books, tools, and toys? Screaming at me to finish what he started?

I stand up from Papa's desk, the doll in my hands. The body is soft, but the face is hard, with removable parts. The frowning mouth pops out like Mr. Potato Head. All Papa had to do to make me happy was flip it upside down, reverse it.

When I flip it, euphoria stirs my feet into an elated dance. I'm happy all of a sudden.

Happy as I take up a scalping knife and stab my likeness in the shoulder. My shirt tears open, and blood soaks my arm. I'm leaking now, and all I can think is how magic is real—how fascinating that is. How feet still work when a shoulder doesn't. How one hand can injure as the other is injured.

If I had confronted the choice to purchase my freedom, I wonder if I'd have said yes to that too. I'm desperate for it now. Desperate to know who I am without his influence, and how much of me can be influenced by my own hand.

"It's your choice to do what you are doing," Papa says. "In my mind, your cousin's sins are not your own. Nor are your father's."

"But you torture me anyway." Jada's sin is shared. Jada wanted to be herself, like we all do. But none of us are anything if not possessed by Papa's legacy, if not carrying on that evil witch's will.

There is nothing illegal about sticking a needle through a doll. If the doll looks like your grandson, and your grandson wakes up with a prolapsed eyeball, the cops would call that a coincidence.

I am tired of doubting my choices out of fear I'll find a gash stinging my leg in the shower. Tired of falling short of breath after failing assignments. If thread must be ripped out my shin and stuffing out my lungs, I want to be the one to do it.

Some of us are built to invent multinational tech corporations. Others tumble whichever way the wind blows, mediocre and unsettled.

I am not the talented tenth.

I am not Black excellence.

I'm just Zeke. Just Zeke.

Just smiling like a doll with a disfigured body.

Where next? Where now?

My lung must survive a stab wound quite well on its own. I've avoided smoking my whole life just so I could live a long one. Or was it because that's what they say you're supposed to do?

I take Papa's knife to my lung. Drill it through the torso of my fake body. So when the final traces of air leak through me, I can be happy knowing I stood up for myself. And Brandy knows the truth—she knows to watch her step smartly because Papa could be watching. She will move this takedown a step further, inherit the rebellion from my father and me. I know she will finish Papa's doll, finish Papa, and break the curse—once and for all.

Amazing how you can be hurt and still laugh.

I wonder if someone hurt that witch, and that's why she took Papa Sr.'s baby. If Papa Sr.'s parenting is why Papa Jr.'s stuck up here, taking his fears of failure out on us. Maybe the reason I can feel so burdened by this family from a thousand miles away is because my imprisonment is a unit of time, not distance.

I hammer myself in the knee, and when my legs buckle, we fall together—me and the doll. We roll on our backs together, mouth bleeding under the attic lights, laughing at the glare as it beckons us up.

No Harm Done

by

Circe Moskowitz

It's Christmas Eve, the snow thick and ghost white, and I'm sitting underneath a dazzling garland, bleeding terribly. I press a napkin against my palm and watch it bloom holly red. Carols howl on the radio inside. I can hear them every time the door swings open and some pale-skinned figure passes my table, smelling of espresso, holding a cup patterned with Santas.

This side of town is jarring. White faces everywhere, signs glossy with fresh paint, buildings free of blemishes. This café, too, is brand new—no flaw to be seen. The tables show no wear. The lacquer shines. The chairs don't creak. A shudder runs through me, travels all the way down to my legs. It's cold as shit, but it's better than being inside with all the chaos. The holidays drive people to hysteria, and I don't want to listen to them verbally abuse the baristas.

Anxiety rears up, threatens to break through, so I focus only on the wound. Seems better now as I lift the napkin—blood clotting instead of flowing—but in the aftermath there's a gory incision all the way from my palm to my upper tendon. Shitty, but also deserved for letting YouTube convince me that I could do knife tricks. The switchblade lies open on the table with a reddened edge.

"Are you Sasha?"

A barista approaches with two coffee cups. I toss the napkin, close the blade, but it's spotted before I can slip it into my pocket. She pales and smacks down the cups, dashing inside before I can get in a thank you. Overdramatic, but whatever. Wham!'s "Last Christmas" is now playing and I hum along, sipping my coffee while the other cup just sits there, unclaimed.

Ten minutes late now. I'm tempted to check Alana's feeds again, to see if she's posted something that might reveal how she's feeling about our meetup. Is she nervous? Excited? Did she only agree out of pity?

When I went digging into my background and tried to track down my birth family, I never imagined I'd find a long-lost sister. My birth parents are long gone (birth mom dead by alcoholism, birth dad in prison for two murders), and the only genetic connection I have left on this earth is Alana Harrington.

A twin.

We were separated at birth, and Alana was adopted by some "old money" white family (google *slavery*) in the suburbs. The moment I got hold of her name, I scoured social media, learning everything I could. Alana is their shining token, a constant feature on the Instagram of her adoptive mother (named Brook Harrington, maiden name Mills). She was born into old white money and married more old white money, in the form of Sean Harrington (recently deceased, a tragic car accident). The story, perfectly rendered on her feed, is how God meant for her to not have children so she could help Alana. You know, because they're such charitable white folks, benevolently taking a Black child off the hoodlum streets and helping her reach her full potential, the way only white parents evidently could. (Like, fuck all the way off.) But look at Alana now: track star, amazing grades, heading to Ivy League come autumn.

God's almighty plan.

Anyway, I debated for a while about reaching out. I wasn't sure if she'd even want to know me—it's not like we have anything in common. The older couple who adopted me kicked me out of the picture two years ago, and I've been living in a small icebox of an apartment with four other people, splitting rent, like, three and a half ways, due to one roomie's freeloading boyfriend. I gave up on high school, definitely not considering college. I'm not exactly the epitome of success. I sent her a message, though, in the end. A sister, a *twin*, was not something I could let slip away, no matter how I felt.

So, here I am. Waiting.

Scared shitless.

Just sitting idle is too much, so I pull out my phone, scroll down her feeds. No new posts, but her girlfriend, Casey Hopkins (in a relationship since 2019), says:

> me and the babe wanna take a road trip this june. anyone down to drive across the country and fuck around?

I click on Casey's profile. No posts about college acceptances, or school at all for that matter. Her internet presence is very laid back—not a lot of selfies, but there are numerous shitposts on her Twitter that are funny. That's where it ends, though. Once I scroll further down to a couple years back, there's no more posts, almost like it's been scraped clean. Curiosity itches. What is she like in person? I wonder. And what drew them together? I'm so immersed in my lurking that I've lost track of my surroundings.

"Hey," comes a soft voice.

I look up.

Alana.

It's even more disconcerting seeing her in the flesh. This girl—my mirror—who, up until a couple weeks ago, I didn't even know existed. But here she is, all dressed up for the occasion, wearing one of those costume elf dresses paired with candy-cane-stripe tights and heeled boots. A reindeer headband twinkles on her head, a constellation of LED lights. The poster girl for holiday cheer. Meanwhile, there's me, dressed in all black, with not so much as a piece of jewelry. I suddenly feel underdressed.

I haven't followed her on anything yet. Partly because I was worried that she wouldn't follow me back, but mostly because it felt premature, considering we hadn't actually met yet. Worst case scenario? She doesn't want to know me, even though we shared a womb in our infancy, and I just keep going as I have. But honestly, that turn of events is already devastating, and I only did it to myself—got attached to the idea of knowing her by spending so much time on her feeds, immersing myself in her life. This is exactly why I need to stop lurking on people. I get my hopes up for no reason. Fucking sucks.

"Hey," I say. "I got you a coffee."

She blinks. "Thanks."

It's a peppermint mocha, but she doesn't ask what it is. She sits across from me, analyzing me the way I'm analyzing her. There is the round face, the corkscrew curls, the eyes so dark they could be black. We are nearly identical, but I think she has a bigger upper lip than me. She takes a sip of her coffee, staring hard.

"I'm sorry," she says. "It's just weird."

"Did you . . . tell your family about me?"

"I wanted to meet you first." Alana shrugs uneasily, making the little bells in her ears jingle. "My dad died, and things are just . . . a lot right now. I don't know. What side of town do you live on?"

"South side. Over by that big park? It's not really a good neighborhood, so, can't see you ever being there."

"Oh, I see."

"Honestly, I was lurking on you a bit."

She smiles, bashful. "Me too. But you don't really post a lot, I was kinda disappointed."

"I'm not exactly living the high life. I work at a dollar store and get stoned on the weekends."

Alana laughs. It's bird sweet and light. *She* is light, like nothing in this world could ever hold her down. Envy burns through me. "You should come hang out with me and my girlfriend sometime," she says. "She'll want to meet you."

And there it is: another meeting extended like a rare branch, blooming with possibilities. I'm scared to jump on it too fast and put her off. It's irrational, I know, but I'm so used to people leaving me behind to consider anything else.

"What's she like?"

Alana's expression softens. "She's the kindest person I know, but she can also be, like, such a badass. She doesn't take shit from anyone, even me. I love her."

That last part she says so simply, and yet she means it with her whole heart, I can tell. A faint jealousy hangs over me. It's not that I want what she has exactly, but I can't help but compare my life with hers. What she has and what I don't.

What I'll never have.

"Your family is cool with you being a lesbian?"

"Of course."

"That's cool. Mine wasn't. My adoptive dad told me I was going to hell."

"What an asshole."

"Exactly." I hesitate. "You're happy, then?"

Alana considers me for a long moment. She pulls out a cigarette and lights it, gives a weary cough as she inhales. Her shoulders tense.

"Smoking is bad for you."

"Tell me something I don't know," she says, not unkindly. "But I guess I'm happy. Are you?"

"I don't know."

She nods like she gets it, flicking the ash off her cigarette. "It's been weird for me at home . . . knowing this. I don't know—I've had a twin sister my whole fucking *life*." She shakes her head. "And . . . I always had this sense, you know? A dark cloud over my whole life. I could never figure out why. Why did it feel like something was always missing, like there was this great big empty space? Nothing would fill it, no matter what I did. And now I know why." Her voice finally breaks. "Now I know why."

A dark cloud. A great big emptiness. Is that what I've been feeling all this time? I'm nearly seized by this need to reach across the table and grab her hand, just to make sure that I'm not having some elaborate hallucination, but I clench my hand into a fist, pulling away.

"I get that," I say instead.

"Yeah."

We stare at each other. She's the first to look away. Her eyes widen as they drop to my hands, curled around my cup. "What happened?"

I follow her gaze. The gash on my hand looks no better. "Cut myself."

"With what?"

"Does it matter?"

She looks a bit thrown off by my tone. And to be fair, I am abrasive. I have never known how to be an easy and open person to speak to. The silence surrounds us, everything still except for the cheerful music floating out from the café.

"I never go out," she says suddenly, breaking the silence. "I'm always so busy with Model UN and choir . . . I mean, my mom keeps me busy. Are you in school?"

"No."

She frowns. "So, you're just working then?"

"Pretty much."

"But . . . what's your dream?"

"My dream?"

"Yeah, like what do you wanna do? What do you want for your life?" When I say nothing, she continues. "Like, I really wanna be a lawyer. I feel like that's where I could make a difference. More so than in politics, anyway."

"Politics are in everything."

"That's not the point."

"Then what is?"

She sighs. "It could be anything, big or small. Something you really want, you know?"

"I dream of being okay, I guess. Maybe happy, the way other people are. But mostly I'd just like to be okay one day."

The way she looks at me, it's like she's really seeing me, for the first time. Or maybe it's just *all* the seeing happening at once, an overload of perception: The way she holds her shoulders and her voice, higher than mine, more girlish. And how everything she says almost sounds like a question, like she's afraid of being punished. She has this elegance to her, an arcane softness that doesn't belong in the world.

My face, my opposite.

What might we have been if we'd grown up together? How might we have spent birthdays? What things might we have bonded over, fought over? Friends, girls, borrowed clothes? Or would we have been just the same—divergent carbon copies? I don't think I really felt it until now, the sadness. All that lost time is a thing to be mourned. I want to speak to it, but nothing feels right, so we just sit there, watching each other, this dreamy hush between us.

A series of crashing sounds break the spell.

Thuds and *smacks* and one loud *smash*. My head snaps to the right. Two men wrangle with each other against the long café window. I jump out of my seat and back away until I hit the curb. The two men thud against the café window again, and the glass shatters, sending them tumbling to the concrete. Everything is loud. People are screaming, retreating against the walls, while John Williams's "Carol of the Bells" howls over the grunts of the wrestling men.

I am frozen.

Raspy sounds emerge from the man on top, building into a feral screech that is pure animal. Mouth wide open, he leans down and sinks his teeth into the other man's face. Away comes skin. He plunges into the neck. Out comes an esophagus. I can't move. Too loud. My head is buzzing.

The man abruptly stops eating the other. Blood is on his chin, flesh in his teeth. His eyes land on me. Instinct kicks in, sends me running across the parking lot. I don't know where I'm running—there is only one thought: *away*.

"Sasha!"

Alana is beside me. I hadn't even noticed that she was there. We have reached the middle of the parking lot. She's on the edge of hysterics, but I am so detached from my body, like I'm in a terrible trance.

"My car's over there!"

Ahead of us, at the end of the lot: her luxury ice-blue Jaguar.

Behind us: the shopping center, carnage unfolding. The cannibalized man has risen to his feet, as though his neck isn't half-gone. He attacks a woman, who tries to get away, but it's too late. So much blood.

We're running again.

"My house is close," she gasps. "We can go there, figure out what the fuck is going on."

We stop by her car. My head is still buzzing. The frenzy at the shopping center has yet to draw closer. But the moment I look up and meet her eyes, I see what I've missed. It's happening too fast. "Alana!"

A woman with bloodshot eyes sprints in her direction, letting out a feral shriek. Alana runs from the driver's side toward me. She knocks into my side, and we're a tangle of limbs as we both flee around the car, then away from it. The woman bounds over the trunk as if the motion is nothing, landing on the hood with both feet.

Alana cries out. I've somehow ended up in her way. She shoves me to the ground, and my head hits the asphalt so hard my vision goes fuzzy.

Then she trips and falls too. Her keys land on the ground, skidding in my direction. She screams as the woman jumps on top of her, teeth snapping at her shoulder. Alana's hands go around the woman's throat, trying to fend her off.

She needs my help.

This girl, my mirror. *She needs my help.* Alana turns to look at me, terrified and desperate, the woman's teeth inching closer, fists whaling at her sides. My hand twitches toward the blade in my pocket.

"Help me!" she screams.

I could help her.

But I dive for the keys.

Alana's scream turns to a wet splutter as the woman teeth break through her hold, closing on her jugular.

I unlock the door just as the woman pounces off Alana's body. I slam it shut. The woman pounds against the window, fast and loud like a drum, screaming at the top of her lungs.

Another second and Alana gets to her feet. Her eyes are hazed with red, her mouth oddly slack. The bone and muscle of her neck is exposed, blood soaking the front of her dress. She shouldn't even be alive in this condition. None of them should be. But there she stands, this hideous undead thing. She lets out a wild shriek. My ears ring.

I start the car.

And I get the fuck out of there.

———

My roommates don't answer when I call, and I refuse to let myself panic, but the vision of Alana's neck split open terrorizes me. I can't stop thinking about the way she changed. My ears are still ringing, sharp and turbulent like the screams.

A shudder goes through me. Tears threaten to spill over, but I swallow them down. I can't panic. *I can't panic.* I have to stay focused. What's the next step, Sasha?

Next: get home.

I stick to the right, looking for where I can enter the freeway. But when I get there, cars are lined up at the entrance, not moving. A bunch of large men in green camo are holding submachine guns, blocking the ramp. They walk up and down the line, each with a severe set to his jaw. A woman sticks her head out of her car to complain, and one of the soldiers raises his gun, yelling out a hostile admonishment. The ringing quiets.

I try to back out Alana's car, but a line has formed behind me. The traffic on the left is also held up. I cannot move. I'm stuck. I let out a frustrated groan.

Alana's wallet sits on the passenger seat. My fingers shake as I reach for it and flip through her ID and license. Her face, my face, *our* face— gazes back at me.

She's dead. I barely knew her, and now she's dead. I left her there.

Don't panic.

I look through her glove compartment, which is a mess of lip gloss and tons of random receipts and mail, including one college acceptance letter that has her home address. Not far from here, perhaps a mile, no more than two.

A soldier approaches. We lock gazes. My heart quickens as I roll down the window. "Excuse me?" I say.

He comes to a stop by the car. "Yes?"

"What's going on? Why are we being held here?"

"We'll get you on your way here soon, ma'am."

Annoyance, heavy on my chest. "That doesn't answer my question."

"Like I said," he repeats. "We'll get you on your way soon." As he turns away from the window, someone starts screaming. He cranes his head to scan the horizon behind, and I follow his gaze. Then I see it.

One of the undead is sprinting in our direction. I roll up the window, and the soldier aims down his sights, immediately pulling the trigger. He shoots and shoots and shoots, then lowers his gun, backing away. He turns and runs. Ahead, the other soldiers are piling into Humvees. There is a rising sound like thunder.

Pandemonium.

So many undead rush forward that I cannot count them all. They climb on top of cars, hurling their fists at the doors. They pull someone out of an open window onto the asphalt, ripping away a hand, then a shoulder. A few others sprint in that direction, piling on top of each other, all of them grasping for a chance to feast on flesh. A bottomless nightmare, damnable, without end.

Footsteps rumble on top of the car. I sink lower in the seat. A head slides into view, upside down on the windshield, eyes locked on mine, something rabid in them. They arch their skull back and then bring it down hard, hitting the windshield. Again and again and again.

Others start crowding around the back doors. Outside, the Humvees are long gone. They left us—they took their weapons and left us. My ears are ringing again, and I can't breathe. I have to get the fuck out of here. I slam down on the gas, and the undead on my windshield goes flying, hitting the ground. I slam into the car ahead. It scrapes forward just barely. I back up, try again, but I don't get very far. More undead climb on top of the car.

The passenger window shatters. Hands reach for me. I scream and whip open the driver's side. Screams follow me as I bolt around the cars. Everywhere my eyes fall, someone is being eaten, and undead are roving round, looking for something else to consume. There are five with their eyes set on me, in pursuit.

Across the roadway, through the intersection, two cars are turned over and smoking. Ahead of me is a convenience store with a bougie front wrapped in Christmas lights. I shove through the glass doors.

I run right into a Christmas tree. It tips over and I skirt around it, sprinting through the checkout lanes and down the aisles. The screaming is so close. My lungs burn. I shove the cart behind me, and the undead, so focused on getting to me, smash right into it. It slows them only briefly. I keep running. I make it all the way to the back, in a narrow dark hall, where there are two bathrooms.

I'm inside the first, door locked, them banging so hard the door shudders. I turn, see a small window. I look around for something I can use to break it open, but there's nothing. The bathroom is stark, polished, barren outside of a mostly used up roll of toilet paper. I kick down the toilet seat and stand on top of it, clenching my already-wounded hand into a fist, and then break it open. Pain explodes in my hand as knuckles are decorated with blood and glass. I struggle to heave myself up, dangling for a dangerous moment, but then I hit the pavement.

I'm panting; my hand is burning; my body is shivering; my knees are soaking wet from the snow. Wild, I scan the horizon, but it is clear. I hear the door finally break behind me.

I run.

I end up off the main roads, finally, and on a quiet backroad surrounded by thick trees and large houses, some verging on mansions. I'm still very much in the suburbs. Every noise, every brush of wind, has my heart pounding. I am pretty sure that I have reached Alana's neighborhood. A few minutes of walking and I arrive on Honor Boulevard, which is shielded by a big black gate. Peeking through the bars, I see big houses running down either side of the street, and my eyes are drawn to a familiar blue house at the very end. I've seen pictures of that porch on her mom's Instagram.

There was this one shot where Alana was sitting on a white wooden swing, holding the family Labrador, both caught in snapshot happiness.

The caption read, "We had to say goodbye to Max today. Keep us in your thoughts and prayers." I remember staring at that photo until my eyes watered, lost in Alana's goofy grin.

That image is soiled now. I remember the way she looked at me—her desperation in that last moment, begging for my help. I am frozen on the street and can see nothing but her eyes, hear nothing but her screams. My ears ring. It's hard to breathe.

Don't panic.

An uncomfortable feeling hooks into me as I stare at that beautiful blue house. I shouldn't do this, but I need somewhere *safe*. I can't stay out here. Who else will take me in, give me shelter? I'd be operating on the good will of strangers when hell has broken loose. I am so far from home, and I have no car. Where else can I go?

I am out of options.

I start climbing the gate.

The house is huge. Like, it's not even fair how huge it is. Pictures didn't capture it. I'm drowning in white suburbia. The roof is coated in snow, and the windows glow warmly in the gathering dusk. My body is numb from the cold, but my heart becomes an unrestrained creature as I approach the front door.

It opens before I even get there.

Alana's mom rushes to me. My trips to her Instagram feed make her instantly recognizable, but it is surreal to see Brook Harrington in the flesh. She's got pale hair and blue eyes so clear it's eerie.

"Alana?"

She has come to a stop, looking carefully over the state of me. I almost open my mouth and confess everything. The words are there, on the tip of my tongue. The guilt crushes—but the fear crushes more. Safety is the single desperate beam of a lighthouse, and I am so scared and so fucking tired. Those screams are ringing in my head. I don't want to fight anymore. I don't even want to stand. Something colossal inside of me has broken, and I don't think it'll ever be right again.

"Hey," I whisper.

I am wary of what comes next. Skepticism? Is my voice off? Do I sound like Alana? But there is no awkward lull for me to climb over because Brook immediately envelops me in her arms. She hugs me so tightly that I almost start crying. My limbs feel strange.

This hug isn't mine to accept. This is for Alana and she is dead.

I let her die.

And now, here I am—this imposter—standing in her place. But if I tell Brook the truth, that I'm not Alana, that I'm her twin, what then? Would she even believe me? Or would she think I'm out of my mind? Worse, would she consider me responsible for what happened to Alana and turn me away, left to face only the undead, shrieking at the sky?

The door opens again, revealing another figure, taller and stockier. *Casey.*

There's no way I could have missed it on her feed, which means she never posted about it—but her long waves are gone. A mussed pixie cut frames her pale face instead. She's wearing soft joggers, a loose shirt.

"Babe? What happened?"

Brook lets go of me, and Casey comes closer, taking my hand in hers. Her brown eyes are so kind, searching my face with deep concern.

What happened? Where do I even begin?

They guide me inside, and holy fuck, it's so warm. Brook sits me down in front of the fire, wrapping a blanket around my shoulders. She handles me with such care, like I'm a delicate piece of glass. I don't know what to do with this comfort. Unsettled, I steel myself against it.

"We were going to come look for you," says Casey.

"I'm glad you didn't," I say. It's not a lie. "Have you seen what's going on?"

"I just saw that they were blocking off the roads. Some kind of out-break? They were being pretty vague on the news." Casey falters. "What did you see?"

I tell them about the man and the woman. How they killed people and then ate them. How those people rose again. Undead. Hungry. *Those screams.* A childish part of me wants to curl into myself and weep. But I need to stay calm. I need to keep it together. *Don't panic.*

Brook puts a hand to her heart, horror-struck as I finish the story. She is silent for a long moment. Then, she says, "I'm going to call your uncle. If they open the roads, we should go stay with him. Why don't you get a shower and change? Try to . . . unwind? I'll make you something to eat."

Eat. I almost start laughing.

I can't get the sound of her screams out of my head.

Casey offers me a cautious smile as I move toward the stairs. When I reach the first step, Brook says, "Where are you going?"

"Um, to shower?"

"You don't want to use yours?"

"Mine?" I repeat.

Brook tilts her head, perplexed. "The pool house?"

"Oh, right. Sorry, my brain is all over the place."

"Of course."

"I'll come with you," Casey says, guiding me to the front door.

I look to see where Brook has gone, but she's still standing there, watching me.

∞

That's how I end up in the pool house, which has clearly been renovated into a living space for Alana. It is twice the size of my apartment, no exaggeration.

Her walls are draped with fairy lights, and she has a giant canopy bed. It belongs in one of those wild bedrooms I'd see on a Pinterest board. My hands trail over everything: her expensive perfumes, her designer clothes strewn over the back of her vanity chair. She left this room in the sort of state that says she'll come back.

She'll never come back.

"Did you see her?"

I forgot about Casey, still there. She watches me so closely it makes my skin crawl. "What?"

Casey hesitates. "Sasha. Did you see her . . . before everything happened?"

My name in Casey's mouth is a shock, but a necessary reminder. This safety could be taken away if I'm not careful. "No."

"Is she okay?"

"I have no idea. She didn't show."

Casey frowns. "Maybe you should message her . . . make sure she's not . . . well, you know."

I despise everything about this conversation. I don't want to talk about myself in the third person. I don't want to dwell on any of it. I think Casey senses my discomfort, because she stops prying and sits on the edge of the bed, holding her hand out to me. "Come here."

When our hands meet, it's electric. She brings me into a hug. There is such deep familiarity in her touch that my body can do nothing but respond. This affection unwinds my limbs and makes me feel real again. She places a tiny kiss on my forehead.

"I missed you," she murmurs. Then, another kiss.

This one on my lips.

I pull away abruptly, my cheeks hot. I am a tangle of both guilt and magnetism. I am not Alana. This is wrong.

"What is it?"

"Just feeling . . . off."

"I'm sorry," she says, looking guilty. "I'm pushing you too much, aren't I?"

"It's not that."

"Are you sure?"

"Yeah. I just . . . need that shower, I think."

"Sure thing." Casey quickly gets to her feet. "I'll be in the main house, okay? Take your time." Her eyes fasten on my chest. "Where'd you get that shirt by the way?"

"I don't remember."

"Never seen you wear it."

My heart races. "It's old."

"Okay," she says, examining my face. "Sorry, wasn't trying to give you the third degree."

My hand, tightened into a fist, relaxes. Casey exits with grating leisure. Even though she and Brook seem to believe me, they didn't see it for themselves. They don't understand. They think that this will pass us over quickly, everything back to normal. But they're wrong. This feels different. All consuming. Irreversible.

The door shuts, and I'm alone. The silence is oppressive. The front door creaks, and my heart skips in my chest. I move against the wall, afraid it's the undead. They've found me again, in this house.

I slip out my blade, easing forward, and peek out the window.

But there's no one. It's just the wind and the house, so unfamiliar in its ordinary locomotion. It takes me several seconds to move again. I try to calm the pace of my heart. To stop seeing my sister, the bloodied monster. The way her eyes changed—from desperate girl to something feral, hungry, barely human—everything she was left in that moment, never to be seen again.

Alana's bathroom is colored in cream and marble surfaces. There are so many mirrors and lights. Fancy products line the cabinets, high-end brands I've only ever seen in magazines. I never knew there was so much one person could have. It is difficult to understand possessing so much— and to make sense of the appetite that curls inside me at the sight of it.

When I'm out of the shower, I stop in front of the mirror, see the girl reflected there. I see her eyes, mine. Her throat red. *Help me.*

What happens when you're not willing to die for another?

The price is only that you bear it. This, then, must be why it can be so much easier to sacrifice and so much harder to survive. We are not built for this kind of agony.

<hr />

They are in the living room watching the news. Brook has laid out a bowl of noodle soup for me on a tray. I keep the blade in my pocket, but every now and then I thumb the hilt, just to make sure it's still there.

I pull out my phone to check my feeds. One of my roommates, Andrea, has finally texted me—"where the hell are you? are you good???"—and statuses are coming in rapidly. Many people are too scared to make a joke out of the situation, but there are just as many who do, because nothing is free from becoming a meme. There still doesn't seem to be a concrete answer, aside from speculation. Some say a plague, others say it's the government, and some say it's the aliens that have been in our heads this whole time. Those who have seen the undead firsthand have taken to social media to speak their truth. Have even posted videos and streamed the chaos online. Seeing the word *zombies* trending on Twitter nauseates me.

Casey asks, "Where'd you get that phone?"

"Picked it up off someone. I lost mine during . . . everything."

Brook says, "Your uncle says as soon as it's safe to go, we can stay with him. I want you to start packing."

"Okay."

"You two should get some sleep." She turns off the television, rubs her eyes. "I'll bend my no-bed-sharing rule. Just this once."

I frown, not sure what she means. But her wry smile gives it away. *Oh.* She means me and Casey.

"Goodnight, girls. Please behave."

Sharing a bed is not as awkward as I was afraid it might be. Casey knocks out pretty fast. But I have trouble doing the same. It takes me hours to fall asleep, and when I do, the undead are there waiting for me—Alana in the middle of them, her neck arched in a raptorial way, hands reaching for me. I wake when dawn hasn't broken yet, covered in sweat. I lay there, unsleeping, until Casey finally stirs.

In the main house, Brook greets us with a hug. "Merry Christmas, you two," she says, soft, and she passes me a warm mug that smells like peppermint.

"Oh, wow."

She laughs. "Did you forget?"

"Yeah, I did," I say, too exhausted to lie.

A look of sadness creases Brook's face. But she shrugs it off just as fast as it comes. "Forget about the world burning for a moment. Just have some cocoa and open your presents."

And what a privilege that is. She didn't hear those screams.

The gifts are overwhelming: a brand-new gaming console, high-end makeup, wireless earbuds ("You said you lost yours, right?"), and a Dior coat, which I know had to cost thousands. In total, at least a year of my rent, given so freely, like it's nothing. Afterward, we watch a couple Christmas movies, and I wonder if it was always the plan for Casey to spend the holiday here at Alana's house. Where is her family? She hasn't mentioned them even once and I want to ask so badly, but that would be suspicious.

We keep an eye on the news, but there are no new developments. The lockdown is here to stay. People are allowed through checkpoints only after swabs are done to ensure they are not infected. This will be done by cops and military. I can imagine just how aggressive they'll be. I tell Brook it worries me.

"Why?" she asks. "They'll take care of us. That's their job."

"Maybe."

"I'm confused. What do you think could go wrong?"

"Not everyone is rich and white," I say, before I can stop myself.

Brook's expression wrinkles a little and then quickly smooths. "You seem upset, honey. Why don't I make you more hot cocoa?"

She gets up and heads into the kitchen, doesn't hang around for my answer. Casey waits until she's out of earshot and then leans in closer, saying, "That was very sexy of you."

I stiffen. "What do you mean?"

"Challenging her like that," she answers with a big smile. "Normally I'm the one who's gotta do it. Good for you. How did it feel?"

She means it as a compliment, but I don't feel flattered. It occurs to me that Alana didn't have these kinds of conversations with her mom. Maybe she never had to. I was so busy being jealous of her lifestyle, wishing her problems were mine, that I didn't consider the true nature of being raised in whiteness when you are anything but. Was every day spent questioning her own sanity? The reality of living in her own skin? How much longer can I keep up this ruse? Alana was a product of her environment, as I am—but where she was a sweet and passive creature, I am a lonely animal who cannot be caged.

"Do you think she'll be mad at me?" I hedge.

"Nah. You know Brook. She'd rather forget about a problem than deal with it." Casey sighs. "Don't stress, babe. Soon you'll be out of here. You'll be at Yale and free of all the bullshit."

And where will you go? I wonder, but I do not ask. Casey's eyes flutter shut, her hand wrapped around mine.

When I was a kid, I quickly learned that the love of my adoptive parents was conditional.

They were an older Black couple who led a church group every weekend. They had these big holidays where they invited over all their Christian friends. Unspoken though it was, there was an expectation to behave a certain way and be a certain way. I remember the first time I talked back to my adoptive dad, Pierce, he hit me hard across the face. I could still hear Silvia cooking. She hadn't reacted at all. I sat there, feeling the sting, and from that point on I learned—not to feel differently than I did, only to hide it better.

A few months after I turned sixteen, they caught me with a girl. If it had been a boy, it might have been more of the same. House arrest, maybe, or another beating. But I was a girl and she was a girl, and that was the sin of all sins. A conclusion to any love they might have had for me. Pierce threw me out on the street, and I bounced around for a while. I was lucky enough to have a friend who let me crash on her couch while I found a job and tried to figure shit out. I stopped going to school—gave up really, as there was nothing for me within those walls. There was grief, but I had no room for grief. The only thing left was to survive or be pulled under. I've floated through this life with no kin, but I've held onto hope that maybe one day I'd find some. A place where I could belong.

I wonder if that's a foolish notion.

I wonder if maybe I haven't paid enough.

Will it ever be enough?

—◦◦◦—

At around eight, Brook asks me to come hang out with her on the porch. I am light headed with nerves as I sit beside her on that wooden swing— wondering if she's finally put it together, seen through this facade. Did she know that Alana went to meet me yesterday? If she's figured it out, maybe I should consider it a blessing. Maybe I should return to that bloodbath and meet my fate. But I can't bring myself to do it.

Brook stares out at the street for a little while, studying the delicate snow shower. "What do you think about roses?" she asks.

Roses? For what? I stare at my feet, tense, wracking my brain for an appropriate response. To my relief, she goes on: "For the party . . . I was thinking white roses . . . but then I thought that might be a little *too* much. So maybe tulips? You only graduate once, so take your pick. Anything you want."

A deep sadness settles inside me. Not for myself but for Alana. I have been waiting for the other shoe to drop, for her to notice, but she doesn't. In a vicious second of clarity, I realize that Brook doesn't know her daughter, not really. Doesn't acknowledge the color of her skin, doesn't question why she is suddenly speaking out of turn, doesn't realize that sitting in her place is an imposter. I could really get away with all of it and she would never know.

"Tulips," I say, after a long moment. "Tulips are nice."

We sit there for a while, watching the snow fall. Brook reaches over and squeezes my thigh. And then eventually, we head back inside. As we do, I think about the ease of all of this, what Alana had. The ability to sit on a porch and watch the snow fall as the world is burning. It's despicable. I should hate it.

But I don't.

———∞———

When we settle back inside, Brook puts on *Christmas with the Kranks* and tries to no avail to order takeout, even though nothing is open and there's a whole apocalypse happening outside the gates. I focus on Jamie Lee Curtis in a Christmas sweater and try to stay calm.

After giving up on takeout, Brook says, "Can y'all help me find the landline? I want to talk to your uncle."

Casey sighs. "Yeah. Babe, can you call it? I'll go hunt."

"I don't remember the number."

Brook tells it to me, and I call it with my phone. I don't even hear it go off, but Casey comes back a few minutes later, holding the receiver in her hand. Brook quickly dials a number. The other end rings only a couple times, before I hear a gruff voice go, "Hello?"

"Hey. We're going to be on our way in the morning."

Casey sits down on the couch with her legs crisscrossed, facing me. She's so close I can feel her warmth. "Have you messaged Sasha?" she asks.

"No," I say, annoyed by the question because I can't eavesdrop on Brook's conversation when she's talking to me.

"Don't you want to know if she's okay?"

I stare at Casey then, and she stares back. There's something off in her voice. No, something *more*. Does she finally see through me? Does she know? My heart races.

"I'll message her later."

"Right."

"What's wrong?"

"Nothing," she says.

But she turns away and doesn't look at me again.

———∞———

Later, in the pool house, I start packing a couple duffle bags. Casey is still quiet, lost in her thoughts. I miss the sound of her voice—I realize now how talkative she is—and I hate this sudden silence. How it's making me question everything. I've messed up. But I don't know how. I go over each interaction and can't figure it out.

"Want help?"

I'm so fucking relieved that she's said something that I just nod. She watches me, though, when she gets up. She can't know, right?

She would have told Brook.

Right?

She stops beside me, starts folding one of my—Alana's—shirts.

"Are you . . . okay?" I ask.

She stops folding. "You lied."

"What?"

"About not meeting Sasha. You lied."

I blink at her. "I didn't—"

"You have her phone. I saw her name on the landline. The caller ID."

Fucking hell.

Does she know? No, she didn't say I *was* Sasha. She only said that I had Sasha's phone. My heart is in my throat. *Don't panic.*

"We did meet."

"Okay," Casey crosses her arms. "What happened?"

I could tell the truth here, finally just do the right thing—*confess.* But if I speak it now, what will it help? What good will it do? In the end, it will only harm us all.

"She died." My body starts to shake. Alana's screams ring in my ears.

Casey's suspicion dissolves in an instant. "Oh my god," she whispers, cupping my face. "I'm so sorry." She just holds me. I don't fight it. I don't pull away. I lean into that embrace, feel her warmth, her heartbeat. It quiets everything.

I have never felt safer.

We end up cuddling on the bed, duffle bags abandoned. She tells me this story about when she was little—how she and her brother used to collect dragonflies in jars. It doesn't take me long to realize that her brother is dead. She knows what it is to lose a sibling, like I do.

That is something we have in common.

Me and Casey.

Not her and Alana.

I think about Alana's life, beside mine. I wonder if I would have fared better here. Or maybe it would have been worse, with well-intentioned racists and forced respectability. A shining token, soaking in a weak trickle of protection that could turn lethal at any minute. Was I better off? Was she?

Truth is, I'll never know. Maybe that can't be properly measured.

Maybe it doesn't really matter.

———⌘———

When midnight hits, she says, "You need to finish packing."

"Are you coming?"

Casey smiles softly. "You know I can't. Mom needs me."

"Have you . . . talked to her?"

"In a shocking plot twist, she was cool about me staying, but she's getting anxious the longer I'm here. With everything going on, I don't blame her."

Casey reaches over me, grabs the remote for the TV, starts searching for a movie for us to watch. I love the arch of her neck. I wish we were cuddling again. There is a low groan, the sound of the door creaking. I flinch, my eyes going to the windows.

"It's just the wind," she murmurs. "You're safe."

Safe. That's all I want.

She's back to looking at the movies. In a sudden burst of delight, she says, "Wanna watch this? Sounds kinda gay." Then she pulls out her phone. "What's your word?"

"What?"

Casey halts. "Your word . . . what's your word?"

What the hell is she saying? She stares at me, waiting, and I stare back. Her eyes go very round as her jaw drops. "Oh my god."

Her tone has changed abruptly, her entire demeanor. She gets off the bed, moving away from me.

"You're not Alana," she says. "You're Sasha."

Silence.

"I'm not—"

"You *are*. Stop lying to me!"

"I'm not lying!"

"Then what's your word?"

"I don't . . . what . . . I'm—" I struggle with the words, wrestling with what I should say next.

"It's a game we play. Me and Alana do it every night. Look at you! You don't even know what the fuck I'm talking about!"

"My memory is just all over the place, after what happened—"

"Stop. Lying. Where's Alana?"

"I *am* Alana."

"No, you're not! God, why didn't I see it before?" Casey's expression is pure disgust—at me, and at herself too. "You're not like her. You're not like her *at all*. Where is she? Is she . . . is she *dead*?"

I'm screwed.

I'm so, so *screwed*.

The words rush out: "There was nothing I could do. Those things—they came so fast, okay? I should have told you the truth. *I know*. But you would have turned me away—"

"And that gives you the right to lie? To take advantage of me the way you did?"

"I didn't take *advantage*!"

"I thought you were her, so I kissed you. I *touched* you." I step back, but she matches me, getting in my face. "You took advantage of her death, and you took advantage of me. You evil *bitch*."

The tears are spilling over now. I can't stop them, and I can't stop shaking. "I'm sorry," I whisper. "I was scared of what you would do."

She's crying now too. She angrily wipes away the tears. "This is so fucked up. Why didn't you just say something?"

I don't know. How the hell do I answer that? How do I say, as fucked up as it all is, I feel at home with them, the way they loved her, the way they could never love me? All my life, I have been chasing that feeling. It was nice to have it just once. Even at the end of the world.

But Casey doesn't know me. She doesn't know what I've been through. She only sees me as an imposter. A threat.

Nothing else.

"Please. Believe me. I'm so sorry. I never meant for it to go this far."

Casey nods, but the motion is too careful. Like the second she gets the chance, she's going to rat me out to Brook for being a lying weirdo. But that's not what I am.

I miss when she looked at me like she loved me.

But she didn't love me. She loved Alana.

"Please," My voice breaks as I stand here, begging, and I hate it. "I meant no harm."

"Okay," she agrees. "No harm done."

But I can hear the strain in her tone. I know where this will lead. She will tell Brook—and everything will be taken away.

I force a smile. "So, we're good?"

Casey nods faintly, steps closer to the door. "Yeah. We're good."

The moment she turns her head, I'm on her.

I pull out the blade. I know how well it cuts. It sticks in her so easy. I stick her again and again and again. There is only the moist sound of her flesh, her screams as she tries to shove me away. But it's too late. I've taken her by surprise.

And I can't stop.

There is so much blood. It's soft and warm, like how it felt when she held me. It pools around her body.

Eventually, we both stop screaming.

—✦—

I bury her body out back. It takes me hours to conceal everything. To shower off the blood. To burn the clothes in the fire. To mop up the floor. By the time I'm done, I'm exhausted, and dawn is peeking through the windows. I sit in the entryway with my bags, knees pulled up to my chin, watching the sunrise through the glass door, until Brook comes.

She kneels beside me. "Hey, what's wrong?"

I can't answer.

There are no words. There is only this pain, weighing on my chest. If only I could have made her understand. I didn't mean for any of this to happen. I never meant to take it this far.

I just wanted to be safe. Loved.

Sobs rake through me violently. Brook takes me in her arms, stroking my head. "You're going to be okay," she whispers. "You're going to be okay."

She says it so many times and I want nothing more than to believe her. To fall into this delusional world of hope that she lives in. It feels better than what I left behind.

She looks past me, around the house. "Where's Casey?"

"She left."

"Oh, *oh*. Is that what's going on?"

"She's just gone."

"She didn't say why?"

I shrug. Brook sighs. "I see. Well, maybe this was for the best. You were going to be leaving for Yale soon anyway."

"You think Yale is still happening at a time like this?" I can't hide the skepticism in my voice.

"If they get this under control sooner rather than later, I think we'll be just fine."

Maybe's she right. But I think about the undead and can't imagine they'll go easy.

Now would be the time to tell her the truth. I have dug myself so deep. Bricked myself in with lie after lie. I could tear it all down.

I would lose this.

But my sister is gone and there's no bringing her back. Even if this all started with a lie, the love is true. Isn't that enough? Does it make me horrible to simply live for the both of us? We were half of each other, weren't we?

Brook reaches for my hand. "I'm sorry about Casey."

"It's okay," I say. "It's okay now."

Her fingers run up the side of my palm and down again, then over my knuckles. She turns her head to gaze out the door. Outside, the car is running, and the sky is pale with clouds, snow beginning to fall again.

Brook lets out a soft sigh. "You're not Alana, are you?"

Everything around me, in that moment, crumbles like a building on its last legs. I hunch into myself. I've been running and fighting and running and fighting, trying to evade this. But I'm tired, and I can't evade it anymore.

I wait. I wait for the punishment to come.

"Look at me," says Brook.

I look. Those blue eyes seize me. We remain there, holding each other's gaze. She knows. There are no more lies between us, no more illusions. But then the moment passes, and her expression smooths out, once again untroubled.

"Are you ready to go?"

At first I'm not sure I heard her correctly. She stands, grabs one of my bags, and heads out the door. I get shakily to my feet, watch the back of her blonde head as she pops the trunk and places the bag carefully inside.

You're not Alana, are you?

I grab the other bag, carrying it out to the car. Every part of me shakes, anticipating retribution. But when we lock gazes again, I see nothing of her prior lucidity. She is light again, as if it never happened. And in this moment, I understand that she will go on pretending. She will look past it, as if I'm not a lie. Like so many terrible things in that beautiful house, it will be silenced and forgotten. My sister was a bird caged in this life. But what if I'm not the bird? What if I am the cage itself?

I gaze out at the horizon, and when I get into that passenger seat, it's like I've laid all the terrible weight to rest with Casey, four feet below ground.

Even with death behind me, death ahead, I am safe again.

We start driving.

Acknowledgments

All These Sunken Souls wouldn't be possible without its authors and their magnificent contributions. So my first thanks must go to Kalynn Bayron, Donyae Coles, Ryan Douglass, Sami Ellis, Brent Lambert, Ashia Monet, Joel Rochester, Liselle Sambury, and Joelle Wellington. What an incredible journey this has been. I'm so proud of these stories and honored that I got to work on them with you.

I am forever grateful to Natascha Morris, who championed this book, and Alicia Sparrow, my editor, partner, superhero, et cetera, as well as the entire team at Chicago Review Press: Frances Giguette, Jonathan Hahn, Candysse Miller, Connor Deeds, Stefani Szenda, and Benjamin Krapohl. Also to Sarah Gavagan for the kick-ass cover art. Thanks for working so hard on this book. Thanks for bringing it into the world. And thanks for making it look so damn awesome. You're all superstars.

I'd also like to give a special shout-out to Zoraida Córdova and Rebecca Podos for answering my million questions about editing anthologies and for believing wholeheartedly that I could do this, even when I didn't. I don't think I could have found the courage without you.

Thank you to my family, forever, always—though "thank you" does not suffice. You have given me everything. And to my besties, Ana Fiamengo and Zo Jacobi, who are my favorite people in the world.

Finally, to Jordan Peele. If you know, you know.

Contributors

Kalynn Bayron is the *New York Times* and Indie bestselling author of the YA fantasy novels *Cinderella Is Dead* and *This Poison Heart*. Her latest works include the YA fantasy *This Wicked Fate* and the middle-grade paranormal adventure *The Locus*. She is a CILIP Carnegie Medal nominee, a three-time CYBILS Award nominee, a Locus Award finalist, and the recipient of the 2022 Randall Kenan Award for Black LGBTQ fiction. She is a classically trained vocalist and musical theater enthusiast. When she's not writing, you can find her watching scary movies and spending time with her family.

Donyae Coles is a horror author who has been published in a variety of short-fiction venues. She devotes her free time to her other great love: art. Her debut, *Midnight Rooms*, is forthcoming from Amistad. You can find more of her work on her website, https://donyaecoles.com, and follow her on Twitter @okokno.

Ryan Douglass is the author of the bestselling horror novel *The Taking of Jake Livingston* and the poetry book *Boy in Jeopardy*. His work is set to appear in forthcoming anthologies *Night of the Living Queers* and *Poemhood: Our Black Revival*. He is an Atlanta native currently living in Los Angeles, where he can be found scoping out bakeries or getting lost in the wilderness.

Sami Ellis is a queer horror writer inspired by the horrific nature of Black fears and the culture's relation to the supernatural. When she's not the single auntie with a good job, she spends her time not writing. You can follow her @themoosef on Twitter or check out her words in her debut novel *Dead Girls Walking* (2024).

Brent Lambert is a Black, queer man who heavily believes in the transformative power of speculative fiction across media formats. As a founding member of *Fiyah Magazine of Black Speculative Fiction*, he turned that belief into action and became part of a Hugo Award–winning team. He resides in San Diego but spent a lot of time moving around as a military brat. His family roots are in the Cajun country of Louisiana. Ask him his favorite members of the X-Men and you'll get different answers every time. His reading and writing tastes can be summed up as "the weirder, the better."

Ashia Monet is a novelist and essayist from Pennsylvania. As a lifelong fan of myth and poetry (especially Sappho), her fantasy novels explore various forms of magic and monsters. If she is ever missing, please search for her in tiny coffee shops, at home playing video games—or, perhaps, on a sudden trip to a city she mentioned being interested in approximately once. Online, she's @ashiamonet on Twitter and @ashiawrites on Instagram and Tiktok. Her website is https://www.ashiamonet.com.

Circe Moskowitz is a fiction writer with a penchant for the macabre. She is a cocreator of the forthcoming graphic novel *Good Mourning* and the editor of *All These Sunken Souls*. Her work has also appeared in the critically acclaimed anthology *Reclaim the Stars*.

Joel Rochester is your friendly neighborhood chaotic bisexual, with a taste for the magical and macabre. He's an award-winning content creator, whilst also possessing a BA in creative writing and English literature from the University of Winchester. Between playing video games, browsing the nearest bookstore, and writing new stories, he possesses an eagerness to embark on new adventures to undiscovered worlds.

Liselle Sambury is the Trinidadian Canadian author of the Governor General's Literary Awards Finalist *Blood Like Magic*. Her work spans multiple genres, from fantasy to sci-fi, horror, and more. In her free time, she shares helpful tips for upcoming writers and details of her publishing journey through a YouTube channel dedicated to demystifying the sometimes-complicated business of being an author.

Joelle Wellington is the author of the YA thriller *Their Vicious Games*. She grew up in Brooklyn, New York, where her childhood was spent wandering the main branch of the Brooklyn Public Library. When she isn't writing, she's reading, and when she's not doing that, she's attempting to bake bread with varying degrees of success or strengthening her encyclopedia-like pop culture knowledge.